BLOODLINES
Legacies of Madness

I0691239

Terry L. Vinson

BLOODLINES
Legacies of Madness

DOUBLE DRAGON

CHAPTER ONE
The Bad Seeds

The young man leaned against the side of the large brick structure with a heavy scowl covering his pasty-white face.

"I cannot believe we have to spend four hours listening to this nonsense, and then write the essay besides," he barked, shuffling his Gucci dress shoes from side to side on the grassy lawn. The girl standing next to him brushed her long dark hair to one side and adjusted her wire-rimmed glasses, which seemed a bit too small for her chubby face.

"Quit your bitching, Jerry. It's just a simple essay, and at least it's the final assignment of the semester."

He turned to her, his lips pursed. He raised a hand, opening his mouth to argue, then was cut off abruptly by an older man who crossed in front of him hastily.

"Okay people," he began, his arms held high as to attract attention. The man was prisoner-of-war thin with short-cropped hair that was more white than gray. A thin line of perspiration trailed down the right side of his face.

"The bus has arrived and will be pulling up to the back of the auditorium any minute. The seminar should last no more than three hours. I'll be grading your essay on both facts given here and your own opinion on the subject matter. Pay close attention to these people. They have some fascinating stories to tell." A tall, lanky young man holding a large yellow folder stepped up and raised his hand, waiving it enthusiastically.

"Professor Carpenter, will all of them be speaking tonight?" The older man sighed, his shoulders slumping a bit.

"Yes, Marvin. Like I've told you people before, each of Dr. Dante's patients is a direct relative to the subjects covered and each has a story to pass on. They've each had…problems of their own since the incidents, and are presently receiving treatment." Another of the twenty or so students had slowly surrounded the professor when the bright headlights of a large yellow bus cut two distinctive lines through the crowd. The bus passed them slowly and pulled around the structure to it's rear. The professor strolled towards the front entrance to the large brick building, a faded '*Macintosh Middle School Auditorium*' sign hanging just above the double doors.

"Creepy place. I wonder why they picked it to hold the seminar," one student whispered to another as he scanned the badly cracked sidewalk leading to the entrance.

"Cheap digs, my man. I'm sure they go where they pay the least," another replied with a shrug.

"Seminar hall on campus was booked solid, obviously," another chimed in. Within moments, lights lit up the small hallway just to the right of the foyer.

A clicking noise followed, and the doors swung open with a loud creak. The man who greeted Professor Wilton Carpenter smiled shyly and held out his hand in greeting. Professor Carpenter took the man's hand and then turned to instruct the students.

"Okay, folks. Everyone sit near the front of the stage and do not talk once the presentation begins. I'm certain you will find this extremely informative as well as exhilarating."

The other man smiled as he knelled down to set the stoppers on each door.

"You are correct, Professor. I can guarantee your students will be mesmerized by what my patients have to say."

As they entered the spacious but obviously ancient auditorium, a chubby girl with a pair of thick-lensed glasses hanging from a chain on her shirt smirked aloud, feigning disgust.

"Jeez, when was this place built, World War I? It reeks like mothballs and rat droppings."

The thin girl beside her giggled, one hand covering her mouth as to muffle the laughter. "Did you see the doctor? He reminds me of that old actor that always plays nutcases. You know, the guy from that Tom Hanks movie 'The Burbs'. Gibson I think his name is.

Little guy, but looks like a real cracked egg."

The lanky, excited young man from earlier stepped up behind her, causing her to cringe slightly before they all selected a chair.

"Henry Gibson. He was also in that 'Nashville' movie from the seventies."

The chubby girl ignored him completely as she sat her notebook down in the empty seat to her right. The other girl smiled and began biting her nails nervously.

"Well, let's just hope Doctor Gibson and his crackpot patients give us the Reader's Digest version of their nutty relatives. I have a Calculus test in the morning I have to hit the books for when we get back to campus."

The inside of the auditorium held fifteen rows of twelve seats, all of which suffered from the faded, chipped paint and wood cracks that time and overuse had inflicted. The tiled ceiling was circular and high, approximately thirty feet at its center, and dark water stains made it resemble a semi-completed crossword puzzle.

The stage itself was fairly small, twenty to twenty-five feet wide and another twenty in length, and the curtains that were tied to each corner were a dull, dim red and held a thin layer of dust, along with more than a few shredded cobwebs.

As the short, troll-like man who had greeted them at the door walked slowly to the dark blue podium at the stage's center, the students seemed to grow silent in unison.

Professor Carpenter, sitting in the middle seat of the front row, nodded politely as the man leaned towards the mic and began to speak.

Squelching feedback echoed through the building for a split-second, then mercifully ceased.

"Good evening, young men and women. My name is Doctor Parnell Dante. I work as the Resident Senior Psychologist at the Browne Institute in Indianapolis. I have worked in this field for thirty-two years, and I have to say it has been many things but never monotonous or boring."

The lanky young man grinned, turning his head slightly to whisper to the girl to his left. "He even sounds like Henry Gibson. I just can't see this guy dealing with psychotic patients with such a wimpy demeanor."

The girl smiled wryly, staring straight ahead as the doctor continued.

"I'll bet he's a real tiger when pissed off," she replied, then repressed another giggle. "Yep. A mad doctor with a filled hypodermic," the student behind them replied, leaning forward while balancing the bulky notebook on his knobby knees.

Professor Carpenter turned suddenly and frowned in their direction, putting a quick end to the banter.

Gripping the sides of the large podium with his small, bony hands, the doctor seemed to be looking over the heads of the small crowd as he spoke.

"I have a rare opportunity for you and your students this night, Professor Carpenter. Nine of my patients will regale to you stories that are based on fact, not science or any other type of fiction. These are tales that concern members of their immediate family, and have affected them in a mostly negative nature since the incidents transpired, or in a few cases for their entire existence. They have come to me and volunteered to share their pain with complete strangers in the hope that it will help them finally discover a tentative peace of some kind in their own troubled minds."

The doctor turned slowly to the left and gestured for the person standing backstage to come forward. A moment later a slim, primly dressed woman possibly in her mid-thirties strolled confidently towards the podium, her long red hair swung back over her shoulders in a thick wave.

"Professor and good students, I would like to introduce you to Miss Laura Willis."

9

A small spattering of applause followed as the woman cleared her throat politely and faced the crowed with a pleasant smile.

"Good evening. As Doctor Dante stated, my name is Laura Willis. My husband, Mack Alan Willis, worked as a Correctional Officer by trade; that is until about eight months ago. Mack was a patient at the institute. He was placed in the violent ward, although in my twelve years as his wife, I never saw one such tendency in the man."

Clearing her throat again, she closed her eyes for a moment, slowly lowering her head. A few of the students glared at each other and shrugged. A few even smiled sarcastically.

When Laura Willis' head arose, the earlier smile had been replaced by a pained grimace.

***

"My husband had been an officer of the state for quite a few years, and although I feared for him each time he left me to enter the gates of the penitentiary, I never envisioned the job driving him insane. This is his story...,"

She took a deep breath and began just as the lights in the mostly empty auditorium dimmed.

CHAPTER TWO
The Tower

It stood fifty-five feet high, it's staggered brick construction giving it the look of being part of an old English castle. When you stood directly in front of it from a far distance, it seemed to be leaning slightly to the left. On foggy winter nights it resembled an ancient lighthouse that had long since been retired from active duty.

There was something about the structure that gave Officer Mack Willis the creeps. He couldn't put his finger on it, but he had been a correctional officer for almost fourteen years, and had pulled tower duty at least a thousand times, probably three hundred or more shifts in that specific tower, but the uneasiness he felt about it never faded. It wasn't as if he had experienced any traumatic events while pulling shifts, in fact, with the double set of thirty foot walls topped with razor sharp barbed wire and electronic sensor alarms along the prison perimeter, Tower duty had become an eight-hour journey into snooze- land. Still, Willis always had a strong feeling of foreboding whenever he climbed the stairs that led him up into the tower, but never understood why such feelings existed. He never mentioned it to the guard he was relieving, but sometimes he thought he saw the same uneasiness in their eyes as they left that particular post.

It was a cold, gusty fall evening as Willis entered the prison grounds and headed for the armory to pick up his thirty gauge. The lunch his wife had fixed was still warming his hands as he entered the gun room.

Bill Ryan, a veteran guard of over twenty-five years, was pulling a shift of signing out the weapons. Willis was always reminded of Archie Bunker when he saw Ryan, who was pudgy, balding, and had the demeanor of an abused bulldog.

"How goes it, Bill? Gonna be a cold one tonight." Ryan grunted, his face a frozen scowl.

"Mack, you youngsters don't know what cold is. Hell, I worked a tower shift one night up in Illinois without the benefit of a built-in heater and glass windows. It was just you and the wind. Hell, it got down to forty below in late January and February.

The whole damn inmate population could have walked out right under me that night and I wouldn't have given a rat's ass."

Willis smiled. He and the other guys on his shift called Ryan "Newsreel" due to his endless stories of the way "Prisons used to be."

According to him, what were once hard ass penal institutions were now 'Wanna-be Lawyer Training Schools' and 'Concrete and steel Holiday Inns.' Mack checked his ammo and then signed out the weapon.

"Well, Bill, this is one youngster that is damn proud to be living in such a technologically advanced society on such a tit-hardening night."

Ryan grunted again, this time a slight smile breaking across his rugged face.

"I hear you, son. I tell ya what though, something in the air tonight. Felt... I don't know.

Something not altogether in place, you know?" His smile had turned into a frozen scowl.

Willis laughed uneasily and felt the hair on his neck instantly stand on end. "I think it's just that, Bill. The wind. Let's hope so, anyway."

His weapon secured, Willis strolled down the paved walkway that led to the main tower. He waived at a few of the officers standing outside the Mess Hall, although he didn't recognize them. Correctional Officer was a job that held a turnover rate higher than any other job in the country. He was used to seeing faces he didn't know. If you lasted longer than six months, you were considered a veteran. Individuals like Bill Ryan and himself were like the Great, Great Grandfathers of the guard.

Willis exited the main gate and walked to the base of the tower.

As he went to insert his entrance key, a strong gust of wind almost blew the keys out of his gloved hand. The prison site itself was ten miles from the city limits, and the surrounding hills and thick foliage compounded the feeling of isolation. Once the gust died down, Willis suddenly became aware of just how eerily quiet it was. His shift started at 6pm, which meant dinner was winding up for all the inmates, and this usually meant lots of loud chatter, screams, and cat calls as they were shuffled back to their cellblocks.

He re-keyed the door and stepped inside, and became immediately aware of the lack of heat inside the walls.

"Aw, great. Real friggin' good."

He heard footsteps above him as he climbed

the steps towards the main tower room. A small bathroom was just to the right of top step as you entered the guard shack. He heard the sounds of the man he was to relieve doing just that. Officer Pat Lawrence had been assigned to the unit only three months ago, his uniforms still slick from newness. He stepped out of the mini-john, which held a toilet only, and smiled the happy grin of the soon-to-be off-duty sentry.

"Mack ol' buddy! Welcome to the land of cold Java and frosty testicles. Can you believe this crap? My prick was frozen to the side of my leg."

Willis walked over to the console, which held one phone; a hot line to the communications center, a felt tip pen and logbook. He placed the rifle barrel against the large window glass, rubbing his arms briskly.

"How longs the heat been out, Pat?"

Lawrence vanished back into the john and flushed the toilet, then reappeared a moment later, smile still intact.

"'Bout an hour after I got here I noticed it getting cooler. It was warm as toast here when my shift started. I hear they're saying it might sleet too. You wearing your long johns under that ugly ass uniform, Mack?"

"Hell, no. Foolishly, I actually expected heated conditions. This pathetic state-issued jacket ain't exactly in the same league as a parka, either. You call it in to maintenance?"

Lawrence was checking his keys and looked back up while shouldering his rifle.

"Yep. Called it in about three. Captain himself informed me that maintenance won't be out 'til

14

around nine or so, so I guess you get to play penguin for a few hours." He started down the steps, then paused, looking back at Willis.

"Mack, you might want to call Com about the lights over in the laundry building. I noticed 'em flashing on and off a few minutes ago. Damn weird. I was fixing to call when you walked in and I remembered I had to whiz so bad I thought it was gonna start leakin' out my ears."

Willis sat down in the 'view chair' as it was called. It was positioned so the view the officer saw was the prison's main gate and the perimeter line all along the front of the site.

"Okie-dokie, dude. Can do. Hey man, check out how quiet it is out there. Maybe they put Quaaludes in the con's tea tonight."

Lawrence stepped back towards Willis, his expression grim and without a hint of the good humor of just moments before.

"Mack, this is gonna sound weird, I know, but humor me. Has it been lightning tonight?"

Willis grinned as he poured steaming hot coffee from his thermos into a 'Scooby-Doo' labeled cup.

"Pat, you know we're not supposed to smuggle booze in here on duty." Lawrence laughed nervously.

"Man, I tell ya, I was sitting there about an hour ago, and I saw this big flash. Hell, it was like somebody had stuck two spotlights in each one of my eyes and clicked them on for just a sec. Weirder than that, a second later I could'a sworn a plane passed over, 'cause a shadow passed above the tower. I didn't hear any engines, but something very damn large flew over."

Willis sipped his Java.

"Pat ol' buddy, over the years my mind has come up with all kinds of strange crap to keep me occupied, most of them pornographic in nature. Don't worry about it, though, it's probably only a brain tumor."

Lawrence laughed and headed back down the steps. "Thanks for your 'moron' support, Mack. See ya tomorrow."

"Not if I see you first, pal."

Willis heard the door close and a key turn, and then felt a rush of colder air enter the small circular room. Every guard was required to pull tower duty when their name came up on the rotating list. It was a duty you either tolerated or despised, but it came with the territory. On one hand, it was an easy shift since it was almost a certainty that you wouldn't be required to do anything but stare out a glass window and write the words "All's quiet/zero occurrence" in a logbook each hour on the hour. On the other hand, you weren't allowed to bring anything in on your shift that might 'distract' you from monitoring the perimeter, i.e., radio, magazine, portable TV. You sit and watched. You peed as quickly as you could and got back inside and watched some more. You crapped as quickly as you could, and got back inside and watched. You called the Com center each hour to verify that everything was quiet and uneventful. It made for an extremely tedious, mind numbingly boring eight hours.

Most officers would rather work the lunch line or even an outside job site in the dead of winter than pull tower duty.

After taking an additional sip of Coffee, Willis scooped up the Com phone and waited for an answer. After three rings, a veteran officer named Potter picked up, sounding slightly out of breath.

"Com, this is Potter."

Willis made a squeaky farting sound into the phone by blowing into his right palm.

There was a slight pause on the other end, then Willis started laughing and heard a weary sigh on the other end.

"Damn it, Mack. Cut the shit, will ya?'

Willis leaned back in his chair and reached into his coat pocket for a cigarette. "How's it hangin', Stan? Sounds like you been chasing down es-ca-pees…"

Potter laughed somewhat nervously. Willis had known this man for years, and he always seemed to be on the verge of sheer panic.

"Aw, we got power outages all over the damn place. Maintenance is short-manned and we got counts coming up in forty-five minutes. Can't count 'em too well by flashlight. Two of the cells blocks are totally in the dark, and the backup generators are on the blink."

Taking a long drag off his smoke, Willis leaned forward, attempting a clear scan of the laundry building. From his vantage point, only the west side of the building was visible, but the windows that he could make out held only blackness. He also noticed a thin sheet of fog drifting in towards the site from the west.

"Other than that, everything's hunky-dory, right Stan?"

"Oh, kiss my ass, Mack. Pat already book?"

"Free as a bird turd. Hey, I guess he already told ya we're thinking about storing meat in this tower for a sideline."

"He told me. I'll get 'em out there as soon as I can, doc. Might be midnight, though," Potter replied with a bit of cheerfulness.

"Spanks a lot, bud 'o mine. Just tell my relief to bring a hammer and chisel to free me from the iceberg when he gets up here at two. See ya, Stan."

He heard Potter bellow instructions to another officer even as he hung up. The fog was coming in heavier a few minutes later. It resembled sea waves headed for some unseen shoreline. The wind had died down from what it had been an hour earlier, allowing the fog line to thicken and group together as it entered the site. It had already coated the ground view Willis had from the tower, and was rising rapidly.

Two cups of coffee and another cigarette later, Willis arose and made his initial trip to the john. He was thinking about just how weak his bladder was becoming at the ripe old age of thirty-six when everything went dark.

"Son of a bitch! Can't even take a miserable leak in peace."

Stumbling out of the small room, Willis paused to let his eyes adjust to the dark, then trudged slowly over to the phone.

He listened to it ring eight times before it was finally picked up. No one spoke for the first few seconds, and Willis could clearly hear loud voices screaming in the background.

"Com...this is Officer Barber."

Willis frowned. He had met Officer Barber once in the mess hall. The word "prick" instantly came to mind.

"Yeah, Barber. This is Mack Willis in the main tower. Juice is out here. What the hell's with the generator's not kicking in?"

He could barely hear Barber's response over the yelling and commotion in the background.

"...not sure. I'm trying to get an outside line to get some more maintenance help in here. Just hold your horses, Willis."

"Maybe we ought to be issued candles when we come on shift, what do ya think? Where's the Captain?"

He could hear Barber yelling at someone nearby, obviously paying no attention to what he was saying.

Mack could feel his face turning red as his blood pressure rose.

"Barber, where the hell is the Captain? A herd of armed elephants just crashed through the main gate. You get that, man? "

There was a pause, then Willis jumped back as a loud pop rang out from the other end before the line went completely silent. He attempted to hang up and re-contact Barber, but got nothing but dead air. He stood and walked over to the window, looking in the direction of the main entrance to the prison, which held the com center at its core. Not even the slightest of glimmers was visible.

There were lamps set up on thick metal poles all around the fence perimeter that were activated by the darkness. Those lamps had gone out sometime after the fog had rolled in. Willis noticed the fog now engulfed the bottom three feet of the prison grounds like a layer of solidifying soup. The pure whiteness of the fog provided the only break in the darkness. Feeling the hair on his arms standing out like pine needles, Willis again gripped the phone in desperation, slamming it down in frustration a moment later.

"Totally unreal. What a goat-rope. Fourteen years and I've never seen anything like it," he whispered to himself, unconsciously holding his rifle tighter against his chest. The rule was specific in its language: a sentry WILL NOT leave the tower post under ANY circumstance, to include a riot situation. It was something that was pounded into your brain from the first day of training. Willis sat in the silent blackness feeling the frustration of a man caught between the proverbial 'rock and a hard place'. The tower was as close to being 'soundproof' as any building not designed as such. The thick brick design did not allow much in the way of distractions from the outside. He looked over the sections of the unit that were in his line of sight for any movement or light. Two minutes passed before he retried the phone, and was again greeted with an eerie silence. He had never known the Com lines to go down, not even in the worst of winter snows or summer thunderstorms. Willis took another quick peek out, then sighed deeply and headed for the stairs.

After locking the entrance to the Tower while departing (and not being really sure why he even bothered), Willis strolled into the fog, which now seemed to be engulfing the entire prison site, then walked towards the main entrance. The fog was as thick as any he could ever remember seeing, and was positioned from his ankles to what he thought to be at least a few feet over his head. He practically ran into the fence before he saw it. Willis knew whoever was manning the main gate was also without visibility, so he didn't even bother to ring the gate buzzer just outside the fence. He used his pass key and double checked it's security before strolling cautiously towards the guard shack.

Willis ducked cautiously into the shack, a fresh group of obscenities preparing to escape his mouth to whoever was unfortunate enough to be on duty to endure them, when he froze at the entrance with his mouth still agape. He felt the pulse at his temples pound as the magnitude of the situation began to sink in. The shack was deserted, it's phone off the hook and silent, the controls to the gate unattended for anyone to utilize.

Despite the cool temperature, Willis felt a bead of warm sweat roll down his neck onto his upper chest. He picked up the dead phone line just to insure it hadn't simply been accidentally left off the hook, and got the same silent treatment his own hotline had provided in the tower. He scanned the small room for the two-way radio that the guard was required to keep in the shack in case of phone problems but found nothing laying on the guards workstation save a half-empty Mountain Dew can and an open copy of Sports Illustrated magazine. There was even a half-eaten Snickers bar sitting near the discarded phone. "Somebody left in mid-bite. This ain't good, Mack, not good... certainly not right."

Willis checked his rifle to make sure it was

locked and loaded, then exited the shack with a nervous sigh.

What in the hell is this all about? Somebody tell me it's a sick practical joke. Somebody's gonna step right out here any sec and start laughin', point a finger at me and shout 'Mack Willis, you're on Candid Camera'. Please, please tell me that's it.

From the main gate, Willis trudged ahead slowly but purposely toward the front entrance to the prison. Next stop was the main Com center and hopefully, some answers. He checked the flashlight he had taken from the tower and made sure the batteries were still alive and kicking.

If it's a riot, why could I hear a canary shit right about now? It's scary quiet. There should be some screaming, hollering, or at least a grunt or two. This damn fog and the dark sure as hell ain't helping my nerves anyhow. Just take it slow, old buddy.....real slow and very, very carefully.

Holding his rifle at his chest in a virtual death grip, Willis almost stumbled on the first step up leading towards the front entrance. If not for the cautiousness of his steps, the blinding fog would have allowed him to plant his forehead directly into the glass door entrance.

As he entered the building, he instantly noticed two things. The fog that had enveloped the site was also, unbelievably, floating three feet above the floor inside the structure. Also, the emergency lights had flashed on in parts of the hallway that led to the Com center. It seemed about every other one was lit up, but the fog inside the building had prevented the floor lights from being visible from the outside. It was a short walk down a slim corridor that led Willis to the outside glass doors of the Com center.

Behind the bullet proof, foot-thick glass walls that held the controls to every cellblock and individual cell at the unit was darkness so solid it was as if the windows had been painted black. Since the only key to the Com center itself was always in the possession of the guard pulling the shift, Willis' only option was to ring the outside buzzer beside the entrance door and wait for a response. The center was soundproof, so he had no idea if the buzzer was being heard or not, or if the power outage had eliminated its use as well. After a nervous moment or two, Willis banged on the thick metal door several times.

No one home, Bubba. Maybe it's just me, but this shit is getting downright strange. Flashlight poised in one hand and rifle held tightly in the other, Mack kept a strained and deliberate pace down the corridor that led to the connecting Cellblock. Willis approached the gate to Block A and this time wasn't shocked at the absence of the guard who should have been on duty there.

He could see the guard stand with its recently manned look and the scattered paperwork, cola-cans, and ashtray that it held, but couldn't recall in fourteen years not seeing a person standing in the space behind the stand itself.

After once again finding the correct key, Willis unlocked and entered the east side of the cellblock. The cells themselves were further down the corridor. The eastside consisted of a community bathroom that held the showers, toilets and wash basins; a TV room with big screen TV and twenty

23

chairs, and a break room which sported pool and ping pong tables. The lighting was more sporadic in the block itself, and Willis now used his flashlight in a waving, circular motion to cover as much space as possible as he proceeded forward. The fog was still covering him up to the ankles, and he forced himself to lift his feet above it with every step to prevent kicking an unseen object that might trip him up. He figured he must resemble a goose-stepping SS troop, and the thought forced a nervous giggle from his suddenly parched throat. Whoa, boy. Get a grip....one small laugh can quickly turn to hysterics if you don't reel in your marbles. Where... the... hell... is... everybody? His light caught a fire alarm halfway up one wall, and he found himself pulling it a moment later. Not surprisingly, total silence was the response. "Good try, Bubba, but no cigar," he whispered, his eyes now focused on the gate entrance to the cells.

"Okay, I'll check A block. Whether I find anything or nothing at all, I book my butt outta here pronto, jump in my Ford and find a phone.....yeah, that's the plan all right."

Another nervous giggle threatening to escape his badly chapped lips, Mack trudged onward, his light cutting a narrow path through what was now almost total darkness. The cell doors were open, which was not unusual considering they were still a good hour from lights out, but the fact that they were completely deserted was more than simply unusual, it was downright macabre. Willis noticed one particular cell held an ashtray with a freshly burning cigarette intact. The cigarette had not quite burned down to the filter, but the two inch long ash

24

trail at the end told the tale. Somebody had laid it down no more than three or four minutes before his arrival on the block. For the third time that evening, Mack Willis felt blood run cold in his veins.

Okay, we have two possibilities here. Number one is that everybody is playing one hell of a game of Hide-n-Go-Seek, the other is that I've slipped on a banana peel, cracked my noggin, and what's left of my sanity has flown the coop. Jesus, now what?

Cellblocks B and C held more of the same. Willis hadn't heard a sound other than the far away creaking of old pipes since he entered the blocks. Rooms had that 'lived in' look, some with clothes scattered on bunks, others with poker cards half shuffled on tables, obviously cut off in mid-game. It seemed as if everyone had vanished at precisely the same moment, leaving objects just as they had been at that particular moment in time.

Yeah, right. Beam me up Scotty, been in prison too long. But, what else could explain this? They had to go somewhere. 500 cons and nineteen guards don't just 'poof' away......do they? Where the hell am I, the Outer Limits? Rod Serling's basement?

Willis walked outside to the adjoining building, which held the laundry room and mess hall. Both were as frighteningly quiet and deserted as the cell blocks had been. He noticed a freshly brewed pot of coffee sitting on a counter top in the mess hall, tendrils of smoke still rising from it in waves. There was only one area remaining to check on the site. Willis felt some of his initial fear turning more into feelings of pure puzzlement. He knew it wasn't a dream, but it had that feel. He realized somehow he was close to finding answers to the situation, and he didn't fear the unknown as much as he looked forward to the relief of solving the mystery. He half-jogged down the walkway that led to the open yard at the rear of the site. The exercise yard was one hundred yards long and fifty yards wide. It held two basketball courts, a large weightlifting area complete with free weights and nautilus machines, and a running track. Inmates spent two hours a day in the yard, some only there to suck down the fresh air, others to work out their frustrations physically. Willis was breathing hard from the sprint as he pushed open the solid metal door entrance.

He stopped cold in his tracks a moment later, his mouth agape. He had to pause and blink quickly a few times just to ensure in his own mind that he wasn't hallucinating. Once he was at least partially convinced he wasn't, Mack Willis stepped forward through the suddenly thinning fog at his boots towards what he had thought (hoped?) for a moment to be nothing more than a mind-bending mirage. The inmates were all there, or seemed to be at least generally accounted for as a whole.

They stood as if in military formation, facing him from the center of the exercise yard. The outside lights of the yard burned brightly, as if running off some unseen generator. They were all watching him intensely as he approached, but none spoke. Their eyes followed him as a child's might a blip on a video game screen. He ambled up to the first row of inmates and halted, facing an inmate he recognized from block B, Pierce Thomas. Thomas was a black male around six feet six and two-hundred fifty pounds of pure muscle and malevolence. His shaved head held a virtual roadmap of scars, born both in and out of the stir. Thomas was a lifer who had served the last thirteen years at the unit, and had gained somewhat of a legendary status for no other reason than that no one had ever reported seeing the man smile. Not once. He now stood erect, almost at attention, displaying a wide, toothy grin that seemed wholly manufactured. His eyes were bright and aware, and the first thing that struck Willis was that he was dealing with a man presently absorbing some quality chemicals of the illegal variety. Mack glanced around at the inmates on either side of Thomas, and they too were smiling and staring at him like as if he were a freshly cooked turkey on Thanksgiving Day.

Damn. They're all wired for sound. What happened here? An exercise yard pill party? Willis held his rifle at shoulder height; the barrel pointed at Thomas' midsection, and noisily cleared his throat.

"Can somebody tell me what in living hell is going on here? Why are you people out of your cells, and where are the other officers?"

Thomas laughed so suddenly and loudly it caused Willis to physically cringe back.

He brought the barrel of his rifle up towards the man's face, his arms visibly trembling with the effort of holding it in position.

"What the hell's so funny, Thomas? Suppose you let me in on the gag."

Thomas' wide grin faded with lightning speed, and was replaced by an angry scowl. "Why, you are the source of the humor, Mr. Correctional

Officer. I never saw you people in this light before. All the intimidation and fear you people dished out towards us seems a tad bit amusing now, that's all."

Willis heard muffled laughter from the other inmates, but it was in a low, harmonic tone that made him wish he was suddenly somewhere, anywhere, but where he stood at that moment.

"Enlighten me on something Thomas, before I take the butt-end of this weapon and 'intimidate' the side of your skull with it. Exactly where are the other guards that were on shift?"

Thomas stood silent, the toothy smile again frozen on his face. Another inmate a few feet down spoke this time, the tone of his voice mechanical, robotic, the words escaping slowly, almost as if rehearsed.

"They were taken for...nutritional purposes by our masters. We offered them the officers as a gift. It cannot remotely compare to what they have given us in return."

Willis felt a nervous tick begin to form in the corner of his left eye.

"Master? And just who might that be? The great pumpkin maybe? Who brought you all out here to the yard?"

Thomas responded wearily, his face now as solemn as a stone. His eyes were distant, like a man trying to recall the details of a hazy dream.

"Things have been changed for us, officer. Drastically altered for the better. The masters came into our lives tonight. They... smelled us here, they said. They sensed our despair in this place that breeds it like flies on a rotting corpse. One of the masters took refuge underground centuries ago on the site the prison was built on, right underneath where the main gate tower stands. He said he came to believe these very grounds became a beacon for them to rebuild their depleted forces upon. They promised to relieve us of both our physical and mental imprisonment. In the end, we knew we had no choice but follow their orders. A few tried to disagree and fight them off. They were like gnats trying to halt a raging bull elephant. I punched one in the face as hard as I could, a blow that would have shattered a man's face. He hardly flinched. I remember being thrown into a wall, then all I can recall after that is sweet, wonderful release." He stopped long enough to glare at Willis and grin.

"You too shall experience the same remarkably soothing relief very soon, Officer."

Willis stepped back, the rifle visibly shaking in his arms, his aim still trained on Thomas' forehead.

"Okay, enough of this horseshit. I want everybody to follow me back towards the entrance. You boys have evidently had a busy night. You obviously broke into the pharmacy first, and now it's waaay past your bedtime."

Willis started backing towards the entrance to the gate, but the inmates remained still, their faces stoic, utterly without emotion.

"Hey, am I talking to hear myself talk? Follow me back out now, unless you wanna stay out here in the cold wind for the next seven hours."

A moment later, Thomas and the two inmates on either side of him broke from the formation and quickly headed towards Willis in a stiff half-jog.

Willis stood his ground for a few seconds,

then dropped his rifle to the side and sprinted madly for the entrance door. He knew he had a good twenty-five foot lead on them, and planned on locking the door and leaving the inmates outside until he could find some help. He was a scant three feet from the door when he suddenly found himself airborne.

He rolled onto his side; his rifle still locked in his right hand like a vise. Leaping cat-like to his feet, Mack stood and faced his attacker.

Thomas stood only a few feet away, but it was a vastly different version of the same inmate from just moments earlier.

"What the hell...," Willis managed, the barrel of his rifle practically touching the other man's breastbone.

"Do not be afraid, Officer Willis, I am here to help you shed the misery of this life and begin anew."

Willis had dealt with Thomas on many occasions in the past, and the only words he had heard the man say during those times were 'sorry asshole' and 'bossy Motherfucker.' To hear this mountain of a man sounding less like a rap singer and more like William Shakespeare was almost as shocking as the physical change that was also now gruesomely obvious.

Thomas' forehead seemed larger now, protruding out over his eyes as if monstrously swollen. Willis was reminded of drawn pictures of cavemen in the encyclopedias he used to read as a kid. He also noticed a dark spot on the side of Thomas' massively thick neck. It looked like a hole had been dug there by a long, sharp object. Small droplets of blood had dribbled onto the man's T-shirt collar.

"Thomas, you're sick, man. C-come with me to the med building. Maybe one of the doctors can…,"

Thomas laughed again, this time revealing incisors that were not only at least an inch long, but so pointed at the end they resembled metal tools that had been sculpted with a steel file.

"No doctors there, Willis. Like we said before, the masters had a use for everyone. They took some for nourishment. They realized the inhabitants of this man-made hell had not experienced freedom of any kind in ages. They deduced we could be set free and do their work at the same time; as to better serve them. Since you arrived too late to depart with the masters, you will provide a different service."

Willis frantically backed up towards the door, but turned slightly to see another of the inmates standing in his way, his back against it, his arms crossed in a gesture of defiance. The man also looked deformed about the face and head, and as Willis whirled back around and saw the entire population of inmates walking towards him in a slow, meticulous gait, he saw they all had the same bloated, comatose look as Thomas. They also all carried the same brand; a small, bloody, dark hole on the side of the neck. Thomas took a step forward, and Willis fell back from the recoil of his rifle. The shot had hit the man full force in the chest, but the smirk painted there never departed his face. Thomas seemed totally oblivious to the large dark hole at the center of his chest or the blackish blood that slowly seeped from it in thick gluts.

Willis dropped the gun to the ground and ran

directly towards the door and the sentry that stood unwavering in front of it. He attempted a body block on the inmate, and instead found himself first violently throttled and then propelled backwards in a spinning heap.

Upon opening his eyes moments later, Willis found himself looking up at literally dozens of faces staring down at him. The mouths that belonged to the faces all seemed to open simultaneously, and the impossibly long, sharp teeth seemed to be sizing him up.

Thomas leaned directly over his Willis' head, spittle dripping form the tips of his incisors.

"Officer Willis, you should be honored. We considered letting you join our ranks, but have decided you can serve an even more special purpose. You will be the first. Soon the next shift will arrive at the facility, and they will be, let's say, the second course. You, Officer Willis, will be our virgin meal as we prepare for the true feast that will ensue when our masters return to re-claim this land."

Mack Willis had time for a single scream before the teeth bore down on him.

**

The lights brightened a bit a few moments after her last spoken word, and Laura Willis backed away from the podium just long enough to cough into her left hand.

"This was the story my husband told the authorities and later the doctors he was interviewed by. He had been found in the prison exercise yard, completely nude and barely coherent. The other officers that had been on shift that night were never found, nor were the inmates. It is listed as the single greatest escape in US penal history. I have my doubts it was a conventional escape at all. Not a trace of any of the missing have been found since. Nothing. How can that…possibly be? You see, I doubted my husband's sanity at first, as had everyone else he graced with the story I have just told. Twelve months later, my doubts have grown weaker. He pleaded to me each day I visited him that he was telling the truth, and lord help him, he seemed like the man I married in every other sense. I believe he did encounter a strange entity or entities of some kind, possibly… alien in nature, but obviously he is the only living human who will ever really know. At least…he was."

As she paused, the complete silence in the structure seemed eerily fitting. A student released a muffled cough, and it seemed to echo through the building like a thunderclap.

"Mack…passed away a month ago tomorrow. Actually, that's not the correct way to phrase that sentence in my opinion, he was murdered, plain and simple, although State officials claim otherwise. The medical staff said he was displaying "homicidal tendencies" and attacked one of the nurses. He was clubbed repeatedly, shocked with stun guns, and beaten senseless. He was in a coma for a few days before passing. The administrator of the institute stated that Mack was suffering mentally from violent delusions and physically from anemia and the beginning symptoms of an unknown virus similar to AIDS. I was kept in the dark concerning the autopsy, as the copy I was given I'm sure is a fabrication." Fresh tears rolled down Laura's jaw and she paused to wipe them with a handkerchief pulled from a small purse at her right side. She resumed after a heavy sigh. She seemed to have aged five years in the time it had taken to conclude the story.

"I...see Mack sometimes. He... comes into my bedroom at night. I look up and he's just... there. His smile is the same, but his other features seem bloated somehow. His fingernails are too long and... pointed. He never speaks to me in these dreams. Just stares at me as if to say "W-where were you when I needed you?" I've found I have no interest in seeing or...dating anyone else. It's as if Mack really isn't dead and I'm still waiting on him to walk through our front door and ask me what I'm cooking for dinner. I loved Mack, but I so want to get on with my life. I...don't know what happened to him and all those other people at that prison that night. No one knew but Mack, and I find myself believing his wild story more and more each day. The prison site was closed and has since been torn down, I hear. I refuse to drive anywhere near it. I want to move to another city, another state. But I'm afraid if I do...Mack won't be able to...find me."

She bowed her head and again wiped the corners of her eyes. She walked tediously from the podium without looking back out towards the crowd.

"Th-thank you for listening."

No one reacted for a moment, obviously not knowing how exactly, then a small group of the students clapped a half-dozen times before ceasing.

Doctor Dante met Laura halfway as he was making his way back to the podium and gave her a quick hug, whispering softly in her right ear.

He seemed a bit shaken as he neared the podium, rubbing his temples with both hands, but regained his composure as he stepped behind it.

"Laura Willis is a special, special woman, folks. She will reclaim her life, of that I can assure you. Our next speaker is Mister Jonathan Willow. Mister Willow is seventy-three years old and the oldest of my patients at the institute. He is a veteran of both World War II and the Korean War. He speaks slowly but very distinctly. Give this man the respect his patriotic past deserves. We would not be sitting here in the land of the free if not for men like Jonathan."

The man had an obvious limp, favoring his left leg as he made his way precariously towards the center of the stage. He was a large man with broad shoulders and a barrel chest, a 'Miami Dolphins' baseball cap pulled low until his eyes were barely visible underneath the bill. His arms were long and thick underneath the blue T-shirt he wore. He cleared his throat loudly before he spoke, his head tilted slightly to the right. His large hands hooked over the sides of the podium in a death-grip, the old man's husky voice reverberating loud enough to cause a few of the students to openly wince.

"My name is Jonathan Willow. I appreciate your time. I'm a bit of a rambler, so if I get to babbling on too much, just chuck a shoe at me and get my attention." A few of the students giggled at this, although some chose to smirk and mock them for doing so. The old man took a deep breath and began.

"My great Grandfather's name was Henry Willow. His wife's name was Molly. In the state of Kentucky and throughout the south those names are synonymous with murder and something much worse. My Grandfather and his family were forced to relocate from the south to the Midwest just to escape the family legacy. They found they weren't trusted, and in some cases were treated like circus freaks by the locals. I myself have been the victim of hounding by the media in the past twenty years or so, and have done my best, god help me, to distance myself and my family from my very own heritage. The story is not a pretty one, nor is it for the weak stomached, but here she goes...."

CHAPTER THREE
Served With A Little Grey

Something was slaughtering Peterson's troops. A few hours after Corporal Wilson didn't report back from perimeter duty, Sergeant Conroy and a few other men found Wilson, or at least his upper body, dangling from the thick lower limb of an ancient oak tree. Actually, more like 'impaled' from a thick oak limb might have been more accurate. This was the sixth man in the last three days found mutilated in the thick, hilly woods they had taken position in since the last battle near Shiloh.

Captain Wilt Peterson had never particularly liked Tennessee. Being a native of Kentucky, his neighbors to the south were natural rivals regardless of the conflict they now fought that brought them together as allies. They had been told to hold position until further notice by HQ, but he was teetering on making the decision to move the unit ten or twenty miles to the north, almost to his home state's border.

Peterson had been a carpenter by trade when President Davis called upon his fellow southerners to take up arms, and he could have never envisioned himself leading anyone into battle, much less being responsible for the lives of over seventy men. He had been discussing the bug-out with his second in command, Second lieutenant John Meyers, who now walked into his tent, his face ghost pale.

"Captain, the men have expressed to me a desire to leave the area as soon as possible...I..,"

Peterson waived him off.

"Understood, Lieutenant. I've decided not to wait on HQ for orders. I see this as a dire situation that calls for immediate action on my part. I won't let any more of my men get...butchered. Tell the men to pack their gear. We'll break down tents in the morning and head north."

Meyers sighed in obvious relief. He placed his mud stained gray cap in a chair beside the Captain's desk and sat down slowly on a table used for mapping.

"What... who do you think it is, sir? Union sniper squads?" he asked, the color returning to his youthful face. The Lieutenant was barely twenty-one, a recent college graduate from Officers candidate school.

This had been his first field test, and it was taking its toll. He was trying desperately to look older than his years, but his attempts at growing a bread and moustache were failing miserably. He looked more like a teenager with dirt on his face. "Not sure, John. I've never seen anything do that to a man, at least nothing human."

Peterson sat back at his makeshift desk, rubbing his worn eyes with gloves that had once been as white as country snow, but were now brown from dust and red from bloodstains.

"Had an uncle killed by a grizzly once. Hell, even the bear left more to bury. Whoever it is, I sense they are not killing our sentries to reduce our ranks, but for the pure evil pleasure of it, to send a message. My god, poor Randall had one of his arms shoved almost entirely into his rectum. What kind of man does that to another?"

Meyers stared at the ground, shaking his head from side to side.

"Wish we could find the bastards sir. I know this is the right decision, but Sergeant Conroy wants permission to set up one more search party before we leave."

Peterson forcefully slammed one gloved hand onto his desk, causing Meyers to jump back slightly.

"Hell, no! Yesterday's so called 'search and destroy' left Corporal Evans with his head peeled like a half-eaten grape. Conroy is as blood hungry as our unknown attacker! Inform the Sergeant to reel in his lust to kill and think about the safety of his men."

Peterson breathed heavily and sat back down. Meyers shrugged his shoulders and glanced out the slightly open tent entrance.

"My apologies, John. The good Sergeant is one of the better combat NCO's in the Confederacy, but his leadership and decision making skills are somewhat suspect." Meyers stood and saluted half-heartedly.

"Understood, sir. I will pass the news onto Conroy and Sergeant Mills. Bug-out at first light."

Peterson saluted back and reached for a cup of already cooling coffee. He knew sleep would be hard pressed to achieve this night, and hoped warm thoughts of his wife and children eagerly awaiting his return from this living hell would be enough to sooth his mind somewhat. He awoke with a small scream escaping his lips. It was still pitch dark outside, and he heard Lieutenant Meyers calling his name from just outside the tent. Still an hour or so before dawn, and another body had been discovered. He dressed quickly and followed the Lieutenant and Sergeant Mills, a grizzled, career soldier who had switched sides when the war had broken out, and who had seen more combat than probably all the men in the unit combined.

Peterson noticed even Mills looked a tad peeked as they strolled south from the clearing of the camp into the deep woods that surrounded it. Only a few other men were awake to accompany them, including a private named Vincent whose age could not have been more than fifteen years, and who looked as if he had just taken a quick trip to hell and was in no hurry to return. Sergeant Mills had to practically carry him along, half- pulling and half-pushing.

The small band of investigators were soon joined by Sergeant Douglas Conroy, wearing only his long john pants, boots, and gun belt. Peterson ignored his presence and kept his attention on the trees and thicket around them. He wasn't lost on the possibility that the killer might have set this up as a trap to perhaps snare the unit commander as his ultimate prize.

Conroy was still yawning as he checked the ammo in his pistol. "Who the hell was it this time? Did any'a the boys see anythin'?'" he whispered to no one in particular. Private Vincent shot him a quick glare, his eyes darting around wildly for a possible assault. Peterson ignored him completely, a tactic that he used quite often when dealing with the brash, uncouth, but undoubtedly combat savvy NCO.

"Goddamn it, what's goin' on?" he finally

screamed. Mills turned on him like a cat that had just spotted a rat out of the corner of its searching eyes.

"Shut your fool trap, Conroy! If they didn't already know we wuz here, they sure as hell do now!" he barked, backing the smaller framed man up a few steps. Conroy had a comical look of shock on his face, causing Peterson to emit a small giggle. He noticed the lieutenant also had a wry smile on his weary face. They continued on an uneven path through the eerily silent woods until Vincent suddenly halted dead in his tracks, almost causing Mills to fall forward from his own momentum. Vincent didn't say a word, just pointed to a large pine tree about fifteen feet to their left. He refused to go forward with the other four men, just stood with his mouth agape and his lips quivering.

Peterson and Meyers flanked the thick-based tree from the left, and the two Sergeants from the right. They all met at the same moment at it's rear, and the gasps escaped their mouths in an almost perfect harmony.

"Holy sweet Jesus," Peterson managed. Meyers took a few steps back, then to the left, the early morning coffee he had consumed only half an hour earlier now deposited in some nearby weeds.

Conroy leaned over the body, his rugged face set in a frozen scowl. "I ain't never seen shit like that done to a man ….ever…," Mills joined him, but remained upright.

"I've heard some of the Choctaw tribes further west are damn good at this kinda thing." Peterson finally managed to take a step forward and keep his gaze focused on the body. He turned back and yelled over his shoulder at Vincent, who hadn't budged a single inch and whose arm and hand were still set in a pointing motion. "Private, who the hell is...was this?"

Vincent paused, then swallowed hard. His eyes were deep in their sockets, his hair sticking out in all directions. Peterson thought he resembled a madman frozen into an eternal pose of stark fear. "Jim...J-Jim Avent, sir. He was tenting with me. He...t-told me he was goin' to take a shit...he never came back. Me and P-Private Lomax went out to see what h-happened...," He gulped hard once again, his arm finally falling back down to his side.

"Lomax f-found him first and high tailed it back 'fore I knew...by the time I saw 'im, I couldn't find Lomax neither."

Peterson glanced back down and caught a whiff of seeping blood and punctured bowel. It was a smell he knew only two well since the war had begun. He had seen heads blown apart by rifle fire, legs shot airborne into trees by cannon explosions, even a man's midsection sliced like a pig at a slaughterhouse by a sword's blade. He had killed in combat more than once himself, and had been wounded three times, but this was different. This was on a whole new plane of insanity. It made the atrocities of war look positively wholesome by comparison.

Private Avent had been stripped completely naked and skinned. Only his feet held any actual flesh. The remainder of his body was stripped like someone had taken a razor and slowly, methodically shaved it down to muscle and bone. His entire frame was a red, mutilated, pulped mass of ravaged flesh. Meyers leaned with one arm propped against the pine. His words came out labored.

"Captain, correct me if I'm wrong, but wouldn't it take hours or even days to do this much damage to any one man?"

Peterson shrugged. The fear that had gripped his gut as they had left the camp had been replaced by sheer disgust. He again turned in the direction of Private Vincent, who was now down on two knees, his chin lowered to his chest.

"How long ago did all this take place, Private?"

Vincent didn't look up, but responded "About an hour ago, sir. That's all. One...hour..," Conway grunted and turned to the Captain.

"Aw, bullshit. No way a man could be this messed up in that short'a time, sir. The kid has horse droppings for brains."

Mills joined them. "Sir, he came screamin' into my tent a little over an hour ago, it's true."

Conway grunted again and spat, only missing the mangled head of what had been Private Jim Avent by a few scant inches.

"I still say that's horse shit. That body..," The Captain cut Conway off and turned to Sergeant Mills.

"Sergeant, see that a detail, an armed detail, is returned here to retrieve the body. Have them bring an unused tent to wrap it in. We need to evacuate this area as soon as possible."

Conway was now facing the Lieutenant, who was walking back slowly the way they had come.

"Damn it, Sir, we need to find the low down sombitch who did this. They're playin' games with us and I don't like it one bit." Peterson, who had been behind the Lieutenant and Conway, ran ahead of them and stopped dead in Conway's path.

"Personally Sergeant, I don't give a rat's rear end what you like or dislike. You heard my orders. Help carry them out."

Conway kept his glance over the Captain's head, his hands trembling.

"Yes sir, Sir. Yore the boss."

Peterson stood his ground for another moment, then turned and led them away from the coppery stench of the recently slain.

Men react to stressful situations in different ways. Some turn to humor to break the mood; others prefer to sink deep into their own personal shells; and some let the frustration of the situation transform them into hostile, enraged individuals looking for a light to their inner fuse. As the camp itself was being torn down and packed away, Captain Peterson saw all these reactions simultaneously. A few minor scuffles broke out among some of the troops, but nothing major, and he ensured his senior NCO's were there to supervise every detail of the move.

It was in times like these that Peterson missed his last second in command, Lieutenant Casey Brookens. Although he thought Meyers to be a competent officer, his inexperience was a glaring flaw, but one Peterson did not fault him for, since he himself had worn similar boots just a year or so earlier. Casey Brookens had seen combat in Mexico and the wide ranges of Texas and Arizona while working as a US Marshall. He was a hard- drinking, hard-fisted, hard-headed bear of a man who stood over six feet five and weighed in at around two-hundred and seventy pounds. Peterson leaned heavily on Brookens' counsel and advice during his first few months as a unit commander. They had mapped out and fought many battles together in the mountains of West Virginia and the rolling hills of Alabama and Mississippi. Although totally opposites in personality, they forged a deep friendship over the year and a half they had been assigned together. Brookens was loud, rowdy, and strongly opinionated, just as Peterson was quiet and reserved. They played off each other well and the men sensed this and felt confident within their command.

The unit was being reassigned to what HQ considered a 'vital perimeter' point just a few miles west of Charlotte, North Carolina just a few months earlier. The men and horses were to the point of exhaustion by the time they reached their objective. They had been traveling for four straight days from just west of Memphis, and were crossing a large pasture surrounded by thick pines when the shot rang out so suddenly no one had time to react. The sniper had obviously targeted Peterson, but must have settled for Lieutenant's bars once the Captain's were too difficult to get a clear shot at.

Brookens had been riding just a few feet ahead of the Captain, and the shot caught him in the center of the forehead, sheering off the top of his head in an explosion of bone and blood. Peterson had fallen off his horse and ducked behind his fallen comrade. Another shot never came, nor was the sniper ever found. Peterson realized another inch of clearance and the sniper would have bagged a different quarry. It took all the will power he could muster not to weep in front of his entire unit as he held his fallen friend to his chest. He made sure Brookens body was shipped to his home in Texas and a military funeral with full honor guard scheduled for his burial.

Within a few hours, all wagons and horses were packed and Peterson waived them forward, hoping that along with the stomped-out campfires and fresh boot tracks, the trail of slaughter was also being left far behind.

Peterson had sent out sentries on all sides and in every direction. He wanted to ensure not only that they weren't being followed, but that they weren't riding into some elaborate ambush to boot.

As they traveled slowly ahead and the rolling hills began to flatten out, Peterson felt some of that morning's tension begin to subside. He glanced over to Meyers, who also seemed to be getting some of his color back. Meyers noticed his look and smiled.

"Captain, I can't deny I fell one hell of a lot better with that stretch of woods behind us. Where exactly are we headed?"

"There's a camp set up near a small town called Walker Flats. We'll report in to a Major Stone and give him the details. I'm sure they have plans for us from there." Peterson sighed and grabbed a quick hit from his canteen, then poured some over his parched face. He couldn't remember water tasting quite as good before.

They had been traveling for over nine hours, and as they neared the crest of a steep hill that was layered with tall, wavy weeds, Peterson halted the unit and waived Sergeant Mills forward.

Mills rode up quickly, his eyes instinctively scanning the area as he neared his commander.

"Yes, Sir. Getting ready to camp?" he queried, a huge wad of tobacco stuffed into his right cheek.

"I believe so, Sarge. Send out a few of the men to round up the scouts to the north and have them come on in, then send someone in to scan the area just past the hill up ahead."

"Will do, Cap'n." Mills started to ride off, then paused. "Sir?"

Peterson had turned away to speak to Meyers. He answered Mills without turning back around.

"Yes, Sergeant. A problem?"

"No sir. Just wanted to let ya know, we're all relieved as hell to be outta there...you know...where we were this mornin'...,"

The Captain grinned and looked back at Mills, a warrior of old who had seen many sticky situations in his time, and who Peterson realized was probably a little embarrassed to be admitting such a thing as fear.

"You know what, Sergeant Mills? I'll bet you and the men are not half as relieved as I am."

Mills smiled back, showing gaping holes where his front two teeth had been before someone's knuckles had done some unplanned dental work years before, then rode off quickly towards his men.

Meyers rubbed his eyes with his stained gloved hands and stared ahead as Sergeant Mills and three other men rode past them towards the top of the hill. "How many men did we send ahead, Captain?"

Peterson took a drink from his canteen, spitting out most of it before grimacing.

"Four. We had two sentries to the rear and one each to the east and west. They positioned themselves no more than a mile from our perimeter.

Damn, it would be nice to find a fresh water source. What's in my canteen tastes like it's been there since we camped in Huntsville."

"I'll have the men scout out for some once we set up camp," Meyers replied, "hopefully it will be safe to do so."

Peterson nodded.

"Right. John, I still for the life of me cannot figure out what kind of foe we were facing back there. The tactics they used would be more fitting for a pack of rabid animals than human beings, not to mention the sorry state the bodies themselves were left in."

"I've racked my mind about it too, sir, although I'd actually rather forget the whole mess. Unfortunately, I do have some death notification notices to write and mail off."

Peterson lowered his head and sighed. "I'll give you some aide on those later on, John." He looked back up after first hearing and then seeing Sergeant Mills riding back down the hill towards them.

Mills halted his steed and loosely saluted Peterson.

"Good pasture just ahead, sir. Large farmhouse ahead a' that. Talked to the farmer and his wife. They said it was fine with them if we use their pastureland. Hell, they even said they'd feed as many of us as they could later on."

Peterson nodded and gave the order for the unit to move ahead and start sitting up a stronghold. He felt like he hadn't had a good night's sleep in months.

The farmhouse sat at the far end of a spacious pasture, which had obviously been used for hay at one time, but was now being occupied by various species of weeds and grass. It was an all-log cabin with a fresh water well on its right side and a small plank barn to its left. Both structures didn't look more than a few years old, but the well itself looked ancient.

Peterson had rode up to the house with Meyers to greet the family who had so graciously offered their land for the units use. The man who met them at the door looked to be in his mid-forties, balding, and slightly on the chubby side. He introduced himself as Henry Willow.

He cheerily led the soldiers into his living room and offered them a cup of coffee.

"Let me see if the wife's got some water on the stove, men, then I'll let ya meet the whole blamed clan." He wandered off into another room, leaving Peterson and Meyers standing in the sparsely furnished living room.

"Nice little homestead, huh Captain?' Meyers started, acting like a man just proud to be posed under a permanently constructed roof again.

"Real quaint, yes. Makes me lonely for my own, actually." Peterson glanced around the room and took in it's simple decoration. Hand sewn quilts covered a fairly large padded sofa, and under

49

their feet lay a shagged carpet rug that covered the entire living room floor from one side of the room to the next, corner to corner. It was, in fact, too long for the room, as it was folded into layers as you walked into the next room. On one wall hung a gun rack which was conspicuously bare, while on another hung a large bear skin once worn by a very large grizzly.

Willow re-entered the room with a warm smile and two cups of steaming coffee. His wife, a thin, pale woman who he introduced as 'Wilma', followed a step behind and offered up two pieces of chocolate cake. Peterson and Meyers sat on the couch and sipped their coffee while Willow and his wife rested on an adjoining wooden table facing them.

"I do everythin' I can for our confederate boys. I got two sons myself. They're out back right now, be in directly. Yep, you boys are fightin' the good fight," Willow smiled through teeth that Peterson noticed were shaded with dark stains. The smile was also obviously forced, but it never waned, despite the insincerity. Oppositely, Misses Willow never spoke, but Peterson noticed she seemed to have a nervous tick that forced her to be constantly ringing her hands together. He tried to ignore these things as he looked over and watched Meyers practically devour his cake.

"What kind of farm you have here, Mr. Willow, if you don't mind my asking? I didn't see any livestock in the pasture," The Captain asked. Willow's grin grew larger, much to the chagrin of Peterson.

"Actually, we only moved into this little

homestead 'bout a month ago. I plan on makin' a go of it with cattle. I farmed corn when we lived in Arkansas. Done a' bit a pig farmin' also. Wanted to try somethin' new here, you know?"

Ms. Willow stood up suddenly and took a few steps back in the direction of the kitchen. "I have something cookin' in the kitichen. Cap'n, I would like to invite you and yer hand here, along with five or six others to supper tonight.

I wish we had enough for all, but I think that'd clear our supply." Peterson smiled and nodded to Meyers.

"M'am, We'd be proud to. I'll bring two of my NCO's, that's non-commissioned officers, also. We do appreciate all your hospitality."

Meyers added "yes, I'll second that. I haven't had a home cooked meal since Moses was a pup."

Willow laughed and stood up himself, patting Meyers on the shoulder as he began following his wife into the kitchen.

"Good, good. Hey, y'all stay right there. I'll go see what's keeping my boys."

Peterson rose to place his cup on the table when a loud knock shook the front door.

He glanced at Meyers, who shrugged, then walked over and opened it. Sergeant Conway stood in the threshold, his face covered with large beads of sweat.

"Cap'n, we found the north perimeter sentries horses 'bout a mile north a' here, but not the Privates that used to ride 'im. The horses were grazin' on some corn stalks, and all the privates' gear was still hitched to 'em."

Conway's eyes darted from side to side in a

paranoid manner that never failed to annoy Peterson to no end. He wished for Conway to speak in a lower tone, and reached to pull him into the house just to lower the man's volume.

"No sign of them at all?" Meyers asked, now standing himself.

"Nope. Hide nor hair. Sirs, this shit is getting downright scary, if ya don't mind me sayin' so."

Peterson glanced outside the still open front door, watching his men mull about in the distance.

"Let's not let this get out to the men just yet, Sergeant. It seems our unseen enemy might still be with us, or maybe not. Many things could have happened to those men. Do you understand, Conway? I don't want any more rumors started that lead to my whole unit driven mad by paranoia."

Conway took a few deep breaths and nodded agreeably.

Meyers asked "What about the other sentries we had out? Any report on them as of yet?"

"East and west reported in just fine, sir. Reported no trouble at all," Conway replied, looking like a man in search of a drink a tad bit stronger than coffee.

Peterson kept his voice to a whisper and leaned towards Conway.

"You, Lieutenant Meyers, Sergeant Mills and I will be dining here this evening. Do not speak of our troubles to this family, Conway. I don't want them thinking they are in danger by having us nearby, understand?"

Conway shook his head vigorously up and down.

"Got it, sir. I'll put on my best manners," he replied with a grin, causing Meyers to laugh out loud and even Peterson himself to flash an involuntary smile.

"Not sure that eases my mind, Sarge," Peterson quipped before instructing Conway to get back to the men.

A moment later, Mr. Willow came back into the room sporting the same unwavering smile. He was accompanied by two young boys who looked to be in their late teens; both of them about a foot taller than their father, but based on the perpetual grins on their collective faces, they were definitely their father's sons.

"Men, these two strapping youngsters are my sons, Willie and Bart," Henry Willow bellowed proudly.

Peterson and Meyers stepped forward and shook the boys' hands.

Before anything else could be said, Mr. Willow motioned for the boys to depart, and they shambled off with their shoulders slumped.

"Good boys, but I have to keep 'em workin' or their minds wonder. Have 'em clearin' a field behind the barn where I plan on plantin' some black-eyed peas and cucumbers."

Peterson picked up his hat and began slowly stepping towards the door.

"Well, Mr. Willow, we'll be back in a few hours. We have to go check on the troops." Willow smiled "Yep, I reckon you do at that. Well, you just prepare yourself for some good eatin' tonight."

As they exited the house and headed for the camp, Meyers turned his head towards the barn, paused, then turned back to Peterson.

"You smell something, Captain?" he asked with one raised eyebrow.

"Now that you mention it, yes. Didn't he say they were 'thinking' about some livestock? Smells a little like they already own some."

Meyers nodded. "Yes sir, something rank is in the air near the barn, but I don't think it will affect my appetite for supper."

"Me neither, John. Me neither."

A few hours later, camp was set up about two hundred yards from the farmhouse and the men were settling down to their own dinner of beef jerky, cabbage soup and tin cups filled with homemade grape wine. Peterson usually didn't allow the alcohol, but he felt a little guilty about the meal he would be consuming that evening, and decided the men deserved a treat of their own. He shaved and changed into a cleaner, more civilized smelling uniform, then went over and met with the other three invitees for dinner. He was not shocked to discover that everyone but Conway looked positively tidy and presentable.

Conway on the other hand was not only still wearing the same stained, sweat-swelling uniform, but also hadn't bothered to shave. He had bothered to down a few glasses of wine, however, and reeked of it as they all made their way to the farmhouse. Peterson didn't bother to say a word to him, realizing such an effort was a waste of breath.

He figured with what they had all been through in the last few days, even Conway had earned a break from being scolded.

Mr. Willow met them at the door before they

had even raised a hand to knock. The smile was still plastered on his chubby face, and again Peterson wished the man would cease flashing those hideously rotten teeth.

As Henry's wife put the dinner on the table, Willow and Conway seemed to be striking up a friendship, a development not surprising to Peterson in the least. Henry Willow sat with his elbows on his chin, head cocked slightly to one side, while being regaled in tales of Sergeant Conway's battlefield heroics. Sergeant Mills turned a deaf ear to it, since he had more than likely sat through each story himself a few dozen times.

The meal consisted of what looked like roast beef in country gravy, fresh corn on the cob, buttered muffins, and more of the same chocolate cake that had been served earlier.

Once the eating began, talk was at a minimum. Peterson noticed Mr. and Mrs. Willow mostly just sat and watched them eat while hardly touching their own plates. They seemed genuinely pleased in being able to simply watch the soldiers enjoy the bounty they had provided.

Only when desert was being ingested did Mr. Willow break the silence. "So, Cap'n, what are you fellows doing in these parts, anyhow?"

Peterson belched and excused himself with a smile. "Well, we're basically just going north for new orders."

Willow looked at him quizzically. He was studying the Captain's cake, which was the only surviving item remaining on the plate.

"Not gonna eat that cake, Cap'n? Molly made that up special tonight. Fresh and moist, it is. I see all the others are lovin' it.'"

Peterson looked around and indeed Mills, Meyers and Conway were all digging in ravenously. He leaned back in his chair and sighed.

"Not my choice, Mr. Willow. Allergic to chocolate, actually," he paused and thought suddenly *Molly? I thought his wife's name was...something else.*

"Where are those strapping sons of yours tonight? Surely they don't miss many meals."

Willow paused, his eyes darting to his wife and then back to Peterson.

"They...uh, had to go finish some work in the barn. They ate earlier." Meyers suddenly coughed harshly, then quickly drank some water.

"Sorry, must have blazed the wrong trail."

Conway almost swallowed his cake whole, and was in the process of reaching for his drink when he began to cough as well. A moment later it subsided, but his face remained locked in discomfort. Mills began to hack as soon as Conway grew silent. Peterson caught a glimpse of both Mr. And Mrs. Willow looking at each other, flashing brief smiles that faded in a single blink.

Peterson suddenly felt chill bumps form on both arms as his scalp began to tingle. Meyers was the first to collapse. He fell from his chair onto the floor in a fit of coughs and gags. His eyes were huge as his splayed fingers found his own throat. Peterson leaped to his side and was trying to turn him over in an attempt to punch him in the lower back, and didn't notice Mr. Willow walk over to the front door and carefully place a padlock through an inside latch. Mrs. Willow also rose from her seat and literally sprinted into the kitchen.

Peterson was frantically slapping his second in command on the back while watching haplessly as his two top NCO's joined them on the floor, both of them racked with harsh, choking coughs. Sergeant Mills had a thick layer of white foam on his chin and his eyes looked dangerously close to exiting their sockets.

Peterson looked to Henry Willow, now standing in a defensive posture in front of the bolted front door. His smile seemed impossibly wide, more like a child's exaggerated drawing of a fictional monster than a living, breathing human being.

"You son of a bitch. You've poisoned them. Why in god's name?"

Willow laughed with mad glee, grasping a straight razor at least six inches long in his left fist.

"Why else, Captain? There is the money factor. Money, plus all the rebel meat we can consume."

Peterson dropped Meyers, who was now breathing in short huffs, and reached for his revolver. He never saw Mrs. Willow standing at his rear, nor the rolling pin that she used to knock him to the floor.

Sergeant Douglas Conway, a veteran of countless gun battles, knife fights, and bare fisted brawls, crawled towards the front door with the speed of a wounded slug. He was pulling himself along with his right arm while attempting to pull a knife from his left boot with the other. Henry Willow giggled at the pitiful escape attempt, and calmly reached over and slit Conway's throat until the man's head was lying face up between his own shoulder blades. A dark crimson coating immediately flooded the front door in a fine mist. Mr. and Mrs. Henry Willow ignored the gasps and weak movements of Lieutenant John Meyers and Sergeant Perry Mills, and proceeded to dismember Conway with a bone saw, only pausing to lick their fingers periodically, their eyes glazed over with maniacal lust.

***

Peterson awoke with a scream. His vision was initially blurred but slowly began to clear, and he realized something warm and sticky had been thrown into his face.

A moment later he cursed the gods that he had regained consciousness. He was tied to a post in the middle of some sort of storage room or cellar. Henry Willow and family, including the prodigal sons, were standing a few feet in front of him, all seated neatly at a large round table. Their lips and chins dripped crimson; their hair matted down and slick. The table was covered in shredded, obviously raw meat, and they had their heads buried in it like competitors in a Cherry pie-eating contest. The thick, putrid smell within the room was unbearable, and Peterson turned his head as much as the ropes would allow and threw up.

Mr. Willow peered up at him and smiled. Pieces of ragged, half-chewed meat hung from his teeth in pulpy strings.

"Look who finally woke up, dear. Howdy Cap'n! How you feelin'?"

Peterson spit at them, his head aching not only from the blow he had taken but from pure, primal rage.

Mrs. Willow arose from her seat and carried over a plate filled with dripping raw meat and flung it at Peterson. The meat bounced off his chest, dropping at his bare feet with a sickening thud. It was then that Peterson realized with stark terror that he was totally naked and painted in blood.

"I guess the reb lost his appetite, dear," she quipped devilishly. Peterson managed to calm down enough to speak a half-minute later. "Why did you follow us...just to kill me? A few of my men?"

Willow bellowed, sending fresh meat flying into the plates of his sons, who seemed oblivious to everything around them. Their eyes were hollow sockets filled with no true human emotion. Peterson felt like urinating but found his bladder had nothing to release.

"Let me tell ya the whole story, Cap'n,'" Willow started, pushing his plate away and leaning back, his entire body drenched in fluids.

"The union boys were either gonna line us up and shoot us or use us as some kind of a 'secret weapon'. You see, they caught us in West Virginny munchin' on a few of their own, and it pissed 'em off plenty. But, there was a general up there that decided we could be...what was that word that fancy pants used...'utilized'...that's it."

Willow rose from his chair and walked to a corner of the room, which Peterson now deduced was a cellar. He recalled the living room carpet that was too large for the floor. Too big for the floor but perfect to cover soaked-in blood stains. His mind reeled. He knew he would die this night, but still found it strangely vital to find out exactly why.

"Don't feel too special, Captain Peterson. Yer just the third of many southern commanders we've...uh...had to dinner, ya might say.."

Willow continued, now removing something from a nearby wooden crate with both his arms.

"We been followin' your unit since North Alabama a few months back. Before that we dined with a Colonel Jenkins, and 'fore that, a Captain Banks in Macon. The yanks think takin' out the unit commanders, the leadership, breaks the morale of the units. Hell, we don't care. We just like the travelin'....the money...and the meat," he shrieked loudly as he neared where Peterson was bound, a large handled object grasped tightly in his sticky-slick hands. Mrs. Willow and the boys were laughing mechanically, as if on cue.

"We knew you'd run north. We simply followed your scouts, a tasty pair they were, by the way. The farmhouse was a perfect set up, don'cha think? Too bad for the old farmer that lived here, but hey, he and his wife were sadly expendable. We have part, uh, parts of them hangin' in the barn. That's where the boys do their best work, you know," Peterson finally saw clearly the object Willow held, the discovery of which allowed sweet release of his bowels, soaking his thighs in his own moist feces.

Henry Willow's ever-present smile suddenly transformed into a leer born in pure lunacy.

"I've seen them boys strip a body down in twenty minutes. I taught 'em well. Captain, most folks would call us freaks or ghouls. But I'm just following a family tradition of meat eaters. As you can see, the yanks desire to beat you rebs knows no morale bounds. Your unit will find the scraps hanging in the barn tomorrow, but by then me and the little family will be long gone."

He raised the sling blade high over his head and paused one final time. "Seems there's this Major down near New Orleans that is next on our menu. "Hell, I always was partial to Cajun food."

***

For just an instant in time, a bursting flash of light first present and then clicked off like a lamp void of burning oil, Peterson was staring straight up at a body tied to a pole.

The legs, arms and torso were shiny with a cherry shaded liquid that flowed downward in thick, seemingly endless streams. He focused on the naked, hairless chest that held a small scar just above the right nipple where a union bayonet had once pierced his own flesh.

The body had no head. The stump of a neck that remained gushed forth like an overflowing well spring. Peterson's eyes peered down before mercifully clamping shut for the final time.

He found no oxygen supply available to allow for even the most pathetic of screams.

***

The old man's voice broke as he had spoken the last few words of the tale, and he hung his head for a full thirty seconds before lifting it again.

61

"That story was passed on to me by my Father when I was nine years old, devoid of a lot of the blood 'n guts, of course. The reason he told me at such a tender age was to explain the reason I was constantly being teased at school and didn't understand exactly why. We moved from the south not long after, and I grew up and worked in the Midwest.

Henry and Molly Willow were captured and brought to trial in the town of Riggs, Montana in the summer of eighteen and seventy-six. They were convicted of thirty-six counts of murder and hung after a trial that lasted only six hours. My Grandfather and great Uncle were brought to trail a few months later in Cummings, South Dakota.

They were acquitted on the grounds that they were minors at the time of the murders. My grandfather was convicted of murder a few years later after knifing a man to death in St. Louis.

My Uncle was shot by Federal officers just outside of Houston a year later. He had kidnapped a rich heiress and had demanded a large ransom.

They found her cut up and rotting in the basement of the deserted house he was captured in.

My own son is, as we speak, waiting to meet his maker on death row in Alabama. He slaughtered his young wife and my two grandchildren with a pickaxe for no apparent reason. As far as my wife and I knew, he had never laid a hand on anyone in his life. He was a...gentle man, or so we thought. My wife passed on last year, as much from a broken heart as anything else."

The old man lurched forward suddenly, causing the podium to tilt forward a few inches. A few of the students openly gasped, along with Professor Carpenter, who leaped from his chair as if to attempt a mid-air rescue before halting when the podium steadied itself.

The old man groaned loudly as Doctor Dante helped him gingerly off the stage. A few of the students began whispering to each other as soon as both men were out of sight behind the curtain. Professor Carpenter shushed them with a finger to his lips before re- taking his seat.

It was a full three minutes later before Doctor Dante reappeared at the podium. His face was a bright shade of red, and his hands were visibly shaking.

"Mr. Willow apologizes for his abrupt departure. I have been treating this man for over two years, and he puts up a better fight against depression than most are capable of, and with a minimum of medication." The next speaker introduced himself as Bernard Winthrop. He was a chunky, middle-aged man who was balding on top and sported a thick walrus mustache.

He spoke in a slightly shrill voice and his words came out in quick spurts, the exact opposite of the elderly man who had just been helped off the stage minutes before. Several of the students were beginning to show the first signs of restlessness, despite the fascinating subject matter being presented. The man wore cowboy boots that seemed a size too large for his feet, and tapped them nervously on the wooden stage as he began his story. A barely noticeable facial tick caused his right eye to blink spastically every thirty seconds or so.

"Folks, I am here to speak of my only son, Barry. Barry committed suicide when he was barely twenty-two years old. My family misses and thinks of him each day, despite the fact that the incident took place almost eight years ago. Bear with me as I tell his story through the eyes of a man he considered a mentor of sorts...,"

CHAPTER FOUR
Top Gun

How do I begin this exactly? Let's start where all stories begin...at the beginning. The names Brooks; Clarence Brooks. I work...excuse me, worked as an assistant football coach, Quarterbacks my specialty, at Winston State University for six years. I graduated from State myself almost nine years ago. I quarterbacked the team in my junior and senior years. Pretty damn good, too, if I don't say so myself. Of course, being somewhat talented at the Division Two level of College ball is like being the egghead in a class of imbeciles. When the school offered me the job working alongside my old coach, Bill Rivers, and his staff, I just couldn't find a reason to say no. Lord, how I wish now that I had.

Winston State had been suffering through some lean years, with four straight losing seasons, including a 3-8 season the year before I arrived. Coach Rivers had axed a few of his assistants soon after that season ended, and I was one of the fortunate (at least at that time) ones hired to help bring back respectability to the program. Hell, the worst record we had suffered through while I was a player was 6-5 in my freshman year. Bill had been the head coach for fifteen years by the time I arrived to join his staff, and had taken the team to the Division II playoffs six times, but all the glory years occurred in the first ten years of his tenure. The athletic director, an uptight little bookworm of a man named Willingham, had supposedly hinted to Bill that either the W's started coming but quick, or the hiring of a new head coach might be on the not-to-distant horizon.

Coach Rivers assigned me to work with the quarterbacks and receivers, since he was leaning towards depending more on the passing game in the coming seasons. Winston State had historically been a team that depended on the running game, including the year I was the signal caller, but with the lack of success in recent years, plus the fact that Bill had recruited more for speed recently, he figured a change in philosophy was in order.

The team's fortunes didn't change right away, despite the new blood on the staff. We went 4-7 my first year back on campus, and 5-5-1 the second. It was during my third season at the school that a toothpick thin freshman Quarterback arrived on campus named Barry Winthrop. None of us knew at the time how drastically some lives would later be altered by this young man's presence. Other schools hadn't exactly heavily recruited Winthrop. At six feet three and barely one hundred and sixty-five pounds, he looked more like a member of the school band than a future signal caller. Bill had heard Winthrop had thrown five touchdown passes in a state high school playoff game a few months before, and decided the young man was worth a look. Coach Rivers drove down to the small town the boy resided in and reported to us that the boy was far too fragile looking, but he had shown good arm strength and running speed. He told me it was going to be my job to bulk the walking string bean up. When I got my first look at

Barry, I knew it was going to be a hell of a challenge. I came real close to expressing to Bill that he had just thrown away a perfectly good scholarship.

Mr. Winthrop and I got to know each other pretty darn well that first year. He didn't take one snap in an actual game the entire season, as Roger Dickey had a fine Senior season at QB, tossing sixteen TD passes and leading the squad to a 7-3-1 season, the school's best in seven years. We missed the playoffs by one loss.

Being fed a steady diet of high calorie, lot fat, carbohydrate laced foods, and also being bombarded with as detailed a weight workout program as I had ever put together, Barry managed to put fifteen additional pounds onto his walking-stick physique. I found the young man to be quiet, polite, and mostly soft-spoken, but he was also one helluva hard worker. He also had a competitive spirit that made me believe he would be the starter at Winston State by his Junior year.

As it turned out, he realized his potential a year earlier than I had predicted. He came to the spring workouts in fine shape, still too thin, but definitely with a more durable and solid look. He beat out the other two QB's for the starting job with his pinpoint throws and scrambling ability. Coach Rivers congratulated me for my progress with the young man, but insisted that I see to it that Barry bulk up another fifteen pounds or so before the fall.

Try as we did, he began the season at a too slender one hundred eighty pounds. Coach Rivers worried that Barry wouldn't last the season without suffering an injury. Behind Barry's consistent play, we got off to a 5-1 start that year, but in the seventh game he suffered a slightly separated right shoulder when he was hit out of bounds after a scramble. He had led the conference in passing at that time of the injury. He didn't take another snap that season. The offense went into the tank and we ended the year a disappointing 7-4, again missing the playoffs.

It was just a few weeks after our last game that year that Bill informed us that a Doctor Willard Rusman would be joining the staff as team physician. This took all of us by surprise, not at the man who was being hired, who none of us knew from Adam, but that the school would actually pay out the funds to provide us with a team sawbones. Bill told us it had caught him off guard, as well. He said 'Ol' Skin Flint' Willingham had come up with the idea, saying it was about time The Winston State Tigers 'joined the 21st Century' with their sports programs. Coach Rivers asked me to work with Barry during the off- season and once again see if there was any way I could add a few pounds of padding to his thin frame.

Despite the extra weight training and 6,000 calorie a day diet, to include various weight gainer and muscle builder powders and supplements, he walked into spring drills at an even one-eighty two. I just shrugged at Coach Rivers, who shook his head in disbelief.

Barry had another great spring, and despite his lack of size, I had a feeling he was going to have a huge season.

In our workouts together, I had finally seen Barry begin to loosen up a little. He had his goals, but playing football was simply fun for him, and the scholarship a way for him to get a degree in Business Management. The kid had his head screwed on remarkably straight...at that time, anyhow.

To say the least, Barry did nothing to ruin my prediction about his Junior year performance. He threw twenty-one touchdown passes and rushed for six more, breaking school records for most passing yards, completion percentage, and total yards by a Quarterback. The team went 9-2 and had their first trip to the Divisional Playoffs in almost a decade. Barry ran for two TD's and passed for one, leading the team to the second round, where we lost despite his three hundred plus passing yards. We ended the year at 10-3 and ranked 18th in Division II. The school and surrounding community had rediscovered their love for the game. Barry was named as an Honorable Mention Division II All-American once the smoke had cleared. It had been an exciting year, but at the same time, I had a foreboding feeling about what all had transpired behind the scenes.

***

It had been around mid-season that I had noticed the subtle changes in Barry. Some were merely physical. He had started the year at one-hundred eighty-two pounds and ended it at around one-ninety. Coach Rivers had been thrilled he put on any weight at all, especially during the season, when players tend to lose body weight. I had been a little mystified by it. Barry had started spending more time with Doc Rusman than with myself, and the good natured and sometimes downright shy young man I had begun to consider my younger brother was suddenly becoming more outspoken, louder, and a bit...arrogant. Now, I understand that confidence can be misconstrued as arrogance. I was a QB myself, and you have to have at least a little swagger about you so your teammates can learn to follow your lead on the field. But there is a difference between the two words confidence and arrogance. I initially chalked up his new behavior as a natural response to the success and attention he was receiving during his fine year, but it did upset me, nonetheless.

I didn't see Barry but once or twice during the off-season, both times in passing on campus, but he had seemed a little aloof to me. I felt some natural disappointment at our inexplicable falling out, but didn't dwell on it. As the winter turned to spring, the buzz around campus was that the team could be looking at an undefeated regular season and a top five ranking with Barry at the helm and a total of eighteen returning seniors.

***

I vividly remember walking into the training room the first day of spring drills and almost not recognizing the huge boned, thickly muscled individual who was in the middle of a low, muffled conversation with Doc Rusman. It wasn't until he walked up to me and spoke that I realized it was even him. His weight was now an astounding two-twenty, a thirty-eight pound gain since the end of last season. He was larger than every linebacker on the squad, and not far from sizing up with the offensive and defensive lineman. When I asked him how he had managed the gain in such a short time, he simply smiled, flexed his huge biceps and pointed at Doc Rusman. The Doc shrugged his shoulders and said Barry was just 'going through a late growing spurt' and that a regimen of jogging and aerobic exercise, along with a heavy dose of free weights and the right vitamins and supplements had contributed to the growth. To say the least, I was skeptical.

I approached Coach Rivers about the possibility that Doc Rusman was giving Barry steroids and the Coach blew it off, bringing up the point that none of the other kids had shown any dramatic growth over the winter, and they had also been working with Rusman on a specialty diets. Coach assured me that he had mentioned the same thing to Rusman, who had laughed it off, saying that Barry was just going through a natural growth spurt. A growth spurt at age twenty-one was a little hard to swallow, to say the least.

What our coaching staff witnessed that spring should have warned us of the events to come. No one changes into the physical monster Barry Winthrop had become over such a short period of time without some type of chemical enhancement. He was like Joe Montana, Barry Sanders, and Lawrence Taylor all rolled into one. When he wasn't running through or around our defense, he was throwing pinpoint sixty-yard bombs. I have to admit his amazing showing blinded me as well as everyone else on the coaching staff to the possibility of something not being quite right. After all, he had been a very good quarterback last year. It wasn't like he had gone from a total klutz to being the best quarterback in the state overnight. I think we all wanted to believe Doc Rusman's theory that the right mixture of exercise, diet, and supplements, along with the natural growth of his young physique, were the secrets to this incredible transformation. We all blew off the negative vibes we were feeling.

Barry was a becoming nationwide sensation by the third game that year. He had, in the previous two games combined to throw for over eight hundred yards and seven TD's, while also rushing for over two-hundred and four more scores. We had won both games by scores of 44-20 and 47-18, both over what were previously considered to be contenders for the conference title.

ESPN had mentioned his four-hundred forty-six yard, five-touchdown performance in the second game in their College Football Scoreboard show that week. College Sports Magazine had contacted the school to do an article on our super QB. We had even heard some NFL scouts would most likely be roaming the stands for our next few home games.

My personal feelings of happiness for Barry and the team's success starting going south the day prior to that third contest of the season. I was in the training room separating some old pads that had been piling up, and I heard someone yelling from the weight room. I strolled in there to check what was going on, and found the source of the screams was Barry. He was working out alone, something we discouraged due to the possibility of injuries when not using a spotter. It seems his wailing was out of joy instead of pain. He was jumping around and laughing like he had just won the Powerball Sweepstakes. I was about to ask him the source of his jollies when I glanced at the weight bench. The bar was bending at both ends with all the weight it was being forced to hold. I asked him how much weight that was, and he grinned at me and said, "Just broke my own record, coach. Five-fifteen."

I laughed at him playfully, and I recall his facial expression quickly changed from joyous to enraged. Before I could say anything else to him, Barry hopped back down under the weights and pounded them up and down one time. I just stood there frozen. I'm sure my mouth was hanging open. I didn't know what to say. Here was a kid I saw having a tough time benching two hundred pounds just a year earlier. Now he was lifting more than any of our offensive or defensive line players could ever dream of. I remember after he finished the repetition, he jumped up and gave me an arrogant sneer and said, "don't ever doubt my word, Coach." He left the room then, leaving me to glare at the weights still shaking on the bar.

The next day, a few hours before the game, I told Coach Rivers what I had seen in the weight room, and that I believed Doc Rusman needed to be seriously interrogated. He assured me that after the game, he would sit down and discuss the ever-changing physical condition of our star quarterback with the good doctor.

Barry was his usual spectacular self that

night. He passed for over three hundred yards and three scores, and rushed for another two TD's. We won going away, despite a late collapse by the defense, 45-27.

The following Monday, game film review day for all involved, Coach Rivers and myself cornered the Doc in his office. He once again adamantly denied Barry's use of steroids or any other illegal muscle growing substance, showing us the results of a urine test he had personally conducted on the young man himself a week earlier. I was skeptical about his 'personal' testing, and he must have sensed this, as he advised that we carry Barry down to a local clinic and have him tested there. Coach Rivers declined this offer politely, too politely for my taste, and as we left the office, I could feel the Doc's hot stare on my neck. He realized Coach Rivers would always accept the positive in such a situation, as long as Barry was All-World and the team was winning, it was only natural. I on the other hand did not trust the man, and he knew it.

A few days before our next game, Barry weighed in at two-forty. He was now fifty plus pounds heavier than he had been at the end of last season. He was bulkier and more thickly muscled than most of the linemen. The most astounding thing about the growth was, instead of losing speed and quickness, which is normal when you add that much pure muscle, Barry had been timed faster in the forty yard dash during recent drills than he had been the week before. Coach Rivers joked that if this kept up, we might think about letting him play defensive nose guard when the other team had the ball. I was not amused at the situation in the least. In fact, I was becoming damn worried.

I had heard from more than one of the other players that Barry's attitude and personality had taken a sharp turn towards psychotic since spring drills. They all reported his moods ranged from boy scout to axe murderer, depending on what moment you spoke to him. I could have ignored these statements, chalking them up to jealousy, envy, or simple personality conflicts, if it weren't for the number of incidents that had been brought to my attention by so many different members of the squad. I myself had noticed the changes, including the weight room episode, but had chosen to overlook them just as Coach Rivers and the rest of the staff had. I felt it was definitely time someone spoke to Barry about matters.

We won our next two games 38-13 and 30-24. Barry threw three TD's in each game, and rushed for over one hundred yards in the second victory. He was now getting some national exposure on ESPN, as one of their draft gurus had mentioned Barry as one of the top ten Senior QB's in the country 'that no one knew about'. What the rest of the country didn't see was how he was turning into a monster right before our very eyes.

After the narrow six point win, in which the opposition scored two late TD's on long pass plays, Barry had supposedly verbally abused the members of the defensive secondary in the locker room. Neither myself nor any of the other coaches witnessed this, but it was reported to us that he had used various profanities and thrown in a few racial remarks as well. Those were terms I just could not envision Barry Winthrop using. In three years knowing the boy, I had never actually heard him curse...ever. His parents were devout Baptists, and had reared their only son as such.

One of the targets of the verbal onslaught said Barry threatened to 'wipe up the floor' with the next defensive player that comes close to costing the team a win with a 'bonehead' play. This incident was the last straw for me. I went to Coach Rivers with the accusations and was more disappointed than surprised when the coach blew it off once again, saying Barry was 'just showing his competitive spirit'. I told the coach I believed we should take Doc Rusman's own advice and have Barry tested for illegal substances at the clinic. I just wanted to make sure. He reluctantly agreed, but the test would be done only after the next game was completed, since it was only two days away and he thought a distraction to Barry this late in the week might hamper his performance. I had no choice but to agree to this.

Barry went off on his receivers the day before our sixth game, going as far as to punch one of them in the chest. It took half the offensive line to drag him off the poor guy, who was approximately half his size. Things were getting nasty.

With pro scouts supposedly scattered throughout the stands, Barry didn't disappoint. He threw four touchdown passes, one a perfectly thrown seventy yard bomb between two defenders, and ran for the winning TD with a minute to play. The 37-31 win gave us our first 7-0 start in twelve years. As it turned out, there were more fireworks in the pressroom after the game than in the contest itself. Barry got upset with one of the local newspaper reporter's questions, something about the added pressure of being a nationwide prospect, and could a 'hillbilly' boy like himself handle it.

Before anyone could even react, Barry had picked the guy up and heaved him over a couple of tables. Coach Rivers somehow convinced the guy not to press assault charges. Our temperamental star's steroid test was only a few days away.

Barry was visibly upset with our request for the test, but he went through the motions. I was more than a little shocked when the test came back negative. Again, Coach Rivers just seemed relieved.

The whole town was alive with the talk of the team. A lot of folks, myself included, thought we had a damn good chance to go far in the playoffs, maybe all the way to the finals. Our pass defense was suspect, but the explosiveness of the offense seemed to make up for it. My only worry was the guy behind the center. Mr.' All-American Psycho' was what a few of the other players had labeled him. They laughed when they said it, but a bit nervously. I had serious doubts that Barry would finish the season, and I wasn't sure exactly why I felt that way.

We rolled the next week, 43-4. Barry left the game early in the fourth quarter with the team ahead 36-7. He had put in another flawless performance, with three-hundred sixteen yards through the air and seventy-two more on the ground. He had three TD passes in the first half, and added a fourth in the third quarter. There was a sour note to the win, however.

Barry apparently didn't appreciate Coach

Rivers 'saving him' for the next game and taking him out early, and passed that opinion on to several teammates in the locker room after the game. A couple of the players had told me Barry had called Coach Rivers a 'stupid asshole' who 'wouldn't be shit without him'. He had also stated that if the coach dared to take him out of another contest early, Barry would see to it he 'lose his job'. A year earlier, I would have laughed at the possibility that Barry would say those things. A few months ago I would have seriously doubted it. At the particular time I was told of the comments, however, I had no reason to doubt the sources.

I found out just how 'over the edge' our star player was just a few days later. I was sitting in with the offense as they watched films from the previous game. After one particular play was rerun in which Barry was forced out of the pocket and sacked for a loss, he leaped from his seat in front of the screen and began belittling the offensive line, calling them 'lazy, untalented shit-heads' right in front of myself and Coach Rivers. Perry Hutchins, an all-conference guard the last two years, took exception to the insults and got in Barry's face. Let me tell you, Perry is one big dude, at least two-hundred fifty pounds of solid muscle, and Barry Winthrop tossed him into the air like so much confetti. It took four other players and me to restrain Barry from continuing the assault. I told Coach Rivers I was going to have myself a little one-on-one counseling session with Mr. Star QB.

***

I sat Barry down in my office and asked him if he was experiencing any problems at home like pressure over his grades, etc. He told me, with a demeanor as calm as I had seen him display in quite some time, that no, it was probably just the fact that his main priority was to get this team to the playoffs and keep them on a roll. He stated that it was possible that he was beginning to let all the outside pressures and small distractions get to him. I spoke with Barry for over forty-five minutes, covering everything from how to deal with scouts to how things were going between himself and Kelli Willis, the girl he had been dating for the past six months. When he left my office that afternoon, I had no idea that the pleasant young man I had just been calmly shooting the breeze with was, in fact, a ticking time-bomb with a very short and frazzled fuse.

The next morning, I discovered two tires on my Monte Carlo slashed. I didn't think anything about it at the time, but now I am almost positive that Barry was responsible for the vandalism. After all that's happened since, there was no doubt he was capable of much, much worse.

The team went to 9-0 the next week after a 35-9 win. Barry tossed three more TD's, one of which was a school record eighty-seven yarder. Despite some reservations from Coach Rivers, he also took every snap from center. We blew out the next opponent also, 51-10, and the Winston State Tigers were 10-0 for the first time in over twenty-three years.

Our next game was against bitter state rival Western University. That game was easily the toughest on the schedule, as it was most years, and one more win was all that stood between us and a perfect regular season. Western had defeated us four years running, including a 23-21 squeaker in the last meeting. They came into this year's contest with a solid 8-1-1 record, and featured a three-time Division II All-American at linebacker named Marcus Lewis, Who had, during the tension filled week before the game, had 'guaranteed' a win for Western. Lewis had also told a local TV reporter, in a clip the whole team was shown repeatedly after that Thursday's practice, that Winston's vaunted offense was 'overrated' and specifically that Barry Winthrop was a 'mediocre showboat' who 'obviously was more concerned about padding his stats than winning big games'. I recall glancing over a Barry as he viewed the clip.

Although his expression remained calm, his entire face had turned a deep shade of red, and the veins at his forehead throbbed visibly.

The team was hyped, wired to the gills, and ready for action by game day. The local media had proclaimed the game the biggest between the two rival schools in a dozen years. We knew the team already had a slot in the playoffs, but remaining undefeated was our goal, plus the thought of our only loss being to Western might send us into the first round of the playoffs on a downer that would be hard to recover from. Western desperately needed the win to qualify for a playoff slot. The excitement as we entered our packed stadium was positively electric, more so than any game I could remember as a player or a coach. None of us attending that game had any idea that within a few hours, we would wish to be somewhere, anywhere else.

I met with Barry, as was our pre-game ritual, a few minutes before the opening kickoff to go over the first page of plays we would be using. He seemed his usual stoic, game day self, his face frozen in a determined state of combat readiness. I really didn't think much about the large band-aide that covered the bridge of his nose. I guess I just figured he had taken a shot in practice the day before. I wish now that I had at least asked him about it.

Western jumped on us right from the start, intercepting Barry's third pass of the game and returning it for a touchdown. They drove eighty yards on their first offensive drive, and we were down fourteen to zip after only seven minutes of play. Our offense got clicking in the second quarter, and Barry's one yard Quarterback sneak cut Western's lead to 20-10 at halftime.

Barry had taken quite a beating in the first half. He had been sacked three times already, twice by Marcus Lewis, who should have drawn more than one unsportsmanlike conduct call for his taunting displays and late hits. I went over a few new plays with Barry in the locker room, and now that I think back on it, he seemed a bit dazed or distracted during our conversation. Hindsight is twenty-twenty, they say.

Barry drove the offense seventy-five yards in our opening second half possession, tossing a short TD pass to finish it off. After the PAT, Western only led by field goal, 20-17. Our kids were regaining their swagger at that point, the earlier

20-3 deficit already forgotten. Unfortunately, our momentum didn't last. A Western back broke a few tackles and ran sixty-five yards for a score only moments later. Suddenly we were down by ten again.

Things went from bad to worse a few plays later. Barry was hit by just as he released a pass, and it was picked off and ran back to our twelve-yard line. Three plays later, Western was up 34-17.

Coach Rivers instructed Barry to mix in a few running plays and try to begin a sustained drive instead of throwing every down, explaining to him that there was still over twenty minutes left in the game and that it wasn't time to press the panic button.

Barry totally ignored the coach, throwing his third interception of the game on the first play of the team's next possession. Two plays later it was 41-17 Western, and the game's outcome seemed sealed. Rivers was furious with Barry, the angriest I've ever seen him in fact, and gave the young man a pretty good chewing out on the sidelines after the last pick-off. From what I had seen, Barry hadn't responded one way or another to the bashing, just stood there with the same expressionless, distracted look I had seen at halftime.

We received the ball again, trailing by twenty-four, but still with a little more than a quarter to go. Barry began slowly picking apart the Western secondary on the drive, hitting five straight completions down to their eleven-yard line. He faked a toss and ran it in from there himself, and took another late shot out of bounds from

Lewis in the end zone. This dirty play did result in a personal foul being called. Some of our lineman went after Lewis on the sidelines, but I noticed Barry just took the late hit in stride, as if oblivious to anything but the scoreboard, and what he had to do to change its present state. This is what I thought at the time. Oh, young Barry had a mission all right, but none of us had any idea how sinister it was. We went for two and failed, still trailing at that time, 41-23.

Western received the ball as the final quarter began, but quickly went three and out. Starting from our twenty-yard line, Barry mixed short passes and trap runs to drive the team down to the Western thirty-three. From there he dropped back and found a receiver wipe open down the right sideline for six. Barry successfully ran in the two-point conversion, and suddenly we were only down 41-31. The crowd was suddenly going nuts again. The problem was, the last drive had taken over six minutes off the clock. Only a little over eight remained, and we would have to get two possessions for a chance to win or tie.

Western managed to grind out one first down, then our defense toughened up and held. We got the ball back on our own twenty-nine yard line with five minutes left. Barry threw an incompletion, then scrambled for fourteen and a first down. A couple of bullet passes to the sidelines gained a total of sixteen more. After a two-yard loss on a sack, Barry threw an off-balance floater that could have easily been intercepted, but was caught instead for a twenty-yard pick-up. I remember thinking to myself at that moment that I was possibly watching a future Pro Football Hall of Fame QB at work. Barry ran for six, then threw a short pass to the tight end for eight more. The team had a first down and goal at the Western nine-yard line with only two and a half minutes left. Coach Rivers called for Barry to throw a slant pass, a play that had worked consistently all year for us down near the goal line. Barry faked the slant, then tossed a perfect lob to the back of the end zone, hitting the halfback coming across. The kick made it 41-38. There was only a minute forty-four reading on the game clock.

Coach Rivers decided to go for the on-side kick, something the team had tried only once all year. We all stood motionless on the sidelines as the kick was attempted. I recall looking over at Barry as the kick was about to be tried, and seeing him sitting alone on one of the trainer's benches. I glanced away to watch the kick just as Barry was starting to reach underneath the bench, possibly looking for a new mouthpiece, I must have thought at that time. I try not to feel guilt that my instincts didn't snap on why he wasn't up on the sidelines with the rest of us for probably the most important play in his college career. What could have been so important to obtain under that bench at that very moment? I try not to, but so far, on most occasions, it just doesn't wash.

Miraculously, we recovered on Western's forty seven-yard line after one of their guys fumbled the kick away. A field goal would tie it, but this club didn't want to even think about that possibility with a minute thirty-nine to go. We still had two time outs and the best damn quarterback in

Division II. A short pass fell incomplete, then Barry scrambled away from a fierce rush and ran down the sidelines for seven. On third down and three, he connected on a short heave over the middle for twelve down to the Western twenty- eight. A time out was taken with a minute eleven left. Coach Rivers gave Barry the next three plays, and the young man, who showed absolutely no outward signs of nervousness in what was easily the most pressure he had even faced on the field in his short life, jogged back into that huddle with a look of total confidence. I could tell by the looks on the faces of the Western defenders that they knew the end was near. I recall even big, bad Marcus Lewis had grown silent since the drive had begun.

A short sideline toss went out of bounds for six, then another for two. On third and two, Lewis broke through the line and sacked Barry for a two-yard loss back to the twenty-two. Worse than the sack, our last time out had to be taken with fifty-three seconds to go, and it was fourth down and four. I stood on the sidelines listening to Coach Rivers give Barry the last play, remembering why I loved this game of football so much. After the play was completed, I realized I might not ever regain that passion again.

Rivers had called for a lob to the tight end on the left sidelines after a roll out, a simple but usually effective eight to ten yard pattern. It didn't quite go as planned, to say the least. No, what our young star QB had in mind had obviously been carefully mapped out days or even weeks before, and the perfect scenario to carry out that plan was staring him right square in the face. He must have been giggling madly inside his helmet at that moment. I stood right next to Coach Rivers and watched, almost as if in slow motion, as Barry took the snap and rolled out to the right, his throwing arm cocked back and ready to fire. He stopped abruptly in his tracks as the protection broke down on that side, and he doubled back quickly to the left. I watched him tuck the ball away and begin his jaunt up the middle of the field clear enough, but unlike some of the players who were just feet away from him, I did not observe him dig his left hand deep inside his uniform pants and remove the object he had stashed there.

When he was clear of the players that were blocking my view of him from the sidelines a moment later, I believe I actually thought I was hallucinating, that is, until I heard Coach Rivers whisper "what the hell?" right next to me. Barry had tucked the ball under his right arm and held the blue steel revolver straight out with his left. The first shot echoed through the packed stadium a split second later, and I watched as Marcus Lewis fell to the grass, blood spilling from between his splayed fingers as his taped up hands gripped at his chest. The remaining defensive players that stood in Barry's path were suddenly running wild in every direction, trying to avoid being fired upon. Barry slowed just enough as he neared where Lewis had fallen to his knees to fire another shot directly into the boy's facemask. Lewis' head snapped back violently, and pieces of plastic and bone sprayed out the back of his head. He fell forward with his arms and legs stretched out like a man attempting an Olympic dive. Barry stopped after crossing the goal line, spiked the ball wildly, then removed his helmet. The security people were still twenty yards away when he raised the still smoking pistol to his head and fired. The top of Barry Winthrop's head exploded upward, and his body collapsed like a puppet with cut strings. I realized a second later that unlike most people watching the drama unfold, I hadn't moved a step since the play had begun. The entire crowd fell silent at once. I believe everyone there thought initially that they were witnessing a very large scale, completely insane practical joke, then the reality of the ambulance's sirens kicked in.

Coach Bill Rivers knelt beside me and wept.

Doctor Willard Rusman broke down under weeks of interrogation and revealed that he had used Barry Winthrop as a guinea pig for a size and strength increasing drug that he hoped someday would 'replace' illegal and potentially dangerous ones such as steroids and be legally sold on the market. He said he had been working on the prototype for over six years, and that the animals he had used to test the drug on in his research had shown no side effects whatsoever. He informed the authorities that he had taken Barry into his confidence and assured the young man the chemical was perfectly safe. He chalked up Barry's personality changes to the drugs initial 'incubation' period, and had thought the effects would lessen and eventually subside within a few months. Rusman was sentenced to one year in state prison and lost his license to practice medicine. Most people, me included, thought he got off damn easy.

I thought the evil bastard should have been

tried for homicide.

They had found Barry's girlfriend, Kelli, in Woorley's woods a few miles out of town two days after his suicide. She had been tied to a tree with barbed wire and shot twenty four times. Ballistic tests confirmed that he had used the same thirty-eight that ended both Marcus Lewis' life and then his own. Twenty-four times, man. This means the young man reloaded three separate times. It's like he was using her body as target practice. It was hard to fathom. The autopsy on Barry revealed fingernail fragments embedded into the wound I had noticed on the bridge of his nose. It seems Kelli Willis had put up a fight before succumbing.

The media circus that surrounded the small town's tragedy went on for almost a year. The football program hasn't, and may not ever recover. The team volunteered to pull itself from the state playoffs after the Western game, and fell to 3-8 the next season.

Coach Bill Rivers had resigned only a few days after Barry's death, sighting 'mental fatigue'. I have heard he has since moved to another state and is retired from coaching.

***

I myself left Winston State also, just weeks before the next football season was about to begin. I'm the head coach of a junior league team two hundred miles away from my old college stomping grounds.

I still have dreams of Barry and the way he died that night, but the madness that covered his face the moment before he pulled the trigger is slowly, mercifully, beginning to fade from my memory.

I'm in the middle of working with a new quarterback at the moment. He has some raw talent, but is too damned frail. Probably can't take a beating unless he bulks up some. But, you know what? I've decided I like him just the way he is.

***

The lights came up and several sighs could be heard, as well as various fidgeting movements.

"My son was a victim of a doctor's lunacy and greed, basically. It's not a new story, but it is one that people always think happens to other people," Bernard Winthrop concluded, his hands tucked inside the pockets of his blue jeans, his booted feet still tapping to some unheard rhythm on the stage surface.

"I keep in touch with Coach Brooks. I cannot say the same for Coach Bill Rivers, however. He took his own life six years ago. His wife says that morning Coach Rivers was calm and in good spirits. He told her he was going fishing on the creek below their house. They found him on the creek bank six hours later, a bloody straight razor in one hand and a picture of my son in the other. It seems Bill never got over it either." The man winced as he paused, rubbing his eyes vigorously before resuming.

"We all have pain to endure in this life. You do not escape it, young people.

You may go most of your life without suffering by its hands, but believe me, your time will come.

My life was contented beyond my dreams before my son's death. Since then I've lost both my parents and my wife, who had a severe stroke two years ago and never really recovered. The Gods of Pain and Misery search you out and eventually, you will succumb. Hate to bear such news, but it needs to be said. I Thank you for your time."

Professor Carpenter stood stiffly, stretching out his arms and yawning loudly, setting off an epidemic of the same among the students.

The young man approached him from the middle isle, his face a study in determination. "Professor, I have to drain the lizard or we might have a flooding problem in here real soon," he said, a nervous smile covering his acne ridden face.

"Go on, Sanders, and take Bryant with you. He's gesturing like a madman back there and the expression I can read is similar to yours. Get back as quickly as you can, and next time lay off the beer before a seminar, okay? Smells like Miller Time in here." The young man's face reddened, and his eyes lowered as he strolled silently away.

A moment later a new speaker appeared; a low squeaking noise evident from the wheelchair as he made his way casually towards the podium. He was a rather large man whose wheelchair seemed two sizes too small for his ample girth. He had a black headband tied around his forehead and grayish hair hanging past his shoulders in the back. His red T-shirt read, in bright yellow letters, 'Don't feel sorry for me....God had his reasons' stenciled across his broad chest. He had a Fu Manchu style mustache that started out thick under his nostrils, but grew thinner as it made its way towards the tip of his scarred chin.

Doctor Dante followed closely behind the man, pulling the mic from its stand and handing it to him with a sly smile, then strolling quickly away just as the stage lights dimmed once again.

The man's voice was a horse whisper, each syllable of every word annunciated in a deep southern drawl. Feeling a bit embarrassed and strangely uneasy, Professor Carpenter felt a cold chill run up his spine at the sight and sound of the man, although he was beyond explaining exactly why. The Professor felt a sudden pressure in his bladder region and decided he would have to 'water some flowers' himself after this specific speaker's story concluded.

"Good evenin', folks. My name is Matt. The story I have to tell concerns my sister and her family and the living nightmare we experienced in the hills of Alabama about five winters back. We had one helluva storm hit that year, one the south and most of the east coast wasn't used to dealin' with. I ended up wrecking my vehicle and losing the use of my legs from frostbite, and believe it or not, I consider myself damn lucky. Sit back, get comfortable and I'll explain why…"

CHAPTER FIVE
Tundra

I remember like it was just minutes ago. My Uncle Matt stood looking out the kitchen window and laughed like a kid my age when he saw the first snowflake fall. He ran outside and started trying to catch the flakes on his tongue. Uncle Matt was kind of a flake himself, actually, but unlike my other two uncles, he was a kick to be around. He always went out of his way to attend my basketball games (although I rarely played), my football games (I never played), and even drove me over to Atlanta last year to see a Braves game. We haven't heard from Uncle Matt in about two days. I can only hope he found a place to hole up in, although I can tell by my Mother's face that the odds aren't good. Grandma is sitting in the living room with the hood of her jacket covering most of her face. I can still hear her crying inside it.

I've seen more crying in the last twenty-four hours than in my entire life up to this point. I try not to dwell on what is going to happen if it doesn't stop soon. I really, really wanted to reach my 16th birthday next month. I know I should be more concerned about my Mom and Grandma, and my sister. I wish I could be less selfish about it. It's weird, but I used to love the idea of a white Christmas or a good healthy snow in January to get out of school for a day or two. Now as I peer over the top of the double glass doors into the dunes of frozen white waves that entomb us, all I feel is nausea.

I had left school that day and had heard the rumors about a possible flurry late that night. Growing up and living in East Alabama, I had seen probably a grand total of three inches of snow my entire life. I faintly recalled being about six or seven when I saw my first flake. It had been a half inch that turned to slosh almost immediately, and my sister and I had tried in vain to build a snowman in the front yard, but wound up with what looked more like a 'snow midget'. My Mom and her boyfriend at the time got a good laugh out of it, anyhow, before it melted into mush right before our disappointed eyes.

On this particular day, there was a pretty good buzz on both the local stations and the weather channel that a cold air surge that was already dumping a foot of snow near Knoxville might dip as far as Winslow. Now, living in Winslow for a grand total of 15 winters (the last five or so I can actually remember), I had heard this song and dance before. My mom snickered at the notion when the local weatherman, Chuck Walters (the man had a toupee that resembled a dead squirrel parked on his noggin) got all wide eyed with the possibility of 'some accumulation'.

My hometown, Winslow, Alabama, (population 3,257 people, and at least that many livestock), sets only twenty miles to the west of the Georgia line, and eighteen miles south of Carson, which is our 'sister' city and biggest sports rival. Carson is a regular 'concrete jungle' compared to Winslow, with a population of around 6,000. I mean, we all knew they had 'arrived' as a city when they opened a 24-hour Wal-Mart Superstore and a brand new six-screen theater with stadium seating. Well, 'Chunky Chuckie' as all the kids called him, was spouting off that Carson might see as much as three inches of the white stuff by that next morning.

My best pal, Brad Prescott, who had been christened 'the elephant man' by our teammates on the basketball team, had clapped me on the back and remarked something about 'see ya next week' when the snow rumors had begun. Brad and I had started our own little club on the team titled 'Bench Warmers Association' or B.W.A, since that pretty much was our job description. Brad had received his latest nickname (they seem to change in junior high every other day) while undressing to shower after our first official practice a few weeks earlier. It seemed my pal had grown a few inches over the summer, and I don't mean his overall height. I can't say I wasn't a little jealous at his gain, so to speak, but all of us just played it off and planted the nick on him for our own evil pleasure. I had been hanging around Brad since he and his family moved to Winslow from Nebraska a few years back. A lot of the kids were getting on his western based accent, and I made the decision to take the poor kid under my wing and teach him the basics of 'southern speak'. It took him a while, but now he speaks with the distinctive 'Bama drawl, minus the 'redneck' influence that I always blame on Georgians, Tennesseans, or any other state the Crimson Tide plays (and mostly dominates) on the gridiron.

My pal was convinced we would be out a few days, even if only a few flakes fell, since the school board in this area of the country gets mighty nervous when it comes to busing kids in bad weather.

I may be fifteen and taking college courses, placed in the 'accelerated' class because of my A average, but hanging out with my so-called 'normal' friends has a way of bringing me back down to earth.

In fact, sometimes I wish I hadn't shown such 'rapid intelligence' back in grade school. I see the looks I get from some of Brads other contemporaries. They think of me as a nerd, an egghead. Sometimes I admittedly have to 'dumb down' my vocabulary, true, but I don't want to be seen as a freaky geek.

I told Brad to get his lunch ready and study for the Algebra test scheduled for the next day, 'cause the only snow we'd see was the thick dandruff that fell from Coach Mitchell's head.

Lord God, how I wished now I had been right.

My sister, Angela, who was a year older (but less wise, I oft said) than me, was asking my Mom if she could use the car that upcoming Friday night to drive to Carson. I saw the first flurry through the kitchen window flutter by just as my Mom was asking her what it was she needed to drive all the way to Carson for. My Uncle Matt had been standing over the kitchen sink and howled "Hey! Get out the shovels! I saw somethin' white come down!"

A moment later I was outside with him trying like mad to catch one of the slim flakes in my wide-open mouth. Matt and I tossed the football around for a few minutes before running back inside to report to all concerned that the flurries were coming down a little harder than before. My Mom barely looked up from the Sears Catalog she had been buried in. My sister was huddled in the hallway with the phone cord from the kitchen pulled tight (no doubt talking to 'Perry', the newest 'love of her life'), whispering as if discussing Top Secret information of some type.

Matt just shrugged and smiled wide. The temperature was supposed to get down to twenty that night, another rarity, and he thought we should check on some firewood in case the electricity went off. The fireplace in our living room hadn't been used since I was five, but I have to admit I felt a rush of excitement just thinking about the possibility of having to depend on burning wood for our only source of heat. It would be kind of like camping out indoors, something else I had never experienced.

My Grandpa and Grandma came over to the house about an hour later. They only lived five miles away up on Stone Ridge road, and had been coming home from a church meeting.

My grandparents were the only elderly folks I didn't feel uncomfortable around. I had spent time with them at least two days a week since I could remember, and at times it seemed as though we resided in the same house.

Uncle Matt, who was what my mom called 'In-between wives' lived between Winslow and Carson and raised and sold cattle and pigs. He was in his late thirties, had spent six years in the Army and traveled to places like Japan, Germany, and Greenland. He had brought a bride home from

Japan, and from Germany, and watched each marriage fall apart within a year. He married a local girl a few years back and moved with her to Mobile. After their divorce ('Inevitable. Had to happen', my Mom used was apt to say) he moved back home and started his livestock business. My Mom said Uncle Matt never had kids of his own, and that's why he liked being around me. I always thought of him as 'one of the guys' despite the age difference between us.

I wasn't exactly a 'natural born athlete', and Uncle Matt had been an all-county quarterback in his High School days, so just being able to talk sports and throw the ball around with him over the years at least made me more 'average'.

After my grandparents arrived and sat in the kitchen with my mom drinking coffee (a taste I cannot ever envision myself acquiring), I was inside my room checking out the latest on the weather via the Internet. Uncle Matt had left a few minutes earlier, afraid he might actually get caught on some slick roads on the way back to his house.

MSNBC.com was reporting Louisville had already gotten four to five inches in the previous three to four hours, and further north, it was even worse. Indianapolis had seen eight inches hit the ground in less than seven hours, and Wheeling, West Virginia was getting sleet on top of six inches of snow. The southeast and east were 'getting theirs' as one Minneapolis weatherman put it, obviously enjoying our impending suffering.

I sprinted into the kitchen to pass on the news, and was met by the same indifference from my Mom, but my Grandparents at least showed token interest, although I could tell they too weren't the least bit concerned.

I sat in the living room and switched from the local reports to the weather channel for a half-hour or so, until I heard my mother utter a word that rarely left her lips unless she was either enraged or had just burned herself by the stove. Her 'Damn, look at that' was followed by a low gasp from my Grandma, and a "Jeez, that's something all right" by Grandpa.

I jogged into the kitchen to see what all the commotion was about, and stopped dead in my tracks as I glanced out the kitchen window. Snowflakes as big as golf balls were sailing through the now pitch black sky and hitting the ground with a frequency I had never actually seen other than on a TV screen. I almost accidentally let out a 'Holy Shit', which would have done more than raise a few eyebrows, but instead substituted a 'Oh man!."

I ran outside and let the huge flakes land on my jacket in clumps. It was a mesmerizing feeling, but one that I would learn to fear and then despise a short time later. My sister ran outside a moment later, laughing and giggling like I hadn't heard her do in years, not since she became 'a woman' in her mind, anyway. There wasn't enough accumulated on the ground to make a snowball yet, or I would have creamed her. She was wearing a tight halter top and gym shorts, and wasn't wearing any shoes at all. I guess I would have considered Angela cute if she hadn't been my sister, but as it was, the only description that came to mind was 'snotty pain-in-the-ass'. She had gotten her driver's license a few months ago, but refused to give me rides whenever I requested them, which wasn't very often. She was constantly badgering Mom for the car keys to our very-well used Taurus, which had seen it's better days, but when it came to helping out her younger brother with a ride, it just 'wasn't possible'.

She looked at me and smiled, and I frowned at her in return. Unfazed, she danced back into the house, shutting the door behind her softly. Angela had a friend at school named Wendi Rhodes who I wouldn't have minded getting 'snowed in' with. I was standing in the middle of my back yard, the beginnings of a pretty good fantasy concerning myself, Wendi, and a deserted isle when I was struck in the back of the head by a mixture of snow and pine comb.

I turned just in time to duck the second object, and saw Brad standing at the far corner of our side yard with a shit-eating grin on his goofy mug.

I chased him inside the house, where he quickly waived at my Mom and Grandparents before running down the hallway to my room. I saw Angela roll her eyes at us as she walked by my room, and Brad blew her a quick kiss and winked. She acted out the 'gag me' routine with her right hand and disappeared towards her own room, and Brad collapsed on top of my bed in hysterics. He often told me how he would like to play 'hide the sausage' with my sister, and I usually ended up throwing a blunt object at his skull just to shut him up.

He had driven over in his dad's eighty-six Buick Le Sabre, a vehicle that was more rust than metal, with tires as bald as a shiny new basketball, and got the gas mileage of your basic RV. Despite all the cons, the big pro was that at least Brad had a vehicle to drive, unlike yours truly, who was still in the dreaded 'got my permit' stage.

We sat in my room and glared at the weather updates, which were getting increasingly grimmer as the evening went on. Old 'Squirrel toupee himself', the Chuckmeister, was reporting that up to two inches had already landed in Carson, and that what we were now seeing in Winslow was not about to slack off anytime soon. Brad clapped me on the back with a cheery 'told ya so' and settled back on my bed with the latest copy of Sport Illustrated.

I heard Uncle Matt's voice about ten minutes later, and went out to the living room to see what was up. He said he had gotten about ten miles from his house, and the snow was already slicking the roads pretty good, so once his truck started spinning on some of the grades, he turned around and headed back. Matt walked over and punched Brad playfully on the shoulder, and then both of them ducked and bobbed like they were involved in a heavyweight title bout. Brad had always liked Uncle Matt as well, especially after we all shared in a six pack of Budweiser that my Uncle provided one night last summer. Uncle Matt had sworn us to secrecy about the brews, which we had downed after helping him repair some fences his cattle had damaged. Since that day, Brad considered Uncle Matt 'cool for an old dude'.

As we gathered in the living room and watched the seemingly never ending cascade of large flakes glide towards the quickly whitening grass, Grandpa told us a snow story from his younger days. He said he had been working on a farm in Wisconsin, mostly tending the pigs and keeping the barn cleaned out, when a storm had moved in and dumped a foot on them within a matter of hours. He said it then proceeded to sleet for over an hour after the snow ended. After the sky had finally emptied itself out, he said the road out to the highway was frozen over like a rock, and neither horses nor man could even stand up, much less walk on it. He said six other hands and himself were pretty well trapped at that ranch, and had enough bread and jerky to last two days. He said on the fifth day the temperature broke, and by that time they all had to chip in to pay the ranch owner the money they owed for one dead and mostly eaten cow. He said he never remembered being so cold since, and hoped he never would.

A knock on the door caused me to jump slightly, and Brad razzed me, although I could see the visible goose bumps on his exposed arms caused by Grandpa's story.

I ran over to answer it, and was greeted by Angela's newest flame, Perry, standing on our front porch with a fresh layer of snow perched on his head, creating the illusion of a much older man. He gave me his best 'how ya doin', kid?" Eddie Haskel smile and then blew by me like I wasn't even there. The only dealings with Perry Goltz I had ever had was two years ago in gym class when he and another jock bonehead named Conrad James had pulled my gym shorts down to my ankles during basketball practice. They had accomplished this after screaming, 'check out the cocktail weenie' at the top of their lungs, causing everyone in the gym at the time, including the junior cheerleaders, to turn and glare at me. I don't think I ever have, or ever will, move any faster than when I made like Flash and pulled those suckers up so high I almost gave myself a wedgie. It seemed old Perry had forgotten that little jewel since he started dating my sister. Brad gave him a 'kiss my ass' glare as he strolled by him with the same stupid grin on his face. Angela and Perry made a b-line for her room, and Brad elbowed me and hugged himself while making kissing sounds.

A minute later we all gathered around the TV in the living room and listened to the local news folks tell us that we could be looking at four to five inches by morning, if not more. Schools in every surrounding county were closed, and Brad gave me a quick slap on the shoulder. They were now saying that Charlotte, North Carolina and Louisville, Kentucky were pretty well getting the crap hammered out of them with freezing rain falling in sheets, this after they already had six to eight inches of fresh snow covering the roads. Reports of electric lines down were already rampant in Kentucky, the Virginias, and the Carolinas.

Even our far neighbors to the left, Mississippi and Arkansas, were getting blanketed from snow that had earlier blitzed Texas and Oklahoma.

Brad and I goofed around playing Nintendo for a while, but I found I was too keyed up from the weather to really concentrate on anything else. My Mom suggested Brad stay the night instead of risk driving, and my Grandparents decided to do the same, despite their house being so near.

They would take the extra bedroom, and Uncle Matt would camp out on the couch. This left a slight dilemma with my old pal Perry, who was told he could sleep on the living room floor with as many extra blankets as we could spare. I'm sure old Perry would have much rather 'toughed out' the night in my sister's bed, but knew better than to suggest it, lest he get a broom handle upside his head for his troubles. He agreed to a spot right in front of the TV, and by eleven thirty we were all sacked out as the snow continued to fall in grooves.

Brad kept me awake for another half-hour by farting every few minutes, followed by hoots of laughter which led to even more farts. I told him to cut it out before somebody came in here and stuck a cork in his ass, which just made him laugh harder. He told me he was going to sneak into my sister's room and slip her the 'ten inch python' later that night. I shuddered at the thought, and hoped I didn't have any Turkish prison dreams that night where I was in a crowded shower and dropped my Irish Spring.

I awoke to somebody bellowing from the living room. After shaking the cobwebs out of my ears, realized it was my Uncle Matt's voice.

I put on some sweats and my favorite Crimson Tide shirt and duck walked out of my bedroom, noticing Brad was already gone.

Brad and my Uncle, along with Perry and Angela all stood at the living room window, peering out at various points from the still mostly closed blinds.

It was about the time I got behind Brad and

peaked out of the space he had separated that I felt my breath catch in my already parched throat.

There stood a solid white line halfway up the living room window. Now, the living room window sits about four feet across and two feet up from the floor. The window itself is about three feet high, so despite the fact that Mathematics, even in its most common form, is not exactly my best subject, even I realized what this meant. We had a drift of around two and a half feet sticking up against the front of the old homestead. My Mom stood behind me a second later with her mouth standing wide open, a grin of pure amazement forming at the corners. Uncle Matt was the only one that showed any real concern, since he had livestock to tend to back at his house. I didn't really know what to feel at that point. The initial excitement I had felt was transformed to a form of dread when I noticed over the drift that not only was the snow still falling, it was coming down almost as hard as when the heaviest flakes fell the night before.

Brad of course was beyond ecstatic. He saw a day of playing video games, watching cable, and employment as a professional slacker in his future. I heard Perry babbling something to my sister about somebody 'canceling the game' just as my grandparents joined us in the kitchen. Uncle Matt and I had brought in ten or twelve pieces of firewood the night before, but my Grandpa commented that an expedition for more would be in order first thing that morning. After a quick breakfast, which for Brad and me consisted of pop tarts and milk, we all bundled up and headed out into a winter wonderland that was fast turning into a winter nightmare.

Brad, Uncle Matt and I pushed our way out the back door, which had been pretty well blocked by the drift that had settled there. The snow was up to my knees as we trudged towards the storage building that sat maybe fifty feet behind the house. I was wearing high top tennis shoes, and felt the cold wetness of melted snow at my ankles as we reached the entrance. The drift that had settled in front of the storage building was halfway up the door, and covered the doorknob completely. Brad had a 'Power Rangers' scarf wrapped around his neck and chin, one he had borrowed from my closet (and of course I caught complete hell for possessing), and for the first time since the storm had started, I thought I caught the slightest glimpse of fear in his eyes. Large flakes were hitting all of us in the eyes as we used our hands to claw our way through the drift and get inside the building.

We only had one shovel, so Brad and I took garden rakes, while Uncle Matt also grabbed a small portable generator and an old oil lamp. We stepped carefully into the tracks we had made on our way to the building, and walked back into the house looking like three men who had just completed an Arctic Expedition to the North Pole. Perry was sitting cozily on the living room couch with his eyes glued to the weather channel. Brad and I joined him a moment later, and within moments understood his stupefied look. It was like watching a science fiction movie or a very scary episode of The Twilight Zone. The weather channel studio anchors looked shell shocked as they switched from one nightmarish scene to another. Milwaukee, Wisconsin with two feet of snow in the last forty eight hours; ditto Buffalo, New York; Detroit, Michigan with two feet of snow topped by a solid inch of freezing rain. These reports were horrible enough, but it was the ones coming from regions that rarely experienced Mother Nature's wrath that sent a cold chill down my already half-frozen spine.

Chapel Hill, North Carolina with a foot of snow; Little Rock, Arkansas with a foot of snow and two inches of sleet as a blanket. Over one-hundred thousand people without power in Shreveport, Louisiana due to ice that was coming down in 'spears' as one haggard reporter put it. Birmingham, Alabama was completely shut down due to reports of as much as three solid inches of ice on roads, and basically all of Tennessee and Georgia covered in sleet and ice. Our local station was reporting we had received ten inches so far, with no signs of let up. The meteorologists mumbled about 'massing fronts', and 'cold air surges', their usually calm, at times almost comatose expressions more alert and apprehensive than usual.

Our local guy, 'Old Squirrel head' himself stated that the ten inches were more than we had received in the last six winters combined. He said this with a voice cracking from both exhaustion and exasperation. I had a feeling he was getting a little 'squirrelly' in the literal sense.

Uncle Matt had been talking to Mom and Grandpa, and asked me and Brad to help him get some more firewood in the house. We had an old stack of pine sitting behind the storage building that I was sure had been there since I was ten years old, but it was all we had. It's not like we spent a lot of time each year preparing for hard winter storms. It was far too late to drive around looking for wood, so we would have to make do. I have to admit the 'pioneering' part of the situation was a fun thought at the beginning, but as I watched more golf ball-sized flakes fall outside, it was already a small thrill that was wearing thin fast.

About a half-hour later we reentered the house looking like triplet sons of 'Nanook of the North', and had managed to salvage three good armloads of at least decent wood.

The rest had been so rotten it had practically crumbled in our hands. Brad took the time to belt me in the back of the head with a few softball-sized snowballs. He also did his best to pee his name into the snow. Uncle Matt nailed him in the balls with a snowball just before he got his pants back up, causing my best pal to jump around like he was bustin' a move. I recall laughing, but it wasn't a good laugh. There was an underlining nervousness with everything I said and did. I knew I was not going to be able to shake that feeling as long as the snow continued to fall.

Brad, Uncle Matt, Perry (finally off his slacker butt) and I took turns shoveling the driveway. The rakes didn't quite work out, considering the first time I shoved one underneath a mound of snow and lifted, the handle broke off in my hands. It took us three hours to clear a path to Uncle Matt's truck, Perry's dented and dull Z-28, and Brad's Le Sabre. Mom's Taurus was parked on the street, and it took me an additional twenty minutes to sweep the drifts off of it just so it could be seen at all.

By the time the deed was done, a fresh inch of the white stuff sit where we had begun shoveling, and two foot high walls stood on either side of the driveway. I had seen such scenes in movies, but never up close. Seeing it in person was a whole new ballgame. The snow did seem to be easing some, or it could have been that I was just used to seeing a heavy, steady fall, and couldn't really distinguish the difference anymore.

We ate ham sandwiches and potato chips, along with hot chocolate, for lunch. Mom said we were running low on milk and bread already, and dangerously close to being out of an item that is absolutely essential to the survival of the human race, that being toilet paper. Grandma told us of a three-foot snow she saw as a child living in Mississippi. She said it took the town a full week to dig out of it, and remembered her family was down to eating stale crackers and honey for supper, and had to bring water in from a well and thaw it out before they could drink it. We all laughed as she recalled how cold the trips to the outhouse were. Grandpa reached over and gave her a gentle kiss on the cheek after her tale ended. Fifty-three years of marriage. Hell, I couldn't even imagine living that long.

Uncle Matt decided he had to at least try to get to his livestock, and we all watched him back out of the driveway around three that afternoon. We kept going outside and sweeping away the fresh snow off of our driveway trail, even though it seemed a lost cause. According to the locals, it had snowed an additional three inches since morning, bringing the total accumulation to over a foot since the night before. We watched some idiot wearing what looked like a windbreaker and a 'Jets' cap stand on a frozen, totally deserted interstate in Virginia and remark that 'this storm has taken everybody by surprise." No shit, Sherlock Holmes. All the weather 'experts' were spouting something about the unusual movement, or lack thereof, of the cold front that was inflicting the damage. They all agreed it would have to eventually slack off, but none made any predictions when exactly that would transpire.

The house was slowly but surely starting to resemble an igloo, and Grandpa was openly concerned about the weight of the snow on the roof, which had seen it's better days in a twenty-five year existence.

As we ate a modest supper of Chicken Noodle soup ('Only got a single can of spaghetti O's left' my Mom had announced), crackers and leftover fried chicken from last night's dinner.

I worried about Uncle Matt as Brad and I played a quick game of Madden NFL on my Nintendo. My mind wasn't on the game, and Brad's Redskins massacred my Falcons, 46-24. Matt had left over three hours before, and the phone had yet to ring. I knew there was a great possibility that the power was out up in the hilly country, but not hearing anything was still unnerving.

We got bored with Nintendo, and Brad pestered me to sneak around and check out some free porn on the Internet. I explained to him for the hundredth time since I got my computer that my Mom made sure the 'Kid's safe' block had been installed to prevent such immoral transgressions.

I glanced out my bedroom window and saw the snow continue to fall. It was like an old, tiresome rerun by that time. It was hard to believe how exciting it had been just to see the stuff coming down just twenty-four hours before.

Brad and I played the old 'what celebrity would you most like to have sex with game' as tedium set in. He always wavered between 'Jennifer Anniston', and 'Jennifer-Love Hewitt." My choice was, and always would be, the sexiest women on this or any other world. So drop dead gorgeous it made my chest ache just looking at her. Two words; Jennifer Lopez. I had seen her in a movie a few weeks before, and the music videos she came out with got my blood pumping so hard I thought I could literally hear it beating. Brad still held to the story that he had lost his virginity last summer when his family went to Fort Walton Beach. He told all the guys he met a DDG (Drop Dead Gorgeous) brunette on the beach that took him behind a pier and 'did the deed' with him. He said she had been 'an older woman', at least twenty, and that she 'knew where everything went'. I knew better, however. I had been pals with the guy far too long, and he couldn't bullshit me.

I myself had never even been close, and wasn't in that big of a hurry to rush things. I had tried pot once, and decided I could get dizzy and fall asleep on my own, so another try would be a waste of time and brain cells. I had gotten drunk once (four beers and a shot of tequila) after a pep rally the year before, and ended up barfing my guts out in the back seat of Walt Parks' brand new Ford Probe his lawyer dad had just bought for him. That boy hated my guts ever since, I believe. I wasn't sure I needed to attempt the alcohol thing again anytime soon, either.

We turned out the lights around midnight, and nothing had changed except the once cleared driveway was again underneath another inch of snow. A two to three foot drift had just about covered my bedroom window by the time I glared out of it for the final time that night.

When we awoke the next morning, we discovered there were no lights to turn back on. Since the temperature was reading a less then balmy fifty nine degrees at seven in the AM, it was obvious the power had gone off around three or four. It was twenty-eight with a wind chill of eight outside, so it didn't take long to start feeling like half-thawed beef when the central heat was cut off. Grandpa was already starting a fire in the fireplace by the time Brad and I wondered into the living room, Brad's hair resembling something out of "Bride of Frankenstein." Angela was sitting at the kitchen table yawning while Perry talked to his dad on the phone. My Mom had broken out the hot plate she had found stashed away in the attic the night before, and was slowly heating up some water for coffee.

Brad playfully ran his fingers through my sister's tangled hair, and she slapped at his arms like someone swatting at a bothersome fly. I saw her smile, though, and so must have Perry, who hung up the phone and walked over to her and began massaging her shoulders. I did the 'gag' gesture with my right hand and walked over to where Grandpa was attempting to light up some small pieces of kindling with a page from an old newspaper.

A few minutes later, the fire popped and cracked, thick smoke filling the rarely used chimney. I noticed with no small amount of terror that the kitchen window was pretty well completely blocked by the drift that had been building there now for a day and a half. I wondered why the kitchen had seemed so dark. The back door was only half blocked, so at least we still had an escape route other than the front door. I had put some fresh batteries in a small Walkman radio the night the snow started, and I went to my room to get it, followed closely by Brad, who farted loudly once we got there. I punched him on the forearm and pushed him away as he waived the foul air my way. I laughed hard, realizing what a true maniac I had for a best friend.

The local radio station was off, obviously shut down, but we picked up Carson City clearly. They were saying we got five more inches overnight, bringing the grand total to one foot, seven inches. The forecast was snow ending around noon, the announcement of which allowed everybody in the room to blow out at least one breath of relief before the bad news followed. The cold front was not moving out of the area anytime soon, as it seemed to be mostly stationary, but it was shifting finally. It was being met by a front of slightly warmer air, and that is where the problem was going to arise. All the freezing rain that had been to our east was now making a b-line directly towards us. The announcer, who sounded like he had been on the air for seventy-two hours straight, his voice horse and his words half-whispered, said we could see up to two inches of pure ice fall after two PM. My Grandma gasped and was quickly hugged close by my Grandpa. The next twelve hours were the longest of my life. Everyone but my Grandma took turns tending to the fireplace. By seven that night, we were almost completely out of burnable wood. My Grandpa, Brad, Perry and I had battled the ice cold sleet that hit our faces and hands and trekked outdoors about three to see if we could literally 'dig up' anything else to burn. We found seven or eight more logs we brought in to dry before tossing into the fire. We even pulled out a couple of old chairs from the storage building and broke them up to burn. Our nearest neighbor lived a good half mile away, and old Mr. Myers, whose face displayed a ragged, road map of wrinkles that had earned him the nickname 'Droopy' from the local children, wouldn't be much help even if he was closer.

The phone lines were still upright, even after the onslaught of the first icy rain, but were dead nonetheless by four PM. Not that it mattered that much, since Winslow Electric's line seemed to be permanently busy, and the Winslow Police Department, which consisted of four officers and three cruisers, weren't answering at all. The sleet had started an hour before predicted, and if you looked at the sky and saw it silhouetted, it looked like any other rain ever seen fall from a dark cloudy sky. When viewed on the piles of white below, you realized that miles and miles of hockey rink were being created right before your very eyes.

Mom tried using her cellular phone later that night, but it was dead and obviously we had no way to charge it. The generator we had pulled from the shed was fuel-less, thus about as useful as an umbrella in the eye of a hurricane.

I heard my Grandpa whisper 'Jesus, help us' as he stood a few feet from me looking out at the mostly blocked sliding glass door leading into the snow dune that used to be our back yard. Brad and Perry argued about whose turn it was to shovel the front drive, so I ended up doing it myself while Perry sulked in the kitchen with Angela while Brad played video games in my room. I didn't mind the work. It kept both my body and my mind occupied, and the inside of the old homestead was getting a little tense anyhow. I focused my thoughts on another Wendi Rhodes fantasy while I worked. This one included a warm, tropical island (accent on the warm part), a string bikini that Wendi filled out quite well, and a romantic island dinner by candlelight. A sudden picture of my favorite uncle broke into my thought process, flushing the rest of the Wendi fantasy away like so much fresh sewage. I prayed that he was okay, but it might be days before we found out one way or the other.

Perry had decided he was going to get home if he had to jog, although hoofing it through five-foot snowdrifts covered by a solid layer of ice for six miles wasn't exactly going to win you the Nobel Prize for wisdom. He seemed genuinely worried about his parents, especially his dad, who had a history of heart trouble, and the thought of the old man shoveling snow wasn't

114

easing Perry's mind. Angela begged him to stay, as did my Mom. My grandpa suggested he take plenty of blankets, a few milk jugs full of water, and some energy food. My Mom gave him a half box of Caramel Breakfast bars and four Pop Tarts, along with the water. We had eight jugs of water saved, along with two bathtubs full and a sink full. My Mom was nothing if not a woman who thought ahead. If she had been given any warning of this mess, we would have had enough canned food and bottled water to last out a nuclear war. As it was, we were almost down to using old copies of my sports magazines as toilet paper, and the water would last five more days at the most before we'd be melting snow by the fire and sucking on ice chips.

We did have a few cans of spam, tuna, and deviled ham. She had stockpiled a few boxes of saltines, and if a human being could live off Lays potato chips, we were set.

In the end, Perry bundled up like a man preparing to climb an iceberg, packed his vehicle with all the supplies we could spare, and hugged my sister like they were parting at a train station.

I gave him a light punch on the arm and told him to 'be careful out there', and Brad shot him a bird with a grin (out of Mom's sight, of course, although I'm pretty sure Grandpa saw it). Perry nodded at us and headed out. He warmed up his Z-28 for at least fifteen minutes before backing out. We had dug out a pathway for his tires, even going as far as shoveling out a pathway onto the road itself. He made it barely fifty feet before the tires spun wildly, sending him halfway into a small ditch off the shoulder. It took Brad and me ten minutes to dig him out and shove the car back onto the roadway, which was close to impossible to distinguish from the ditches on either side.

Angela came out and begged him to stay one last time, but Perry just kissed her on the cheek and slowly pulled ahead. We saw his brake lights dip out of sight at the bottom of the hill that led to the main highway a few minutes later. He couldn't have been driving more than five miles an hour, and even then was visually spinning as he dug his own trail through the virgin snow.

The unthinkable happened about eight PM. We officially ran out of toilet paper. The spam sandwiches we had indulged in for supper didn't exactly agree with my stomach, and I found myself wiping as the grinning face of Mark McGwire of the St Louis Cardinals greeted me from the inside cover story of a month old Sports magazine. Big Mac was my favorite player, but hey, a guy's got to survive.

Brad had been hitting on my sister during supper, even if Angela didn't notice. She seemed more than a little bummed out over Perry leaving. My grandparents tried to convince her he'd be fine if he just took his time. My Mom was making fresh coffee when I came into the kitchen and caught her crying. She had been staring out at the block of ice that now completely blocked the window over the sink. It looked like someone had thrown a coat of white paint over it, and even the six large candles stationed around the room did little to brighten up the area.

I hugged her and told her we'd be okay; a line I

was having a hard time believing even as I spoke it. She wiped the tears away quickly and played the 'strong parent', a role she had mastered since my father died when I was two. I saw the look of despair and hopelessness in her eyes, and I think just the sight of her mental condition put a large dent in my own well-being.

We lost all radio contact by eight thirty that night, with nothing but worthless static in the place of actual human voices. Incredibly, the sleet did not run its course. It had begun at around one that afternoon, and by nine PM, was still coming down with shocking regularity. My Grandparents said they had never even heard of a sleet storm lasting this long, and they had lived in Michigan and Ohio back in the 50's and 60's, where ice and snow were pretty much King from November to late February.

The house was becoming a live in freezer. The 'Bama thermometer in my room was reading a frigid forty-six degrees by ten PM. The one on the front porch was reading twenty-seven, and with the ice and snow turning the structure into a large wooden igloo, the temp had nowhere to go but down. The biggest problem was that we were running out of things to burn by the time midnight came around. My grandma was wrapped in three blankets with only the middle of her face uncovered. Grandpa was sitting next to her on the couch, his long arms wrapped around her like he was trying to protect her from an unseen attacker.

My Mother and sister were bundled up in every jacket they owned, and sat at the kitchen table gripping coffee cups with both hands. I couldn't understand how they could drink room temperature coffee, but I guess it was better than anything cool.

Brad and I were giving it the old college try, but the last piece of decent wood had went into the fire over an hour before, and we were down to burning magazines I had pulled from my bedroom closet. It was at least five or ten degrees warmer in the living room as long as the fire was burning, and we were determined not to lose the one semi-comfort we had remaining. No one was speaking. There didn't seem to be a hell of a lot left to say.

The snow and ice had the house wrapped in a tight cocoon, and the faint sound of fresh ice hitting the roof was barely audible in even total silence. I sipped some of the Java just to keep my insides warm, even though I have never seen how people drink the stuff consistently. I guess it's like beer or beef liver. You have to develop a taste for it. I had loaded my cup with sugar and half-and-half, so it was at least edible. I was always a milk or Cola man myself. At that particular moment however, I would have given the kingdom for a cup of steaming cocoa with melted marshmallows.

I volunteered to keep the fire burning until three AM, then Brad would take over until six, and everybody tried to get some sleep. Grandma and Grandpa lay on the couch, wrapped in each other's arms and curled inside various blankets. My Mom and Angela lay on the carpet about five feet from the fire. Brad slept behind the couch with his head buried inside his parka jacket's hood.

I burned everything from The Sporting News 1998 Major League Baseball Preview Issue to Sports Illustrated's '98 Swimsuit Collectors Item (that one hurt a little) over the next three hours. I realized in horror that it wouldn't be long before I'd have to break out the Playboys hidden in the back of my closet, and knew I'd have to burn those at strategic moments when Mom wasn't paying attention. Strange how your mind works. I mean, there we were, tittering on the edge of becoming human Popsicle's, and I was worried about getting caught with skin mags. The really scary thing was, what happened when all burnable material was gone? We might dig up enough stuff to last the rest of that day, but what about the next night? Even if the temperature outside shot up twenty degrees, which wasn't very likely, it would take a good three days to melt the majority of the tundra that had been built up. I remember wishing that Uncle Matt had stayed with us. Even Perry would have been okay. Safety in numbers, they say, whoever 'they' is.

I shook Brad from his slumber at 3:15 AM. He had been farting loudly in his sleep, and the entire living room was stale from the natural gas barrage. I took his spot on the floor since he had warmed up the carpet with his body heat.

I had a fresh pile of magazines for him to burn, and had cleaned out the fireplace to make room for them. My Mom had always called me a 'pack rat' for saving all the sports mags and newspapers since I was ten or so. I told myself if we survived this, I would never, ever throw away anything flammable again.

My grandpa woke me up around seven. I leaned up; feeling like a Mac truck had backed over me, then pulled forward again just for good measure. After a breakfast of pop tarts (the last of the supply) and Java, my grandpa announced his plan. Being that we were pretty well out of things to burn unless we started with household items or our clothes, and also that the food supply was running dangerously short, it was inevitable such an attempt was going to have to be made. He said he thought about it last night, but wanted to wait until the next morning to see if the weather was going to finally break. We could hear, if not see, the sleet still hitting the side of the house as we sat in the kitchen. The temperature reading inside my room was now forty-six, and it wasn't but a few degrees warmer in the living room and kitchen.

My grandma pleaded with my Mom to change Grandpa's mind, and Brad and I even volunteered to carry out his plan, but he argued that we were needed at the house. My grandpa was a kind man, and a sensible one, but once he made up his mind, there was no altering his opinion. He was going to bundle up as best he could and trek over to old Mr. (Droopy) Myer's house to see if there was any food or portable heaters we could borrow. With any luck, maybe Myers' phone was working. We seriously doubted anyone had power or a phone, but it had to be checked. The oil lamp we had pulled from the storage building was in working order if Myers' happened to have any lamp oil at his place. Another long shot, we knew, but at that point any chance was a positive one.

Grandpa put on an additional sweatshirt that I pulled from my quickly thinning out closet, giving him a total of four he wore along with two thick coats. He had worn his Wolverine work boots, with small rubber spikes on the bottom for 'extra traction' to the house, so his footwear was set. He pulled a full-face toboggan (again from my personal winter wonderland supply closet) over his face, and topped that with my junior football helmet, which fit perfectly over his long, thin head. By the time grandpa stood at the front door and readied himself to leave, he resembled something out of one of those old 'Mad Max' movies. He could barely lift or drop his arms due to the thickness of all the outer garments holding them in mid-air suspension, and the two pair of pants he wore gave his thighs that 'Hulk Hogan' look. The only thing held in his thickly gloved hands was a large thermos of hot coffee my Mom had heated up on the now severely over-worked portable hot plate. My grandma hugged him close for the five minutes or so it took us to tug open the frozen solid front door. We had to pour a pitcher of heated water on the inside crack to loosen the ice that had frozen it shut. It finally broke open, sounding like a piece of splintered wood hit by a heavy axe blade, and Brad fell backwards onto the carpet when it flung open, sending me into temporary hysterics. It felt good to laugh. Even my sister let a giggle escape, and I hadn't even seen her crack a smile since Perry had driven off.

We had to pretty much pry grandma from grandpa's body once he tried to step out the door. The sleet was still falling, but very lightly. Once I stepped outside a few steps to survey the nights damage (almost falling on my ass as I walked on what a few days ago had simply been dead grass), I caught the gasp before it escaped my lips.

I've seen nature specials on The Animal Channel and National Geographic that were set in Iceland, Greenland, and all the other ice burg spots on planet earth. They used to pan the camera to give you the full impact of just what kind of frozen hell some animals lived in on a daily basis and some scientists were insane enough to visit for extended periods. The scene I viewed from the front porch of my house in Winslow, Alabama made some of the shots I had seen in Alaska and the North Pole look like the Bahamas by comparison.

Everything, and I mean every single object that had been left exposed outside the house was layered, or maybe submerged was a better word, in two to three inches of solid, shiny ice. The pathway we had worked so hard to keep clear of snow was a hockey rink. There were only a few inches of snow trapped underneath the ice, since we had shoveled most of it away just before the heavy snows had stopped. Looking out towards the road, the only visible part of my Mom's Ford Taurus was the roof, which looked like a large piece of blue ice buried in a mountainous snowbank. The trees had been blanketed in heavy snows, then bent over to the ground by the coating of ice. It looked like a giant spider's web had been expertly spun over the entire landscape. The clouds weren't as dark as the previous days, and just the thought of actually seeing the sun sometime soon warmed me for a brief moment.

I had my doubts, as I almost tripped again just getting back through the front door, that grandpa would be able to make it a mile to our neighbors without falling and seriously hurting himself. I mean, the man was strong, both physically and mentally, but he was also seventy years old.

I pleaded with him (out of earshot of grandma, of course, who had went into the kitchen with Mom) to let me go instead. He just hugged me and said, 'stay with your mother and grandma', grinning through the toboggan with that familiar, 'everything's gonna be fine' smile of his. I hugged my grandpa back hard. He was a good man, and had been a father to me in a lot of ways. I tried not to let him hear me as a cry escaped my throat. I slapped him on the shoulder as he walked out. Angela cried out to him to be careful and to walk very, very slowly, echoing all of our concerns about him falling on the hard ice. My mom stayed in the kitchen, hugging my grandma and doing her best to convince her he'd be fine.

Since the windows were completely blocked, I periodically peered out of the front door to check on him as he made his way down the road. It took grandpa over an hour to half- step, half-drag himself out of my view, which covered a distance of probably less than one hundred fifty yards. An hour to make it a football field and a half. At that rate, it would be another two hours or so before he got to Myers' place, maybe longer. It made my head hurt to think about it. It seemed that Mother Nature had really shot us the double-barreled bird this time. I pondered how bad the situation must be up north if the south was getting massacred like this. I could only imagine New York City buried in sixteen feet of snow, or the White House in D.C. only visible by the top of the flag sticking up from fifty tons of the white stuff.

We had a lunch consisting of the last of the saltines and some slightly sour ham slices. I had brought in some fresh snow and put in one of the sinks to melt, so we still had drinking water. Brad and I would go out later and hammer free some chunks of ice to bring in. He told me he knew he was beginning to wreak under his clothing, since it had been quite a few days since anybody had enjoyed the luxury of bathing. I just told him he always reeked to me, and he tagged me in the shoulder. I know my pal was secretly worried about his folks and little brother, but to his credit he never let on. He realized, unlike Perry before him, that trying to get to them would more than likely see him as the only fatality to come out of the situation. He knew his dad was in control there, and there was little doubt of their safety.

We broke up one of the kitchen chairs after lunch and fed the dwindling fire. My Mom had no choice but approve the dismantling, but her heart hadn't been in it. In my mind's eye I could envision us sitting around in an empty house, all but the clothes on our backs transformed into smoky ash. Angela brought in a pile of Vogue and Teen magazines to burn later that afternoon, the perfume-rich smell of the pages filling the living room. Brad was taking a nap in the middle of the living room floor as she carried the books in, and I noticed with humor and slight embarrassment that my old pal was experiencing what we guys like to call 'a pup tent raising'. The size of the bulge that begged for release from his jeans did not go unnoticed by Angela, who almost visibly cried out in a mixture of laughter and I believe, awe. I secretly wondered if she had seen or maybe even touched old Perry's man hood. If she had, her reaction surely spoke to the fact that it didn't compare with Brad's in mass or length. I turned back to the fire and begin shifting around the ashes, not letting her in on the fact I had seen her ogling Brad's boner. After she left for the kitchen to join my grandma and Mom, I went over and kicked Brad lightly in the side until he turned over onto his stomach.

***

As I look outside it is almost seven PM. The sleet has finally stopped completely, and for the first time in almost four days, a small feeling of relief washes over me. It would take a week of sixty-degree temperatures to completely melt all the frozen rain and snow, but at least no more layers are being added. The house itself is literally an iceberg. It would take a team of excavators using bulldozers and jackhammers to saw it loose from its cocoon.

We are out of just about everything, including all food except for half a package of stale chocolate chip cookies, a cup of milk, and three cans of spam that were probably purchased back when I was wetting my diaper. My Mom sits at the kitchen table, which has become her throne of despair since grandpa left. Angela is bundled up on the couch, her legs visibly shaking under the pelt of blankets that hide them. My grandma is sitting across from my mom, her eyes staring blankly ahead at the kitchen wall. Brad is in our attic trying to find something, anything that will actually light and sustain a blaze.

Nobody has said anything about it, but all of us wonder why grandpa has not gotten back yet. Grandma's eyes tell her worry, though. Mom reaches over and pats her hand every few minutes.

I go into my room and begin pulling the six or seven stashed Playboys to ready them for the 'Joan of Arc' treatment when I hear my Mom scream and a loud thump come from the living room.

I practically run over Brad in the hallway as we both bolt for the source of the commotion.

My Mom and sister are kneeled over a fallen body at the doorway. All I can see for a moment is the bottom half of the person's legs, which are covered in a thin layer of white, and what once might have been black boots but were now the color of something that had been dipped and soaked in Clorox bleach.

I gently push Angela to the side and the rest of the body comes into view. It actually takes me a few heartbeats to recognize the face. The eyebrows are frozen and stick out from the forehead like feelers on a cockroach. The flesh of the face seems to have been roasted over a slow burning grill, and fresh cracks seep clear liquid that would be recognized as tears if they leaked from the eyes. The mouth seems stuck in a suspended grimace that had started as a scream but hung in neutral. It's Perry, but not exactly the same one who left us what now seems like weeks ago to check on his family. Brad helps me pick up his unbelievably frigid body and slide it onto the living room carpet, as close to our dwindling fire as possible. My Mom and Angela pull off (although 'peel' is a better

126

description) his brittle jacket, and cover him with the last of the spare blankets we have. Angela tries to get him to swallow some heated water, and finally he takes a few sips, coughing hard afterwards. I notice he has what looks like dried, frozen blood on his nostrils and upper lip.

After fifteen minutes or so, Perry actually attempts to speak, but only manages a raspy grunt. Angela adds some coffee to the warm water and gets him to sip another half cup. She holds his head as he drinks, and helps him lean up onto the couch a few minutes later. I notice the blue tint of his lips start to turn a reddish color, and his eyes begin to blink more rapidly.

It's another half-hour before Perry is able to sit up on his own, and it's then that I notice the fingers of his left hand. They had been covered by a ragged pair of worn wool gloves, but as he slowly pulls them off, I am the first but not the only one to notice his pinky finger missing. His index finger is curled like an overcooked noodle into his palm. Angela screams and grabs the mutilated hand, holding it up as if she were putting it on display. My Mom runs into the bathroom and returns with peroxide, bandages and wrap. The pinky finger looks like it had snapped off cleanly, like a narrow strip of wood that had been struck by a heavy hatchet blade. There is no blood, just a circular stump just above the knuckle. As gross as that is, it's the sight of the mangled index finger that causes the hair on my neck to rear up. The skin is pitch black, and the digit swings back and forth like a piece of rubber tubing. I feel myself getting nauseous and have to turn away, and Brad gives me a look that said exactly what I was feeling.

Perry finally manages to put some words together, and I wished with every fiber in my body that he had remained mute. My Mom runs from the room towards her bedroom, not caring the temperature everywhere in the house except the living room was now in the mid-thirties and dropping. My grandma sits back down at the kitchen table and begins to pray, her eyes closed but her mouth speaking in a low whisper. Angela just lowers her head and continues to tend to Perry's injured hand.

I go to my room and cry. I try not to. I do my best to hold back the flood that I knew was bubbling behind my eyes, and had been since grandpa had left the house that morning. Everything hit me at once after Perry's story, and the floodgates opened like a dam wall had burst.

Perry had only made it a few miles down the road before sliding into a guardrail and rolling into a ditch. He said he was only driving about ten miles per hour, and a small knot on his head where he hit the steering wheel was the only injury he'd sustained. He said he got out and began walking (he said he fell about every third step) towards the Ramey's house. Jim Ramey is a mechanic who lives about three miles from our house in one direction and two miles from the highway in the other. Besides old man Myers, he is the only inhabitant of the unnamed road besides us.

He said he must have only been a few hundred yards from the Ramey house when the sleet began coming down so hard it was completely blinding him. Despite only walking what he thought was no more than two hundred feet from his car, Perry said it must have taken all of twenty minutes to get back to it. He said he doesn't even recall actually making it back to the vehicle, just waking up shaking from head to toe surrounded by darkness. Perry said he would run the car in short intervals, letting the heat thaw him while he listened to a very faint radio broadcast from Atlanta. He said he had to watch how long he ran the car just to keep from killing himself with carbon monoxide. Atlanta was reporting that from west Texas to the eastern seaboard it was a frozen wasteland, and that the West Coast was being bombarded with flooding that matched the intensity of the blizzards that we were suffering. The president had declared pretty much the whole damned country a disaster area, and the National Guard was helpless to assist because the conditions were all but impossible to travel in.

The battery ran down just after the gas ran out on Perry's Z28, and he said he was forced to leave what had been his safe haven a few hours later, as his clothes were re- freezing to his skin due to the earlier thawing out.

He said he wrapped himself in the blankets that had been laying in the back seat, and kicked his way out of the frozen driver's side door. He said his Z28 was covered in a two- inch thick web of ice as he walked away from it and back towards our house. He said he thought about checking on Ramey's house, but reconsidered since the sleet had stopped, and decided to try to make it back here before any more *precip* hit. Perry said he made it halfway back before the freezing rain began to pelt him again. He said he walked with the blanket covering his head like a shroud, and watched his feet take him forward. He said his entire body was drenched within minutes, then the rain turned to a heavy mixture of sleet and snow. He said he seemed to black in and out after that, his entire body so cold he thought a few times he had quit breathing. He recalled falling a few times on the slick shoulder of the road, and once feeling a strong stinging sensation coming from his left hand, which he had landed on hard trying to break one of his falls.

Perry said he had practically tripped over my grandpa about a half-mile from the house. Grandpa was lying in the middle of the road face up, his mouth and eyes wide open, the latter filled with crystallized shards of freezing rain. I wished Perry hadn't been so damn graphic in his description, especially in front of my mom and grandma. I wanted to tell the dumb bastard to shut up. Just telling us grandpa was dead would have been enough. Maybe in his mind he felt he had to share this horror with someone, or go completely mad as the only one who had to live with the thought of it, but I still think it was downright idiotic.

***

I go back into the living room, where Perry is asleep on the couch and Brad is burning my Playboys. I see the exquisite face and body of Tyra Banks melt in the small flames, followed by last April's centerfold, a breathtakingly beautiful Asian girl with almond colored eyes and perfectly shaped breasts. I no longer have the energy to worry who sees what is being burned. My Mom is out of commission anyway. Your son looking at 'girly magazines' and the tragic death of your father in a sleet storm don't come close to comparing to one another on the old problem meter.

Angela sleeps on the floor, her swollen face looking ten years older than it did just days ago. My grandmother has her head down on the kitchen table, but I doubt she sleeps.

The temperature in the house is going to hit the twenties soon. We'll have to burn more furniture to keep the fire going, and maybe start throwing in some clothing. I'm back in my room and start digging through my dresser for old t-shirts and socks, and hear the now clearly distinct sound of freezing rain connecting with the icy grounds outside. Just to clarify that my over-taxed mind is not hearing things, I casually stroll into the dead silence of the dark living room and crack open the front door.

I frown at first, then the frown becomes a smile, the smile a laugh, the laugh a cry. I fall to my knees and swing the door open, the blustery wind blowing out the candles that provide our only light in what has become our live-in grave, the family crypt.

I begin to crawl outside on my hands and knees, but Brad pulls me back inside, his own mad laughter matching mine howl for howl.

I ask him if he sees. He nods yes. I ask him if the snowflakes he sees are as big as softballs. He nods yes again, giggling like a lunatic. I ask him if the sleet that is mixed with it is indeed coming down so hard it almost dents the ice it strikes on the ground. He again nods yes, his head now swinging wildly from side to side, then up and down, large streams of drool flying from the corners of his mouth like a rabid dog.

I try to ask my best friend another question, but somebody turns out the lights.

***

I awake in total darkness, my breath clearly visible to me as it escapes my mouth in frantic, hurried gasps. My eyes adjust to the darkness and I see I am in my room, lying on my bed. The skin on my chest and stomach is fish belly white, and it hits me with some degree of shock that I am completely naked. It is probably no more than twenty degrees and I am wearing no clothes. My penis is the size of a cocktail sausage and my testicles seem to have taken the high road looking for a warm place to hide.

I leap from the bed and suddenly realize it is the only item in the room save for myself. My clothes dresser, my end table, my TV, everything is missing. Even my McGwire and Bear Bryant posters are stripped off the closet door.

I exit my room and stumble into the hallway, tripping over what appears to be a small piece of shattered wood. I see the light of the fireplace and I step towards it, my head as fuzzy as my body is stiff. All I can think of is getting warm. I see someone slumped over the fireplace, digging into the ashes with a poker. They are holding the poker into the fire, actually suspending it over the flames. There is an object at the end of the poker, embedded on its hooked end.

I stop a few feet from where the person stands, and they sense me there and turn slowly towards me.

Perry's face is half-hidden underneath the blanket as he turns, but he reaches up with one gnarled hand and pulls it free to reveal himself to me. I see with horror he has no teeth, only purple gums as he grins at me and winks with one bloodshot eye. He gestures at the poker and seems to be asking me something, but his lips never form any actual words to give me a clue.

I glance at the poker and do a double take, and the next thing I feel is the warmth of my own urine as it flows down my right thigh.

My grandma's head stares back at me, the ruined stump of her neck still dripping fresh blood into the fire, the overwhelming stench of copper burns my nostrils, and I hear the sizzling pops it causes as it drips slowly onto the heated embers below.

Perry keeps repeating the same words to me over and over as I try to unlock my knees and run.

"I've burned everything I could, and we ran out of food. What choice did I have? Someone has to make it, am I right?"

"I've burned everything I could, and we ran out of food. What choice did I have? Someone has to m-.."

My eyes dart around the living room and I see a pile of bloodied, severed limbs stacked waist high next to where the couch had once set.

I scream and my legs finally began to function. I get halfway down the hall and now see clearly the object I had almost tripped on earlier.

It's a leg. Cut cleanly at the thigh. The toenails are painted in red with sparkling dots. Angela's leg. I turn to see not Perry, but my grandpa standing by the fire. His mouth is wide open and ice is falling out in large, crimson-colored chunks. He has no eyes, just dark circular holes that call to me to come give him a hug. Grandpa wants a hug. I turn to walk towards him. I want to show him I do love him…will always love him.

I get a few steps away from Gramps, and his mouth opens gruesomely wide, a large object forcing its way through the suddenly huge crater that causes his skull to split open like rotted plywood.

Uncle Matt crawls from the cave that was only a moment ago the jaws of my grandfather. Uncle Matt is naked also. He doesn't speak, just takes my left hand in his right and tells me to come with him. He tells me he has found a 'warm place' for the whole family to move to.

He tells me my Mother is already there, and my sister. He says Brad is there playing Nintendo and is waiting for me to join the game.

I follow my Uncle into the dark cave. My Uncle lied. It's cold in here. My Uncle is dead. So am I. They were wrong, you know. Hell is not hot. Not even remotely warm, in fact. No sir, is it colder than anyone could ever imagine.

**

Not even breathing could be heard as the man finally paused, backing his wheelchair up a few

134

feet from the edge of the stage. Someone whispered "Jesus" , and another voice could be heard whispering "I heard about that storm. It was a real shitter, man."

"Yes, young man, it was definitely a real 'shitter' as you say. In all, forty-three people in Northern Alabama met their maker in the eight days it lasted. Another twenty-six in Tennessee and nineteen in Georgia lost their lives. Hell, it took the National Guard a good week to dig most folks out after the snow and ice had finally stopped fallin'. I personally lost my legs and every cow I owned on my farm, sixty-one head I believe it was. I also lost my sister and her family, all but her youngest that is. The story I just told you was drawn from his own notes, written in the two years he spent in the institute after the storm, before he came up missing. I loved that boy, tried to help raise 'im. The doctors think it was a simple case of cabin fever that caused him to kill his mom, sister and Grandma, along with his best friend. I won't go into the details. Number one because I'll be damned if I want to think about 'em, and number two because I don't wanna make anybody in here lose their cookies. The Guardsmen that found the place had to be treated for some problems of their own years later. One told authorities that the house looked like someone was holding their own personal 'weenie-roast' with human body parts. That's all I need to tell ya. You get the general idea."

More whispers rose from beyond the stage as the man paused again to rub his eyes with worn leather gloves that had the fingers cut out.

Professor Carpenter, feeling the urge to not only pee but to possibly be physically ill as well, made a quiet exit towards the restrooms just outside the auditorium's double doors.

"Lamar disappeared from the institute one rainy evening. Just vanished. The place had been locked up tight and all bodies counted the night before. His cell...uh, room was found empty the next morning. His bed had been made and all his institutional clothing had been accounted for. The state sent an all points out and did a pretty extensive search. He hasn't been found to this day. Hell, I almost think aliens came down and picked 'im up. He had pretty much been an alien to me since the day they found my sister crammed in the fireplace of her home, minus most of her head. I'm...I'm sorry. All I can say in finishing is that I try real, real hard every day not to visualize the image of my nephew, or what I might do to him if I we ever do come face-to-face. Thanks for listening."

He turned quickly and wheeled himself backstage, coughing harshly as he went.

Within minutes and without the stage lights ever brightening, a new speaker stood poised at the podium. She was a distinguished looking woman who could have been someone's grandmother but who could have also passed for a middle-aged mother. She was dressed smartly in an ankle length white dress and had her blonde/gray hair tied neatly in a bun.

A few of the students cleared their throats almost simultaneously and then once again grew silent.

Jerry Watkins, his fingers sore from the nine full pages of notes he had already taken, looked around nervously, his beady brown eyes searching the darkened room for Professor Carpenter. He had noticed the professor exit quite a few minutes earlier, and saw the front row seat still unoccupied even as the next speaker began their rendition of what he had already come to think of as 'Tales from the Cracked." Julie, the short-haired and quite attractive redhead who was sitting to his left hadn't even cracked a smile at the pun, but he was determined to break the ice with her before the seemingly never-ending evening crawled towards it's epilogue.

"Good evening, folks. My name is Betty Danley. Doctor Dante has decided the time for formal introductions is past, it seems. Let me tell you a little something about myself. I am sixty-two years young and a retired nurse. I have a thirty-two year old son who is a practicing M.D. and my late husband was a retired Police Captain who passed three years ago from a heart attack.

Our first and only other child was a daughter named Carolyn. Carolyn spent time at a Mental Institute just outside Chicago. She had been a resident there for over six years. Carolyn's problems began early in her teens, and escalated until they bore the incident I will now inform you of. Her depression and instability has become my own since my husband's death, unfortunately. Maybe the telling of the tale will help me cope in some way. Well, without further ado...,"

CHAPTER SIX
Skeleton Cruise

The tall, lanky man sat in the dimly lit hallway and stared at the checkered ceiling tile. He closed his eyes, rubbing his right hand through his crewcut styled hair, then glanced at his watch and sighed. A moment later the office door to his left opened abruptly and he quickly jumped up, his knees popping loudly, and practically sprinted inside. The older man whose name was stenciled on the office door he had just entered sat back down in his reclining leather chair and took off the reading glasses that had been perched on his nose. The younger man stood in front of the man's desk, his hands ringing together nervously.

"What do you think, sir? Did you listen to all of it?"

The older man glanced up at him with a look of exasperation.

"Damned if I know, Agent Clifford. This tape was over two hours long, the majority useless dribble. I have two of our record technicians checking the details now. Sounds a bit like wild fiction to me, if you want complete honesty."

FBI operative Bruce Clifford was a field veteran of over eleven years, and was infamous for his stubborn, borderline obsessive attitude when it came to closing cases. He was also known for his hand wringing, leg shaking, eye darting nervousness, Such habits had earned him the nickname 'Agent Spaz' within the ranks of the agency.

He finally calmed enough to sit down in a chair that faced the older man's desk, although the hand wringing gestures had already hit full stride. "Sir, I believe it will be confirmed the other four people are missing, and have been since the dates Wilkins mentioned on the tape. Call it a gut feeling, but right now it's all I have. This kind of incident has been known to happen before. I read a case study about a group of tourists that were capsized in the Atlantic just a few hundred miles from the coast of Puerto Rico. They were found on an island no larger than half a mile long and two hundred yards wide, alive and well after six months. Then of course there are the countless confirmed tales of lost parties in the Bermuda Triangle. I believe..,"

"Bruce, I know you. I know your 'gut feelings'. They've been known to lead more than a few of our agents on wild goose chases. I cannot spare more than the two I've assigned to you on this matter. Regardless if it's true or not, we already know the outcome. It's simply a matter of notifying the families if we do find the individuals mentioned in the tape. The media will have more 'TV movie' fodder, and that's where it will end."

The older man, his eyes concentrating on the cassette player that sat in the middle of his cluttered desk, spoke to Clifford like a father attempting to console his young son after a bad day on the baseball field.

"Take the cassette and listen to it again. Hell, get Morrison to go over it if he has the time. See if you can pick up anything else useful. I understand the raft held no other clues, and the

139

body is being autopsied as we speak. Let me know when the results come in on the other individuals mentioned on the tape."

Clifford reached over and gripped the player, then stood and quickly headed for the door. He halted just before exiting, and spoke without turning around.

"I really, really hope this is simply a work of demented fiction, sir. But I have my doubts." He strode quickly down the long narrow hallway, past mostly empty offices being that it was after five and the majority had already departed for the day.

He turned a sharp curve past the sixth floor elevators and practically ran into the office of agent Gary Morrison, who was lying on a small couch in the corner of the office. His eyes were open, and he stared unblinking at the ceiling.

"You've got the tape in your sweaty little hands, I presume?" He asked, a small smile stretching across his lips.

Clifford couldn't help but grin himself as he walked over and placed the cassette on the large oak desk in the center of the office. Papers were scattered in makeshift piles in every available space. The computer monitor that centered the desk was almost completely covered, and yellow 'post it notes' blocked whatever free space the files and papers had left.

"Yeah, I got it, and since it's obvious you haven't got anything better to do….," Morrison laughed hard, leaned up and vigorously rubbed both eyes. "Correct-a-mun- do, ol' pal' a mine. I've only got cases opened six months ago collecting white out and cobwebs. The old man wants me to give it a listen, huh?"

"You got it. I have the distinct feeling my single opinion on this little work of art is considered shaky at best. He trusts you, Gar. Hell, even I trust you."

The other man pushed his way off the couch and poured himself a steaming cup of coffee from a large thermos that had been sitting on one of the unidentified piles of documentation.

"Okie-Dokie, Bruce. What the hell, I was starting to feel guilty about only working a 12- hour day anyhow. Turn 'er on."

Clifford reached for the player and paused.

"I was going to stay in here and gauge your opinion as it played out, but I need to clear my head of the whole mess for a while. I'm gonna go down to the break room and get some caffeine, Mountain Dew style. I'll be back in less than an hour. Then you can give me your take on it."

He hit the play button and headed for the door. Morrison sat back down on the couch and reached for a Marlboro out of his right shirt pocket.

"See ya, Chuckles, and thanks for giving me the opportunity to again sleep in my office. It does tend to cut down on gas expenditures, ya know?"

He heard Clifford groan with laughter as the door shut behind him.

Morrison sat back and inhaled deeply off his cigarette as the initial static at the front end of the tape began to clear.

***

Hello, Hello...testing 1-2...the name is Barry

141

Wilkins. I'm recording this for prosperity. It is 6:11 A.M. The date is March 19th, 2002. The planning is over and we are just half an hour or so from sailing off into the deep blue Atlantic. I've decided to keep this audio journal just for kicks, and in case we end up sleeping with the fishes with the crew of the Titanic, someone can at least hear how we got that way. Let me introduce the rest of the crew. The Captain is Lane Wainwright. His first mate is Barton McCall. The ship's cook is also my wife, Carolyn. There is another shipmate who hasn't arrived yet, and I'm not even sure of his name. He better hurry or he'll be paddling to catch us. We are sailing on the 50-foot Schooner 'Pegasus'. What I know about boats and sailing I couldn't write a paragraph on, but it has all the bells and whistles. We have a full kitchen area, entertainment room complete with video games and TV/VCR/Stereo, and individual sleeping quarters which are a little cramped but better than I expected for this price. The Captain assured me it has all the power we will need for the journey, and that he had a new engine installed in her only six months ago. If all else fails, we do have the capability to set the sails and glide. Carolyn and I have been planning this for years, but bills and conflicting work schedules have always kept us from seeing it through. Actually, without the additional funds provided by our other mystery vacationer and fellow sea traveler, we probably couldn't have pulled it off. I hope he shows up soon. I know the Captain informed Carolyn that he had already paid them for the cruise via credit card weeks ago. I can't imagine him not showing up. Must be the traffic. More later.

It's 7:32 A.M. Our other guest's name is Dave Kendricks. Looks about forty-five or fifty. Said he's a car salesman who, like us, has been planning on doing this since he was a kid. Said he grew up in South Dakota and always dreamed of the ocean. Moved to Fort Walton Beach four years ago and has been saving for a cruise ever since. Divorced with kids who are already married and out of the house. Seems like a good guy. Talks a lot, but we're all a little nervous. Carolyn and I have only been living here ourselves for two years from Michigan. The humidity kills us still, but we'll settle in. The last vacation we took was to the Smithsonian in D.C. Went to the Grand Canyon five years back. I'm more stoked about this than both of those combined. I tell Carol were just 'sailors at heart'.

***

8:54. We're on our way. Captain let us stand on the 'bridge' and hold the wheel. The weather is perfect, the wind just a cool breeze. I love the smell of salt water. The boat cuts through the water so smooth it's almost like we're sitting still and the water around us is moving. First stop on our little trek is a small island called Juarez. Captain Wainwright said it is basically just a supply stop with not a whole lot to see for tourists. He said we could buy cheaper once we get to San Juan. We ate breakfast on deck. Biscuits and Orange Juice and more Coffee. I've had six cups since this morning. I think I'm on more of a natural high than a caffeine one at this moment.

***

7:21 P.M. Just had dinner in the 'galley' as we jokingly call it. Baked chicken, rice, rolls, and iced tea. Carol is amazing how she can throw meals together in minutes. We have enough food to last us a month, but already she is concerned about the calorie count. I mean, she weighs less than one hundred twenty pounds and she's five-ten. I myself should get off my 'sea food' diet, you know, I 'see' food, I eat it. I weighed in at two-twenty last week. I see this cruise as a good opportunity to get away from all the two- martini lunches I'm used to at work. I should drop at least ten pounds in the next eleven days, if I lay off the brew. I noticed McCall giving Carol the 'eye' at dinner. He's at least ten years my junior, maybe twenty-five or so, and looks like he works out ten hours a day. I noticed he has a long, deep scar on the left side of his face. Looks like somebody nailed him with a shovel. He's a little too quiet for me. The word 'spooky' comes to mind. Mr. Kendricks on the other hand, seems to be unable to stop talking. He could make a ten- minute speech on the pros and cons of eating hot dogs, I believe. Carol just rolls her eyes when he gets off on one of his tangents. Tonight we'll sleep early and rise early. I wanna see the sun rise over the edge of the Atlantic.

***

March 20th, It's 5:21 A.M. Well, that was a wash. Too damn cloudy to see the sunrise. Had coffee with Wainwright. He's been monitoring the radar in his office and says we might be in for a pretty good toss from the waves this evening. It seems a storm is developing just off the southern coast of Mexico and headed right to us. He said it doesn't sound too serious, but pretty nasty winds will give us our first chance to experience what he calls 'the wobble'. I hope I don't heave later. Carol is just now waking up. Think I'll jump her bones before she can wake up enough to turn me down.

***

11:15 A.M. Has developed into a cloudy, cool day. The wind is picking up, as promised. I was on the bridge talking to Wainwright. I let him know that I did not appreciate his first mate, McCall, so obviously ogling my wife's rear end at lunch today. He informed me that he had just hired McCall on before this sail, that he had lost his former first mate to another job. He let me know he would speak to him. Carol had been doing her best to avoid Kendricks, who in my opinion needs his lips sewn shut. Has really turned into a rather shitty day all around.

***

4:24 P.M. I had been standing up top with Wainwright when McCall came running up, looking like he had a bad case of the runs, and told the Captain that he had just received a radio call about the storm. It's gonna be worse than they originally thought. McCall reminded me of a little kid about to get the crap kicked out of him by the school bully. I thought the big asshole was gonna cry. At least I don't consider him a threat anymore, but his wondering eye still bugs me.

145

6:12 P.M. Radio's out. Wind reminds me of a tornado that came through my hometown once. You can barely stand upright on deck. Wainwright ordered us to our cabins and told us to strap on our life vests. He did this with a 'just a precaution, folks' attitude, but I saw the fear in the man's eyes. Jesus. Carol is in the john. Poor thing was shaking like she was out in an ice storm a few minutes ago. I can't say I'm exactly 'Mr. Cool' myself.

***

9:17 P.M. Not sure when (static) I'll be a-able to record again. The Pegasus is shaking like a Dr. Pepper can in a Twister. C-Cap'n gave us life jackets and has us sitting in the dining area awaiting his word. Generator went out a few minutes ago. Wainwright was screaming for McCall to ready the two life rafts. (loud shouting noises) My earlier joke about the Titanic isn't a damn bit funny anymore. Carol is crying. Jesus, first full day out.

***

9:32 P.M. Kendricks said he heard a loud crack on the left stern moments ago... I think we're in some serious s-shit here, and here I sit without a paddle (nervous laughter). Gotta go, here's comes the Cap'n with that asshole McCall. Already barfed twice. Got nothing else to heave. I...think I just pissed my..(cut off) (thumping noises) (clicking sounds, followed by what sounds like a muffled scream) My watch says it's 3:11 A.M. I'm laying here holding Carol by my side. She's still

146

sleeping. Wainwright and his inept right hand man are roaming around some-damn-where, probably looking for a seven-eleven. Wainwright is trying to 'find some kindling' or some such horseshit. I'm beyond commenting right now on this comically depressing situation.

***

8:11 A.M. Okay, here's the deal. I find myself amazed this is really happening, but as I sat with my feet in the sand in sopping wet clothes looking out at nothing but rolling ocean, it cannot be anything as explainable as a simple nightmare. We are on an uncharted island somewhere between the Florida coast and Mexico, or maybe Cuba, or maybe the fucking Mediterranean Sea, who the hell knows? Certainly not our esteemed Captain, who is too busy trying to figure out how to repair a boat that now sits scattered and practically broken in half all over the beach. We hit the same side of this sand dune a few hours before the damn ship arrived though, so I think we have dibs on naming it. The rafts had hardly inflated before we were basically thrown into them. We must have drifted for hours in hellish waves before we felt the sand stop us. The Captain and his brainless cohort say we must have run against a coral reef during the storm. The boat sank like a rock within minutes of us jumping off. I stand here looking at its front half, which if you stand directly in front of it, gives the illusion of being completely sailable. Some of the food survived and is eatable, mostly the canned stuff. We have enough water for five or six days, ten if we really suffer. The 'island' is basically a large dune with some ragged weeds and bush growing staggered in places. It might be a football field long and two wide. We built a fire last night from some of the brush. That imbecilic moron Kendricks actually starting singing the theme from "Gilligan's Island" to us. Let's just say it didn't break the tension. Carol is sleeping again. She bumped her head pretty hard when we departed the Pegasus. I think she has a concussion. That asshole McCall keeps asking if 'he can help' her. I finally told the shitheel to back off, in no uncertain turns.

***

12:44 P.M. Just had lunch (laughs). Not exactly a meal fit for a king. Two bites of spam on saltine crackers and half a tootsie roll. Well, I did wanna lose weight! Kendricks has finally stopped talking. I think lack of food is starting to weaken his tongue. The Captain and his crew are still trying to get the radio to work from inside what's left of his communications room. No go so far. He told me it's only a matter of days before his contacts in San Juan contact his wife and let her know we never made it. After that, the search will begin. Days! Jesus, what a dream vacation this turned out to be. It's bone- chilling cold at night. We need to keep the fire burning constantly. I suggested we stay awake in shifts to keep it lit.

***

8:48 P.M. Damn, it's freezing. Carol is finally

shaking off the jolt to the head she took. We took a walk around the island, what little of it there is. I saw that son-of-a-bitch McCall staring at us again. If I see him look at her ass one more time, I'm gonna do some 'counseling' of my own. I'm gonna start limiting my time on the recorder. It's a wonder it works at all as wet as it got last night, but I'm afraid the batteries are gonna start getting weaker.

***

March 22nd, 10:12 A.M. Well, not a lot to report. We just had 'brunch' consisting of a potted meat product resembling cat food, and one sugar cookie apiece. The water is starting to run low as well. Wainwright sits around mumbling all the time, and the man looks like he's aged ten years since we landed here in Shangri-La. His first mate paces the island as if with each trip around he might find a way off. That crazy jackass scares me. He never fails to glance at Carol every trip around. Kendricks on the other hand has decided that if we build a big enough bon-fire, basically set the whole island on fire, a passing plane or ship will see us. I think he is the proverbial 'one brick shy of a load'. I comfort Carol that we will be fine, but as another night faces us, I'm having some serious doubts.

***

March 24th, 6:21 P.M. The good Captain and myself got into a bit of a screaming match concerning the psychopathic idiot he has working for him. This morning I went off to look for more

149

weeds and wood to burn, we are running pathetically low, and left Carol to sleep.

When I made it back to her, I caught McCall leaning over her stroking his groin. He backed off as soon as he saw me coming, and later denied the whole incident to the Captain. Carol was still asleep while he did this. I told Wainwright I would not hesitate to kill the man if he did anything like this again. Wainwright told me I was suffering from hallucinations caused by stress and lack of energy due to the food and water shortages. Kendricks wondered off at lunch and no one has bothered to look for him or even shout his name. I think the batteries are really losing it now. I will limit these recordings from now on. Damn, I'm hungry. My kingdom for a grilled steak... (loud static, then a click, followed by a long pause) (heavy breathing) Hello...this is...Captain Lane Wainwright speaking. I confiscated this recorder from...(long pause). I don't have much time, I think. She knows I'm on the boat.

The crazy sumbitch has killed my first mate and Doctor McCall. I...(low sobs) caught...he... his eyes were torn out. One...of them was hanging out of its socket like a m- marble on a string. I'm sure all are dead but myself. The radio doesn't work. We ran out of water sixteen hours ago. Food doesn't mean a thing without water. Never seen anyone go from being so normal one minute to...such an animal the next. The face even changed, it seemed. Maybe it was just my eyes, I dunno. I could have sworn she was a m-..(sudden movement, water splashing noises)...oh Christ, I've been found....if someone finds this, tell my wife Marcie I..I loved her. I don't think I can- (tape clicks off). (Squelching noises) (very weak voice) T-this is Carol. C-Carol Wilkins. I believe it is the 30th of March, but I'm not really sure. It's early in the morning, but I have no idea what time. I don't know how far I can drift in this raft. I just know that without food, and without water, I have no chance staying here. My husband is..is (sobs)...(long pause)..gone. Everyone is...except me. If I don't make it back to the authorities alive, this tape is my testimony of what transpired here. (pause, coughing) We had been stuck there for eight days, and tensions were running high. The food and water were completely gone, and everyone was angry and fatigued. We were getting ice cold at night and burning hot during the day. Barry was running a constant fever. The Captain spent his days on the ruined remains of his (coughs) boat. His assistant, Mr. McCall I believe had a breakdown of some kind. All he did was walk...constantly, around the small island. He stared at me quite a bit, scaring me and inducing rage in Barry.

Mr. Kendricks, whom I believe to be mentally ill, starting camping on the other end of the beach. He went from being a man who seemed to live to talk to being one that seemed to forget how. We kept out distance from the others (coughs loudly). I woke up last night to find McCall on top of me. He was lying on my back and pushing down so hard I could barely breathe (pause, sobs). I looked over at Barry... Kendrick and the Captain were holding him down. I saw...pure madness in their eyes. I watched as Captain Wainwright pulled a long knife from inside his left boot and slowly....(pause)..cut... Barry's throat. The blood sprayed out from the...(clicks off)...so much blood it didn't look real somehow...(clicks off) (clicks on, static; followed by a low male voice, almost whispering) ..and the son of the bitches were raping her. They tied me up with rope from the boat and made me watch them penetrate her. They... took turns, McCall and Kendricks. The Captain just stood there and laughed until I could see tears running out of his eyes. He would clap me on the shoulder and then point at the rape scene, then laugh even harder. (voice gets much louder) I wish...oh lord, I wish I could have done something to help Carol! I would have killed those bastards with my bare hands! She was so helpless! (loud sobs, then a long pause) (back to a low whisper) When they had finished with her, McCall walked over to the sand and picked up a large rock. He...strolled over to my wife and as calmly as you please...b-bashed her skull with the rock. He then looked...(sobs) over at me and grinned. I knew I was dealing with Satan himself then. He handed the rock to Kendricks, and they proceeded to take turns smashing....my wife's face and head with the rock until I couldn't even r-recognize h-her. Her entire head was mashed into the sand (pause) leaving only... a.. large red... smear. Wainwright just kept laughing the whole damn time. I can still see his face. I can see his yellow teeth and his bloodshot eyes. Kendrick then (loud sobs)...Kendrick then turned to me and said.....oh god! He said.. 'let's see if he's as good as his wife'! I was tied, you see. There wasn't a fucking thing I could do. I recall thinking of the movie Deliverance... When they cut me loose to do their deed, that's when I de-(clicked off) (long pause, woman's voice) I took the sharp end of the wood and...stuck him in the throat with it. His blood... coated me in crimson waves. I have to say this, even though it is hard to admit. I enjoyed killing the bastard! After what they did to my husband, heaven help me, I loved it.

No man should be subjected to what they did to him. (sobs) I had to watch those men....(deep sigh). I guess God was looking out for me, because when it came time for them to rape me, Kendrick and McCall went at each other like rabid dogs. Kendrick ripped McCall's throat out with his bare hands. I saw the Captain jump him from behind while he was still choking McCall. The Captain must have used his knife to cut Kendrick's throat, because I saw Kendrick fall down suddenly like a bag of bricks, and he didn't move after that. I had scooped up that jagged piece of wood, I guess it came off the Pegasus when she floated to the beach. I held it behind my tied hands, and when he cut me loose to have his way with me...I shoved it forward with all my strength. I was surprised it went so deep, but I realize the neck is a soft area. His blood...shot out and...splashed all over my face and chest. He grabbed his throat with both hands and struggled for a moment, then fell back and didn't move anymore. I enjoyed killing the son of a bitch for what he helped do to my husband and me. I...never knew people had such bottled up evil in them, just waiting for a stressful situation to fester and then emerge. If I make it back to society, I will be more wary...of everybody. (click off) (apparent male voice barely audible) ..she was the love of my life, and those cre-creatures took her away, but I made them pay, and I loved every second of watching them die. I have no water and no food. This raft won't stay afloat if I run into bad weather. I know I don't have much of a chance, but remaining here is no choice. I will come back with authorities to find my wife's body and give it a proper burial. She des-(voice dragging, sounds like a low whisper)...-serves that. This story must be....told. (clicks off)

***

When agent Morrison heard the last click of the tape, he leaned forward to pick up the recorder and only then realized he had been sitting on the very edge of the couch.

A moment later, Clifford entered the office holding a box clearly marked 'donuts' in one hand and a large mug of coffee in the other. He smiled at Morrison wryly and shrugged his narrow shoulders.

"So, my man, what do ya say? I've listened to it three times and it still sounds a little hokey and a tad scripted, although undeniably scary as hell. What's your take?"

Morrison stood up and stretched, a puzzled look on his haggard face, and was about to respond when his phone buzzed.

"Morrison. Yeah, he's here. Okay, Mills. Yeah, I'll tell 'im."

Clifford was just biting into a frosted donut when Morrison hung up. "Our pal Jake Mills in research. He's got the scoop on your body."

Clifford dumped the remaining piece of donut in an already overflowing trash container and started for the door. He turned to Morrison as he was about to exit.

"You are following me down there, right?" he asked curtly. "Hey man, I wouldn't miss this for end zone Dolphins tickets."

They met Jake Mills in his office on the third floor. The research department was as deserted as the rest of the building at seven PM.

Clifford ran up to the man with the enthusiasm of a boy waiting for an autograph from his sports idol.

"So, Jakey boy, what's the story?" he asked, his eyes glowing as his hands begin to wring. Morrison stood behind him and silently laughed at his colleague's excitement.

Mills, a large black man with what seemed like a permanent scowl frozen onto his round face, barely glanced at the agents before turning to face his computer screen. He replied to them as he typed.

"Well, it seems a Mr. Lane Wainwright does run a tour vessel out of Fort Walton Beach, Florida. Has since 1985. Boat name is 'Pegasus'. His first mate is listed as one David C. Kendricks. Wainwright is a white male, fifty-two years of age. Kendricks also a white male, twenty-eight. Fort Walton Police Department confirms both of them, along with their vessel, have been missing since…,"

He paused as his fingers flew across the keyboard and displayed a separate screen.

Clifford's knee began to shake unconsciously.

"...March 19th, 2002. They were both reported missing by family members on March 22rd, 2002, when they failed to report in from their cruise destination in San Juan." Morrison sat down in a nearby chair and lit up a cigarette.

"Damn. So far, so true," he whispered mostly to himself. After exiting the screen he was on, Mills quickly clicked on another and continued. Clifford still stood over him, and slowly pulled out a cigarette of his own.

Mills frowned, but continued typing.

"No smoking in here, gents," he said, his fingers still pecking away. Both men ignored him and he let out a deep, frustrated sigh. Morrison smiled. He had always liked Mills for his no-nonsense, 'wouldn't know a joke if it hit me over the head' attitude. Mills resumed his pecking.

"Also, a Mr. Barton McCall M.D. was reported missing by his ex-wife on 28 March. It was reported by associates at Baptist Medical in Fort Walton that he had been on vacation since 17 March. White male, forty-six years of age."

Clifford blew out a long cloud of smoke, then glanced over at Morrison, who shot him a quick wink.

"Here we go, Spaz. Now it all depends on you-know-who."

"Yep-per. And don't call me Spaz."

A new screen flashed on the monitor and Mills leaned back in his chair, stretching out his thick arms.

"O-kay. Here's what you've been waiting for. This will sincerely blow your mind. Barry Wilkins, white male. Age thirty-five. Native of Flint, Michigan. He worked as a used car salesman there as well as later when he relocated to Panama City Beach, Florida three years ago. His wife's name is Carolyn, also a native of Flint. Worked as a schoolteacher there but was let go and spent some time in a mental institute in Panama City after the death of her husband two years ago."

Clifford stepped back, his mouth agape.

"Say what? You mean another husband other than Barry Wilkins?"

Mills glanced up at him, his hands wrapped behind his head. "Nope. Barry Wilkins died in a boating accident in 1997. He was deep-sea fishing off the coast of Mexico and fell overboard during a sudden squall. Now, get this; the Wilkins' separated in '96 but got back together after an incident where the wife was allegedly raped at her school in Flint. She joined him in Florida a few months later. After his death, she tried to commit suicide several times. She was treated on occasion for depression over the last few years. I talked to a Doctor Messersmith in Panama City who treated her. It took me three calls to convince him that if he had some information that might help us find her and these other people, he needed to spill. He gave me the 'client-doctor confidentiality' crap for a while, but finally divulged something I think you'll find veeerryy interesting."

He paused with a smile, then continued when Clifford started gesturing wildly for him to continue.

"Well, it seems over the months of her treatment, the good Doctor noticed she would slip into a different personality; her husband's. He said she even showed up at one of their appointments dressed as a man with her hair cut in the same style as her late husband. He also divulged that she had very violent tendencies and flashbacks to her rape. Beyond bizarre, am I right?"

Morrison slapped his hand on his knee and laughed. "Holy mystery solved, Batman!"

Clifford turned to him, his eyes darting back and forth from Morrison and Mills.

"You think...my god. Those poor folks were on a ship with a time bomb waiting to detonate. Welcome to the Schizoid ward."

Mills clicked off his computer and swung his massive chair around to face them both. "Also, just got word from the coroners office. He's confirmed that the body was female.

He said the state of the corpse and the decomposition suggests she was drifting for at least a month after death. The birds and elements did the damage."

Sitting down with a sigh, Clifford's eyes stared straight ahead down the pitch dark hallway ahead.

"She used his voice for most of the tape, so obviously she was disguised as a male. Must have had a complete breakdown once they were stranded. In her mind, they were both on the damn ship. Her rage must have come from the rape flashback. She didn't have her husband with her when the actual situation occurred in Michigan, so her mind fabricated an attack where he was there to help, only it backfired and escalated somehow. Jesus, those poor folks never saw it coming."

Morrison shrugged.

"Well, more than likely they all would have died anyhow. They had already ran out of provisions and obviously weren't gonna get found anytime soon."

Mills turned back to his computer screen and began clearing the windows he had previously opened.

"I'm sure the man upstairs will initiate a search, but seems to me it's the old 'needle in a haystack'."

Morrison stood and clapped Clifford on the shoulder.

"Let's go home, Spaz. I'd like to at least get a few hours of sack time before we do it all over again in the morning."

His shoulders slumped, Clifford walked away shaking his head from side to side.

"Un-freaking real. Just goes to show you, you never know the mental condition of people you meet. Many are just one negative scenario from blowing an inner fuse and going off like a stick of TNT. Scary shit, my man."

Morrison grinned, his eyes wide and bloodshot from fatigue.

"So true, McDuff. Hell, who knows how many here at the Bureau walk that fine line. I know one thing for damn sure, Spaz ol' friend. No Love Boat cruises in this man's foreseeable future."

They both laughed weakly and made their way back to the elevator.

**

Clifford ran across the sandy dune towards

159

the Coast Guard officer that had waived him over. He noticed the man was standing directly over what looked like the shape of a body. It was lying next to pieces of shattered wood that had come from the Pegasus. He leaned down and had to turn his head quickly to avoid vomiting. It was Kendrick. What was left of his mangled face was enough for identification from the old driver's license photo they had received from DMV last week. The man's throat had obviously been cut. Although parasites had eaten away most of his upper chest and neck, the deep slash was still visible at the base of the throat in a clear horizontal pattern.

A moments later he crawled aboard the shattered remains of the Pegasus' front end. What was left of the structure was leaning hard to the left, and he had to sidestep to enter the now wet and musty hallway that led to the crews quarters below deck. The smell of decay was so stout it almost made him physically ill. Pieces of what had been cabinets, doors and walls floated ankle deep all around him.

He noticed all the cabin doors were open except the last one at the far end of the tilted hallway. Clifford was about to turn and head back into the fresh air of the beach when he heard the whispers. He felt a fresh, cool sweat break out onto his forehead. Instinctively he removed his thirty-eight from its shoulder holster and held it in front of his chest like a shield. He took a small step forward and heard a clear, short laugh, followed by a lower, muffled giggle.

Clifford considered turning back and calling in one of the Guard troops, but instead found himself standing in front of the closed door with his left hand posed on the already rusting knob.

He took a deep breath and the door swung open with a loud creak.

Their faces held smiles too wide and toothy for their bloated faces. He noticed the open sores and bruises on their naked, swollen torsos. He understood what caused these types of marks. He had seen 'floaters' before. Dead bodies that had been slowly chipped away at by salt water and the parasites that frequented it. Neither of them had eyelids. They sat up off the bed and glared at him with teeth bared.

"Hello, Agent Clifford," said the man-thing that Clifford recognized from old photos as Barry Wilkins. He held out a torn hand that was missing three fingers.

"Join us," said the other, her face hopelessly disfigured on one side. It looked as if sharks had been taking her apart section by section, inch by inch.

Clifford tried to back away, but found his feet frozen; his legs as useless as the revolver now swinging powerless at his side. As they continued to hug each other and grin at him hideously, he then noticed a detail that had earlier escaped his shocked psyche. He felt his chest burn as the ability to inhale fresh oxygen suddenly escaped him.

They were joined at the side. Their flesh was seared together as if welded into place. There were only two arms and two legs. Only one torso held both heads. The female breast protruded from Carolyn's side. The other side of the chest was hairy and flat. Clifford glanced down with his

161

mouth agape and saw the crotch was shaved and sexless.

He finally managed to turn from the abomination and attempted to sprint down the crooked hallway when he felt the hand grab his shoulder. He was held back by two strong arms and felt the wet, hot breath at his ear.

"We can share things together, and we never have to leave here. In fact, we can never, ever leave..."

***

Clifford fell out of his bed screaming, his hands swinging madly. A moment later, he was standing naked in his living room with a cellular phone in hand, his face stoic and expressionless.

"Jesus, this crap has gone on too damn long," he whispered to himself as the phone rang on the other end.

"Yeah, this is Clifford. Yes, I'm very, very sure. You said you could help me with a transfer. I'm a ten year man, I should have a choice." After a long pause, he sighed.

"Yes, the department branch in Denver would be fine, thanks. Yeah, I understand the move has to be approved and it takes a few months." He hung up a moment later and walked back towards his bedroom.

"Denver. That'll do. Yep. Not an ocean wave in sight."

***

One of the students sneezed loudly just as the last sentence had been completed. The speaker nodded agreeably and smiled.

"Bless you out there," she said politely, and a few low giggles ensued from the small crowd.

She backed away from the podium for an instant to adjust her dress at the shoulders, then resumed.

"Carolyn had suffered from schizophrenia in her teens, but medication and constant counseling had allowed her the prospects of a normal life. We...that is, my husband and I, thought she had turned the corner when she met Barry. He was the best thing that could have ever happened to her. When he passed away in that tragic accident, her mind could not handle it, and the disease took hold once again. She was convicted of the three homicides I mentioned, and most of the story passed on to me by Agent Clifford has been proven by various DNA and forensic testing. I myself am being treated for severe depression, and hope someday I can accept the fact that I truly did all I could for Carolyn.

I long for the day I meet her in heaven, and her mind is no longer infected by that terrible condition. Thank you for your time."

Her back straight and her head held high, she strolled off the stage like an actress receiving a standing ovation.

Jerry leaned back and stretched, then turned and again scanned the darkness for any signs of Professor Carpenter. He leaned forward and got the attention of a slim, blonde girl by tapping her lightly on her shoulder. The aroma of her perfume filled his nostrils, and he felt his pulse begin to race.

"Have you seen the Professor in the last half hour?" he whispered in the huskiest voice he could manage.

She turned to him sluggishly and grunted.

"Can't say I've missed him actually." Her forehead creased a bit and she began glancing around herself.

"Now that you mention it, my roommate's been in the bathroom quite a while."

He grinned and shrugged his shoulders nervously. "Maybe they all just found a place to nap. I think quite a few might have sneaked out to the bus to stretch out."

"Can't say I blame them," she replied just before covering the yawn that was forthcoming.

Jerry was in the process of reaching over with his right hand and properly introducing himself when the next speaker walked noisily out to the center of the stage.

His partially slumped over torso and thick white hair identified him as a man at least in his fifties, but just exactly what his actual age might be was hard to gauge due to the spring in his walk and the agility of his movements. He wore blue jeans and tennis shoes, along with a black T-shirt with the words 'OLD FART' stenciled across the front in white letters.

Jerry leaned up and whispered, "Looks like this one just had a large dose of his medication."

When he got no response from the blonde girl, not even an indication she had even heard him, he frowned and leaned back softly, his face reddening.

The man's voice was low and shrill, cutting through the still air like a straight razor through Jell-O.

"Good evening, young ladies and germs. I just flew in from the nut house, and boy are my arms tired and needle marked."

A few guffaws, some genuine and some obviously sarcastic, echoed through the large room.

"My name is Randall Costner, and before anyone asks, no, I am not a distant relative of Kevin's. Seriously folks, I am here under the supervision of Doctor Dante and am totally harmless as long as no one is concealing any plastic explosives out there in the crowd."

This time not even a giggle was apparent, and the man cleared his throat and tugged at his collar comically.

"O-Kay. That takes care of the humor segment of the show. Like I said, the name is Randall Costner, and I suffer from manic depression. I have since my sister, Margaret, passed away while a resident in the same institute I now habitat. I loved my sister dearly, but to say the least, she had some...reality problems. Allow me to explain...,"

CHAPTER SEVEN
New Blood

Homer had watched with great interest as she had been rolled into the room next to his. As a resident of the Pine Acres Retirement Home for going on six years, Homer had seen 'em come and go like busboys in a restaurant.

He wasn't exactly sure why he was so curious and inquisitive about this latest addition to their little community, or as he often said "societies loss is our gain" to the ones he liked.

He didn't get a good look at her face from the angle he had been standing, but her dark black hair was what first caught his bifocal covered orbs.

Not even a touch of gray there, and incredibly, it looked natural.

Pete McClancy, Homer's last neighbor down the hall, had passed away a few months back. The bone cancer had finally gotten him after years of remission. Pete had been a quiet sort, but Homer had cracked through the man's protective shell a few times and even gotten him to laugh on several occasions. Homer was infamous at the home for spreading laughter and mischief wherever he went. He was seventy-three now, but as healthy as he had been twenty years before. At one-hundred fifty-seven pounds, he was only five pounds heavier than when he had been twenty-five and working on loading docks all up and down the eastern seaboard. True, some of the weight had settled in strangely different places than in his youth, but at least he was still able to see his Johnson when he peed, as well as his feet when he walked.

He was also very proud of the fact that among the seventeen male residents at Pine Acres, he was the sole owner of his own thick, wavy hair. It was as white as a fresh Colorado snow, true enough, but it was also as layered and healthy as when he had been a boy growing up in rural Arkansas.

Homer stood at the half-closed door to this room and saw Billy and Carol stroll by after helping the women settle in. Billy had been an orderly at the home since Homer arrived. He was a pot-bellied forty something with a sour disposition who Homer had long ago labeled as a 'collector', meaning he was only there to put in his hours and grab that check every two weeks. Carol was a young girl who had just come on board a few months before. She was a 'smiler', one who seems to be able to grin even if she's being punched in the gut. "Smilers' worried Homer. You never knew what exactly was behind that cheery outward appearance. She seemed a little too perky in Homer's professional opinion, as well as others in the home that seemed to be extra cautious in her presence.

As soon as the two orderly's footsteps became too faint to hear, Homer stepped out of his room and took a sharp right. His plan was to pretend he had business at the other end of the hall and get a good look-see at the new blood without being too pushy.

He stepped forward, exaggerating the swing of his arms to give the appearance the stroll had begun further down the hall, and turned his head to the right and glanced inside the room.

The woman was lying on her bed, the wheelchair they had brought her in with sitting in the far corner. She glared directly into Homer's eyes as he passed. He felt a chill run up his spine as he took another few steps down the hall. He paused, then stopped completely. He suddenly felt ridiculous. Doing an about face his old unit commander back in the service would have been proud of, he whirled around and stepped back in front of the room's entrance.

Her dark brown eyes were still trained on his as he cleared his throat and prepared to speak.

"Well hello there. The names Homer. Homer Dustin. No, I did not murder my parents over my first name, nor am I a distant relative of "Mr. Hoffman" with my last. And you are?" She smiled, revealing startlingly white teeth that Homer quickly deduced were not of the genuine variety. It still made her smile a killer though, he thought. Her face was that of a woman in her early fifties, though Homer figured she was at least sixty-five.

"Margaret Bonnel. Pleased to meet you, Mr. Hoffman." Homer grinned, bowing dramatically.

"I hope you liked me in 'Rainman', although I personally believe 'Little Big Man' was my finest performance."

She laughed, the pure sweetness of the sound turning Homer's knees to jelly.

"Homer my good man, where exactly do you reside in our little township?" she asked cheerily.

Gesturing with his right thumb towards the next

room, Homer found himself hypnotized by her gaze.

"Right next door, my good lady. As we are gonna be neighbors, I wanted to be the first to say welcome and add we're glad to have ya."

Margaret nodded agreeably. Homer could feel her gaze burning into his own.

"I appreciate that, Mr. Dustin. I'm glad to have you as a neighbor. I am feeling a bit tired, however. Can we delve further into the intimate details of each other's lives tomorrow?"

His feet shuffling from side to side like a nervous teen, Homer felt himself blush.

"Why certainly, Margaret. I will see you at breakfast. They begin poisoning…whoops, I mean, feeding us at 6 AM. Good night and sleep tight."

Her eyes closed as she leaned her head back onto the bed pillow and sighed.

"Same to you, neighbor. Would you mind clicking that light off as you close the door?" Homer reached over and clicked off the light. "No problem, Margaret. Sweet dreams." As he closed the heavy oak door and heard the click of the knob, Homer had to giggle to himself. He hadn't been that flustered in front of a woman in forty years. He walked with a renewed vigor to the break area and watched the Letterman show with a few of the regulars while sipping orange juice from a can. As his head hit his own pillow around midnight, his thoughts turned to his attractive new neighbor. He slept with a sly smile covering his wrinkled face.

He was eating eggs and ham the next morning, listening to Harvey Wilkes latest speech on the evils of republican government when he saw her wheel herself slowly into the dining area. Wilkes was in the middle of 'Communist Plot' number six-fifty three when Homer waived him off and rose from his meal to join her in line. Wilkes was still babbling as he strolled away, oblivious to any and all movement surrounding him.

The meal line was built with wheelchair bound residents in mind, so there was ample room to maneuver for those who needed it. Margaret was reaching for a bowl of mixed fruit when Homer walked up behind her and cleared his throat nosily. She tilted her head back, her thick hair rustling with the effort, and smiled sweetly.

"Well, good morning neighbor. I see you put on the feedbag pretty darn quick for a man who keeps such late hours."

Homer shrugged, again feeling his face grow red.

"My lady, the alarm clock in my belly is as dependable now as it was decades ago. Besides, how do you know I keep 'late hours'?"

Wheeling herself slowly down the line, Margaret only paused long enough to grab a small box of cereal and a cup of milk. She showed all the skill and technique of a person who had perfected the art of wheelchair navigating. "I heard your door open and shut around Midnight. I was just dozing. You really ought to get that door oiled, Mr. Dustin."

Homer picked up a cup of milk himself; stopping short of adding a piece of apple pie to his breakfast menu, then joined Margaret at one of the specially built handicapped tables. These had adjustable tabletops that one could control the height of the table with simply by turning a knob on the table's edge.

"I think I need to oil more than the door, truth be told, Margaret. And please call me Homer. I realized it sounds a might silly off the tongue, but I have accepted the moniker long ago as my own. As I was going to say, I wouldn't be surprised if it was my old knees popping that woke you up. I apologize. Old football injury." Margaret took a sip of milk and a quick bite of fruit, all the while keeping her eyes fixed on Homer's.

"Old football injury? How long ago was this? Were you playing in a 'Professional Seniors league' I don't know about?"

Homer leaned back with his arms now crossed over his chest.

"Oh no. I was a waterboy at Boyer Tech back in thirty-eight. I got run over by the other teams mascot. We were playing the Wilmore Bulls at the time. My knees have popped like fireworks ever since."

Margaret laughed softly until a cough interrupted. It passed quickly.

"A born athlete, I take it. You're from the south originally, Mr...uh, Homer? Your right, it does feel kind of strange just saying it."

This time Homer laughed, his hands leaving his chest and swinging down to slap his thighs.

"I sincerely apologize. I think my parents were torn between Homer and Carlton. I'm actually thankful of the choice that was made. Yes, I was born and spent my first eighteen years on this earth stomping grounds in Hillview, Arkansas, population two-sixty eight, give or take a cow or two. How about you, Margaret?"

"Saint Paul, Minnesota, born and raised. My husband was an ambassador for the Government, so I did a bit of traveling in my time. I will always be a Golden Gopher at heart, though."

Homer sipped his coffee and glanced over at the breakfast line, which was growing busier as the residents shuffled, some literally, their way in. He spotted Wilbur Jinks, a card playing buddy, and gave him a quick nod.

"I won't hold your Yankee status against you, Margaret, as long as you refrain from mocking the 'Colonel Sanders' drawl that escapes my lips from time to time."

She nodded appreciatively.

"Deal. So, Homer. How many residents do they have here in all?"

"Oh, I believe your admittance makes it an even thirty-four. We had up to forty-three at one time, but we've lost some over the past few years. You're the first new addition in almost a year."

After a sip of juice, she glanced back up at him and sighed.

"Well, Mrs. Topkins did say there was a long waiting list. I signed up almost two years back. This place is considered one of the best in the state."

"Well Margaret, let me tell ya, I've been here almost six years now, and I've had exactly one complaint the entire time."

"And what was that, Homer?" He grinned mischievously. "Despite my desperate pleas, they refuse to get the Playboy Channel."

Instead of the laugh he expected, Homer was surprised and a bit aroused at her upturned eyebrow and pout-lipped expression.

"Ah, the wonders of Viagra, huh?" she replied sheepishly.

For the second time in a 12-hour period, Homer felt himself blushing.

He volunteered to give her his personal 'tour' of the place, despite the fact the staff had done just that the night before.

They checked out the rec-room, complete with pool tables, card tables, foosball table, and four different pinball machines. The TV room was broken off into sections, and three big screen TV's were pushed into the corner of each.

The activity room consisted of a free weight area and ten different nautilus machines, along with padded floors for stretching and sit-ups. On either side of this room was a full length basketball court and indoor swimming pool.

The sauna room consisted of two large whirlpools and three two person Jacuzzis.

There was a fully stocked library on the grounds, as well as a park especially built for the residents that encircled the structure on all sides. A jogging/walking trail zigzagged through tall oak and elm trees, as well as thick, lush shrubbery that lined the trail. There were ample picnic tables and benches on the park grounds, and of course everything was set up with handicapped and wheelchair bound residents in mind.

Homer spent most of the day with Margaret, introducing her to each resident they ran into along the way. That night, the weekly bingo game was scheduled, and Margaret agreed to accompany him there after dinner. Homer felt reinvigorated when he was in Margaret's company, and actually experienced what he thought might have been pangs of jealously when other male residents began openly flirting with her.

After assisting her out of her wheelchair and into her bed that night, Homer reached down and gently kissed her on the right cheek. She had stared into his eyes for a split- second afterwards, and in the light of the room he could see the deep worry lines at the corners of her eyes. She had told him her age to be sixty-seven, but she showed no outward signs of being over fifty, the lines at her eyes the only blemish on her astonishingly youthful face.

After the peck on the cheek, he had left her room without saying another word. As he lay back on his own mattress, his mind kept re-running the day they had shared.

Margaret had told him of the car accident two years ago that left her paralyzed in both legs, and of her husband's death ten years earlier of a massive heart attack. They had been a couple for over thirty years and he had left her with a nice house and enough money to live on comfortably for the rest of her years. She had simply decided that the two-story, three-thousand square foot home was too big and lonely for her to finish her days in, not to mention the toll that keeping it clean took on her. They had one son, and he had passed away at age eight with leukemia. After the heartbreak of that situation, they decided to go childless. With her husband's job requiring he travel so often and far away, Margaret trained for and became a registered nurse. She retired from that career after her husband's passing. She had come to Pine Acres for companionship. She had grown lonely of living in a big, spacious house with no one to share it with.

Homer had given her his own 'Readers Digest' version of 'this is your life' as they ate a dinner consisting of baked pork chops, mashed potatoes, and green peas.

After High School, he had helped his father work the family farm until he left home at age twenty. He and a buddy had gotten into the dock workers union and traveled up and down the East Coast working on the shipping docks. He had spent time in the Carolinas, Maryland, and New York State. He was drafted in 1950 and was immediately sent overseas during the Korean War. He was assigned to a unit near Seoul, and fortunately didn't see a lot of combat action. After his hitch was up in '52, he returned to the docks and worked a few years in Florida and Georgia. A man that he worked for in Myrtle Beach set him up for a supervisor's job in San Diego, California. He spent twelve years running a dock there, before coming back home to Little Rock, Arkansas in '69. He latched on with a book and magazine publishing company and was given the job as warehouse supervisor. He retired from that job in 1991 at the age of sixty-three. He had never married, but had come close more than once. There was a girl in Charleston, then another in Jacksonville. He was even engaged to a girl in Little Rock, but discovered she had been seeing an old boyfriend on the side and called the marriage off.

He found out about Pine Acres through a mutual friend who knew he was looking for a good place to hang out a permanent shingle. Being single, as well as what the old timers called 'a skinflint' throughout his life, Homer had saved a considerable nest egg, and decided at age sixty-seven to let someone else worry about life's little mundane problems while he kicked back until he kicked off.

He had made a lot of close friends in his stay at Pine Acres, including some fetching females his own age, but none that made his old heart pump like a man twenty-five years younger the way Margaret Bonnel did. Around midnight, Homer fell asleep with a small smile pasted across his weathered face.

At five-thirty Am the next morning, they found Harvey Wilkes' body. Billy Conroy had been doing his morning grounds walk-through and discovered Harvey lying between two shrubs outside the rec building's west wall. The rumor was going around by about noon that Billy had to be sedated and sent home for the day. Chester McDaniel, a thirteen-year resident of the home, had been mulling around the scene when the ambulance came to pick up the body. Chester was having lunch with Homer and Perry Boone that day and told them he heard one of the 'medics' throwing up in the bushes and the other one moaning and groaning that 'he hadn't ever seen anything like it.' Mrs. Topkins directed the rest of the staff to steer clear of the site, and to ensure all residents did the same, until it could be 'cleaned up'.

The residents were told the next day that Harvey had suffered 'a major stroke' and died almost instantly. Homer had glanced over at Chester McDaniel when this announcement was made and saw him shaking his head vehemently.

Homer hadn't seen much of Margaret the day Harvey had passed. When she hadn't shown up at breakfast, Homer had knocked on her room's door and then gently pushed it open. She was sleeping peacefully, her face a portrait of tranquility.

He had a group basketball game scheduled at eleven that morning, but it had been cancelled after the situation with Harvey. He shot some pool with Perry Boone and Walter Mitkins until lunchtime, but retired from that after discovering he had somehow shattered a fingernail in the process. He then decided to skip the midday meal and again look in on Margaret. She was still in her bed, reading a thick novel, and told Homer she was having one of her 'headache' days, and simply needed to rest.

Homer saw her the next day at breakfast, and thought she looked more radiant than ever, if that was possible.

"Good morning, sunshine. Boy, were you right about that beauty rest. You look fantastic."

She practically beamed as she replied, her eyes almost fiery in their alertness.

"Well, hello neighbor of mine! Yes, I have to admit there are days I have to get my thirteen to fourteen hours of slumber just to feel human the next day."

Homer sipped the steaming hot coffee and winced. He hadn't slept very well after the previous day's events. He had bandaged his busted finger from shooting pool, but it was still managing to throb just enough to drive him crazy. He felt his smile was a bit forced, and the chronic neck problem he had suffered from for thirty years was sounding off in Dolby stereo.

"Did you hear about Harvey Wilkes?" He asked casually.

Margaret nodded slowly, pausing before taking a large bite of eggs and sausage. "Yes. So sad. Do they have any idea yet of what happened?"

"Not a clue. Rumors swirl around here like bats in a cave. It seems, however, that natural causes has been ruled out. I hear they're thinking of hiring an outside security firm to guard us. Just what I always wanted to be a part of, a police state retirement community."

Margaret paused in mid bite, then gave Homer a concerned look. "They believe...somebody killed him?" Homer shrugged, dismissing the remainder of his coffee with a scowl. "I hear the man's head was completely torn off and sitting a few feet from the body. Poor old Billy Conroy was shaking so bad the medics had to give him a handful of Quaaludes. I hear he's taking the rest of the week off just to try and get over what he saw."

Pushing her unfinished food away, Margaret reached over and laid her right hand on top of Homer's.

"I'm sorry, Homer. He was a good friend of yours, wasn't he?"

Feeling his eye's begin to mist, Homer avoided direct eye contact with her and instead stared out the dining hall's wide glass windows.

"Harvey was kind of a loner, actually, but you can't help but get acquainted in a close knit society

178

like this. He and I used to ride the Home's shuttle to the mall and take in a movie, along with some of the other guys. He was a firecracker on political subjects, but pretty reserved otherwise. I hear Ms. Topkins has called a resident meeting at six tonight to discuss what really happened."

After a day spent together that included a long walk, lunch, and playing gin, Margaret told Homer she needed a few hours rest before dinner and the resident meeting. Homer sat on the small couch in his room, listening to a Frank Sinatra CD, and wrestling with the feelings he was building for his attractive neighbor. He glanced outside through the small window over his bed and sighed deeply, a new moistness at the corners of his eyes.

Ms. Topkins, a chubby, somewhat anal looking woman in her mid-forties, called the meeting to attention at straight up six o'clock. All thirty-three residents were present, although Perry Boone was fast asleep in his chair and others seemed primed to join him at any moment. Ms. Topkins slightly mousy voice echoed off the walls of the library conference room, causing more than a few to frown in response. Homer sat with Walter Mitkins on one side of him and Margaret on the other. Predictably, there weren't told, at least not at first, anything they didn't already know. Yes, Harvey had not died of natural causes, but from some kind of attack. Yes, the Blankenship Security Company would be providing part time security services during the night time hours. Then came the part that did open some eyes, even Perry Boone's baggy set.

The local authorities were filing the death under the heading of 'animal attack'. Whispers and low mumbling filled the room almost at once, even some sarcastic laughter.

"What the hell was it, Big Foot?" Lucinda Cruz bellowed in her whiny tone, causing an outbreak of howls.

Ms. Topkins waived off the remarks and dismissed everyone, but not before ensuring them all that 'the staff at Pine Acres will continue to provide the finest service possible to its 'special' residents'. She reiterated the point ad nauseam, but her face revealed just how difficult it was to sell the comfort and 'good living' of a retirement home that was just the scene of such a gruesome, mysterious death.

Later, over fresh coffee in the rec-room, Margaret asked Homer his theory on the apparent homicide.

"Well, my dear lady, I can almost assuredly tell you it was not any kind of animal mauling. The only animals that inhabit the surrounding woods are squirrels, chipmunks, and maybe a small fox or three. None of the above can do the damage I heard about unless Harvey was already dead when the animal went to work on 'im. I truly believe we had some sort of demented maniac outside the grounds that night."

Margaret gasped aloud, her right hand brought to her chest.

"Do you think it's someone who lives near the home, or even…no, that's crazy."

His elbows resting on the table, Homer removed them and leaned over the tabletop towards her.

"What? What sounds crazy?"

She hesitated, then the words came out in a rush. "Do you think somebody here did it? I mean, did he have enemies?"

Homer leaned back and laughed, although a bit nervously.

"No…I mean, no way. Ol' Harv didn't anger anybody. He could be a bit of a grump at times, but hell, we all are at this age. Far as I know, he wasn't the kind to draw the attention of a murderer."

"What about the staff? Or maybe a family member of his? Do you know where he was from?"

Homer held up his hands as if to block off any more questions.

"Whoa there, Nancy Drew. The staff isn't even here after 5 PM at night, just on call. I doubt if one of them would come back to the home to murder him, or have any reason to. Harv could be a horses' ass around us at times, but not a troublemaker with the staff. He had no family to speak of. He buried 'em all. I think ol' Harv was pushing eighty or eighty- one. He didn't have any kids and his wife died ten years ago."

Margaret folded her arms onto her chest. Her eyes were stern and her face drawn tight.

"I can't believe I spend almost two years picking out just the right retirement home, and it turns into a damn 'Matlock' rerun." This time, Homer's laugh was more at ease and natural sounding. "I'd say it's closer to 'Perry Mason', but then I am older than you are."

Margaret excused herself a few moments later, leaving Homer alone to sip Java and once again ponder his true feelings towards her. There was definitely an attraction there, but it was accompanied by a mysterious foreboding he couldn't quite grasp.

The next morning, Homer awoke at around 7:45 AM and peeked out his window. Thick sheets of rain blew across the grounds, and the remnants of what had more than likely been a thick fog earlier still lingered a few inches off of the moist grass.

By the time he brushed his teeth and combed through his tangled hair, it was close to 8:15. At 8:20 he arrived at the dining room, and found it eerily deserted. He usually got to breakfast by six-thirty or seven at the latest, but on the occasions he had arrived after eight, there had always been a pretty good sized group congregating around the coffee pot. About half the residents were late risers, including a few of the regulars he hung with on a regular basis, so he was set back by the absenteeism. He had poured himself some Java and was reaching for a biscuit when the hand came down gently on his left shoulder, almost causing him to drop the biscuit to the tiled floor.

"Sorry I startled ya, Homer."

Homer whirled around to face Perry Boone, whose face seemed paler and gaunter than ever, his eyes sunk deep into their wrinkled sockets.

"Morning, Per. Where the hell is everybody this morning? Was I the only late sleeper or what?"

Perry removed his hand from Homer's shoulder and leaned back, both of his liver spot ravaged hands propped on the heavy oak cane that was his constant companion.

"You mean you haven't heard about Lucinda?"

Homer sat his cup down on the nearest table.

He saw that Perry's whole body was trembling.

"What about her?"

Wiping the moistness from his eyes, Perry spoke with a voice on the verge of cracking. "You know how she loved those late night walks? She told us last night nothin' was gonna stop her from enjoyin' that. She said she paid enough money to this place to be able to do what she wanted. Th-they found...her and a security guard this morning. They was...torn to pieces, Homer. Walter saw the bodies 'fore they wrapped 'em up in garbage bags. He said ya couldn't tell which body part went with what body.." Perry did break down at that point, and Homer moved over to grasp the other man's shaking shoulders. Lucinda had been loud, boisterous, and had to have her way. She was also well liked by everyone who took the time to get to know the person underneath the act.

After a half-hour of searching, Homer found Margaret along the park path, her chair sitting underneath a still blooming oak.

There was none of the usual good humor in her expression as she turned to meet his gaze. "Margaret, are you okay?" he asked quietly, kneeling down on her right side to allow for eye-to-eye contact.

"She won't be the last, you know," she replied, her eyes unblinking and burning into his with a grim intensity he never knew she possessed.

"Wh-what do you mean? How would you kn-.."

"There is a dark force that lives among the innocent here. I have felt it since the day I was rolled into the entrance to the home. I realize now why I stayed instead of running. I'm through running, Homer. I'm...tired. I've never been so tired. I feel for the three innocents. It should not have been them."

Homer stood up, his face frozen in stark puzzlement.

"Margaret, what are you talking about? I know you're scared....hell, we all are, but we have to..."

She glared up at him, tears trailing down her jaw lines in thick streams.

"The other residents should leave the grounds, Homer. It isn't safe for anyone, and they are not the true targets here. He feels threatened since my arrival here, and he's lashing out. It's as simple as that."

Homer threw up his hands in frustration.

"Who feels threatened? What in the living hell are you talking abo..,"

Her face now void of expression, Margaret rolled away quickly, her thin arms pushing her along frantically back towards the residential buildings.

"Margaret! Hold up a minute!" Homer bellowed as her jogged to catch up with her. He stopped a few feet short of pulling even with her chair as she raised her right hand from the chair's wheel and waived him off impatiently.

"Leave me be, Homer. I seek privacy. I will talk to you later in the evening. Don't be mad at me, my friend. I just need to think."

Around noon, all residents were called to the conference room and told they were to be moved to a local hotel for the duration of the police department's investigation into the three murders on the grounds. Ms. Topkins, her voice cracking wildly, apologized for the inconvenience and reiterated the Pine Acres policy that all residents would receive sufficient financial reimbursement for the forced movement. She wanted each resident to pack their essential clothing and medication and be ready to board a bus by six that evening. Homer noticed that Margaret left halfway through Topkins' speech. He desperately wanted to follow her, but decided to wait until after the meeting. The words she had spoken earlier that morning haunted him.

She had sounded like a woman on the verge of breakdown. More terrifying, she had been on the edge of sounding suicidal.

It was almost 2 PM by the time Homer reached his room. He had knocked on Margaret's closed door and got no response. He tried the knob and found it unlocked. She had already left. Her bed was made and all lights had been turned off. As he packed his gym bag with underwear, shaving cream, toothpaste, and his daily medications, he tried to figure out where she could have gone. The bus didn't leave for another four hours. He considered that maybe she had called a relative and had them pick her up. As sad as the thought was, he wouldn't have blamed her. She had been at Pine Acres for three days and three people had been mysteriously slaughtered. Homer secretly wished he had somewhere, or someone to run to. He noticed his hands shaking uncontrollably as he reached to zip up his tightly packed gym bag.

**

At nine PM, Homer jerked awake, almost

185

spilling off the hotel mattress onto the hard wood floors below. He had lain down just to relax his blood shot eyes and dozed off into a deep, dreamless sleep.

He picked up the phone after the third ring, his mind becoming clearer with each passing second.

"Meet me on the grounds, beside the main picnic area. I'll be waiting, my friend."

Homer tried to speak but only managed a low grunting noise at the sound of Margaret's calm, strangely seductive voice. He heard a low click and then the dial tone. His mind, still wrapped in cobwebs from his slumber, raced with possibilities. Why did she not accompany them to the hotel that evening?

Where did she go? Why did she want to meet him on the killing grounds that had become the Pine Acres retirement home? Most importantly, why did he know that he somehow must meet her demand?

He called a taxi from the Holiday Inn's lobby at nine fifteen. He wore a T-shirt and jeans. He paid the driver with moist, sweaty hands as he exited at the front gate of Pine Acres. The gate was locked, and the deafening silence of the area sent chill bumps up Homer's forearms. He walked around the right perimeter of the low Iron Gate that encircled the home, and ended just inside a clump of thick shrubbery. He pushed back the shrubbery and made his way down the dark park trail. He realized with some shock that it wasn't fear he was feeling, but a bizarre surge of excitement. He picked up his pace as he neared the large overhang that was known as the main picnic area. She was sitting underneath the wooden overhang, beside one of the long picnic tables.

He heard her sigh nervously as he neared.

"I knew you'd come, Homer my friend. I think you realized you had to," she murmured weakly.

Homer sat down slowly onto the picnic table, facing her. Her face was still blurry in the darkness, but she had greeted him with the same seductive tone she had used on the telephone earlier. He could feel the pulse at his temples pound relentlessly.

"Where did you go, Margaret? I was, that is, the staff and everyone was worried about you. We all left around six for the Holiday Inn.."

She held up her right hand in a stop gesture. Homer's mouth froze agape.

"It has to end here, Homer. Far too many innocents have died through the years. It cannot be allowed to continue."

Homer reached over and touched her cheek. She cringed back at first, then allowed his hand to settle on her cool, dry cheek.

"Margaret, my dear, you have awakened my old heart in the few days I've had the pleasure to know you. I want you to stop talking this suicidal nonsense! You have so much to give. I…I have so much to give to you."

Homer could feel the warm tears coat his fingers as she sobbed quietly.

"Oh, my poor dear Homer. You are oblivious to it all, aren't you? I truly believe you are. My god, this makes it much, much harder. This makes it…cruel somehow."

Smiling weakly, Homer stood up and backed away a step.

"Oblivious to what, Margaret? You've been talking in riddles since yesterday. Please tell me what this is all about."

Her chair rolling back a few feet onto the concrete, Margaret pulled the object from underneath the sheet that covered her wilting legs. It took Homer a full thirty seconds to decipher exactly what the dark object was, and another thirty to comprehend it was being pointed towards him in a threatening manner.

"Oh, I'll explain everything to you, Homer. You deserve that, if nothing else. I know now you are as innocent a pawn as the victims that you claim."

His hands frozen at his sides, Homer's eyes darted back and forth from Margaret's face to the revolver she held steadily aimed at his chest.

"Margaret, wh-why are you pointing a g-gun at me?" he managed through trembling lips.

"Tell me Homer, when you told me your life story, why did you omit your stay at the Rimsdale Retirement home?"

His eyes grew wide and his brow furrowed, as if the door to a room which held a buried memory had just been roughly pried open.

"You were a resident there for a little over three years, remember? You left there and found your way here. Strange circumstances arose there, I understand. Two residents were found ripped apart on successive nights. It was chalked up to a bear attack on both counts, since Rimsdale was surrounded by thick forests that held such animals. We know better, don't we, Homer?"

Homer's mouth twitched as his arms became

visibly soaked with fresh perspiration. "Rims-d-dale? I do-don't recall..."

Margaret lifted the barrel of the revolver until it was trained on Homer's forehead. He could see her grim, sarcastic grin in the grainy moonlight.

"I had just come aboard as an assistant administrator just days before the killings. I had worked at several retirement homes before my husband passed away, and decided to continue my career out of sheer boredom. I was especially thrilled to get the position at Rimsdale. You see, my mother was a resident there. She was until the night they found her frail, ghost white body sprawled out underneath a large oak tree just a few feet behind the exercise yard. Her head was found lodged between two tree branches. I found it quite strange you were the only resident out of the fifty-six at Rimsdale to depart after the killings. I could not accept as easily as the local law that animals had killed my mother and poor old Mr. Kemp. The killings stopped just as you had left the day after the second one. There wasn't enough left of Mr. Kemp to bury. His remaining teeth had to be used to ID the body. The next day, you left, siting 'unsafe conditions' for your reason for withdrawal from Rimsdale."

His hands now held out palms up like a street beggar hoping for a quarter, Homer's head began to shake from side to side in a gesture of denial.

"In my grief and anger, I did my own little investigation. I have some connections through my husband, and one is with the Federal Bureau of Investigation. He gave me access to your records, Homer. Both military and everything they had on you as a civilian. Imagine my surprise when I found out that Homer Jud Dustin was born February 14th, 1887. I must say, Homer, you look damn healthy for a man of a hundred and twelve. Your military record shows you fought in WWI. I thought at first there had been some kind of mix-up with your dad's records, but everything matched up to you, right down to your social security number and fingerprints. I've followed your movements through the years since. You stayed at a bordering house for almost a year, but left after the unexplained death of one of the borders while you lived there. You were questioned by the local authorities, but of course they released you after a routine interview. Not their fault. How could they possibly know what you are, Homer?"

Homer blinked madly, his whole body beginning to convulse like a patient stricken with Parkinson's.

"What... I am? M-Margaret, what are you talking about? P-Please put down the gun." Ignoring his pleas, she kept the barrel trained on the center of his forehead, her hand as steady as a rock.

"I had almost caught up with you at that home in Charleston. In fact, I was on my way there when I had my accident. Dreaming of the day when I would face you in this position is what kept me going during the years of rehab I had to endure. When I discovered a resident at the Charleston home had been killed during your brief stay there, my suspicions became fact. Of course the local and federal cops are going to again label them 'animal attacks'. They will not, or cannot face the truth that such as your kind exists. I came here not knowing exactly what I would do when I faced you. I actually like you, Homer. The second morning I was here, I waited for the police to leave the area and I executed my own personal crime scene investigation. I found a claw embedded in an elm tree right near where the poor man's torn body was found.

I noticed that day that one of your fingers was bandaged, possibly covering a ruined or totally missing nail. Believe me, Homer, it took years for me to accept the fact that creatures such as you actually exist."

Homer threw his arms up wildly, his face a wide, frozen snarl. He seemed to almost be growling.

"Creatures such as what, Margaret? I'm starting to get extremely pissed off at how vague you're being as you point what I will assume is a loaded pistol at my head!"

Margaret rolled away another half foot or so, her expression a mixture of pity and admiration.

"I'm so sorry, Homer. You've been living this nightmare for so long and didn't even know what was happening all around you. I suspected as much. You were...too nice a man. You have unknowingly carried the curse for decades. God knows how you contracted it. I pity you, but I cannot forgive. I must carry out what I began to do years ago. Your soul is Lupine now, Homer, not human."

The hammer clicked back on the revolver. Homer's eyes closed tightly, as if hoping that when he re-opened them, both the woman and the gun would have been figments of his imagination, and he would be standing alone under the overhang. When he did open them, his vision was blurred somehow. He felt his scalp grown suddenly hot, and his entire body tingled as if electrically shocked.

Margaret gasped when the changes became obvious. His eyes went from brown to fiery red, almost glowing. The hair on his slick arms became noticeably darker and thicker. She gripped the revolver in both hands and took careful aim.

Homer opened his mouth one last time, possibly to plead his case before sentence was carried out, but a guttural growl was all that escaped. A growl that revealed incisors over an inch long. His forehead began to contract and bulge.

His shirt ripped at the breastbone, and long, razor like claws replaced the stubby human nails at the tips of his now hideously elongated fingers. He lunged forward just as the shot echoed, temporarily lighting up the area in a flash of white sparks.

A moment later, two more shots followed in succession.

Margaret wheeled forward and stared into the bloodied face of Homer Dustin, casually removing the silver shells from the cylinder of the revolver and pocketing them in her windbreaker's pocket.

She took the time to weep at the complete shock and puzzlement that his face expressed.

She whispered a single word over his body, then wheeled herself away from Pine Acres Retirement Home.

That word was her mother's first name.

"My sister was to be tried for the murder of Homer Dustin, but they found her mentally unfit before it ever came to trail. She had been spouting on about werewolves and creatures of the night and such, and she ended up spending her days sedated and, on certain occasions, strapped to her bed."

A few scattered coughs and throat clearings emerged from the audience, and the old man stepped back and closed his eyes, his hands still gripping the podium on both sides. When he spoke again, a weariness had crept into his words.

"My family had, as far I as knew, never had a history of mental problems. I tried to chalk up my sister's to the tragic death of her husband, a man she loved more than life itself. I've done a lot of soul-searching as to whether or not I did all I could to help her while she was institutionalized. In the time since her death, my own sanity has slipped a cog. You see, I refused to visit my sister after she was institutionalized. We hadn't been very close since childhood.

I guess I thought walking into the walls of that facility might seem like an invitation for madness to seep into my own mind. The guilt I suffer through now, as I was Margaret's only living kin, is ten times worse than anything I could have heard uttered from my sister's lips. I've attempted suicide three times in the last two years, and I swear to god I don't recall any of the incidents. Somewhere in the sky, I feel my sister watching me. Monitoring me. I can't help but feel she just might be gleefully reveling at my downfall. I hope…I'm wrong."

The spring had left the man's steps as he exited, and the lights of the auditorium lit up to their full capacity just as he ducked behind the curtain.

Jerry blinked a few times to allow his eyes to adjust to the sudden brightness, and then turned his attention back to the blonde girl, who was stretching out her arms and yawning.

"I guess this is finally break time," he mumbled, wanting to slap himself for sounding so tentative.

"Long overdue, I say," she replied without turning around, then glanced casually at her watch.

"We've already been in this rat-hole for two and a half hours."

Jerry's mind raced as he tried desperately to come up with a witty comeback.

"I hear ya. Watching the grass grow rates higher than this on the excitement meter," he blurted as he rubbed his suddenly sweaty hands together.

The girl ignored the remark and stood slowly, her knees popping as she rose.

"Gotta go pee. Save my seat, will ya?" she asked sarcastically, still not bothering to actually meet his eyes.

"Actually, I have to go drain the weasel myself," he spouted, his mouth frozen in a painful grimace after the realization of what he had just said sunk in.

She glanced at him as she strolled away, a look of pure disgust on her heavily made up face.

"Thanks for sharing that lovely sentiment," she smirked.

Jerry smacked himself on the side of the head with an open palm and cursed under his breath.

"Drain the weasel? Drain the freakin' weasel? Way to go, Jer. You're a real study in modern romance."

He pulled himself weakly from the seat and debated whether or not to actually make the long trek to the men's john. He finally decided to go for no other reason than to give his legs some work, when he noticed the next speaker already positioned at the podium.

"Jeez, give me a break," he murmured, although deep inside he couldn't deny the morbid fascination each story contained. He looked around before re-taking his seat and noticed that the dozen or so other students that sat scattered all around him had the same look. They couldn't wait for the next chapter in the annals of insanity that was about to be unfurled.

"Good evening. My...my name is Martha. Martha Brackens."

Her ample girth somewhat hidden underneath the large, pulled out shirt she wore, the woman brushed the long, gray-streaked brown hair from her forehead and placed her hands behind her back as if at parade rest in a military formation. Her voice was muffled somewhat as she placed her mouth too close to the small mike as she spoke. She backed away an inch or two and smiled in embarrassment.

"Sorry about that. This is all new to me. Like I said, my name is Martha. I had a stepson named Michael. Michael Watkins being his full name. My ex-husband and I raised him from the time he was a young child due to his folks being killed in a car crash.

Mike witnessed the accident, and was traumatized by it as he grew up. He had multiple personalities and lived in his own hallucination-filled world most of the time. He was…involved in a string of homicides in his early twenties and was finally captured and placed in an asylum. My ex-husband and I were hounded by the media, who seemed to be placing the blame for the…murders at our doorstep. It drove my husband and I apart after twenty-six years of marriage. I've had some problems coping since…Michael's release. He was allowed to re-join society almost a year ago, and hasn't been seen since. He spent almost four years in treatment, and I am both relieved and disappointed that I haven't heard from him. Here is his story…"

CHAPTER EIGHT
The Thin CRIMSON Line

Watkins leaned over the toilet and threw up for the third time in an hour. He had barely made it to the bathroom in time, and practically tore the stall door off its hinges in desperation. He stayed down on one knee after wiping the vomit from his chin with tissue, his free hand rubbing his temples briskly.

Eight years he had been a Highway Patrolman for the great state of Georgia, and in that time had come upon many a gruesome scene; auto accidents with victims so mangled it was hard to tell what part of the body went where; unfortunate hitchhikers found lying in ditches with throats cut open or bullet wounds in their chest or head; women wandering the shoulder of the road in search of help after being brutally, sadistically raped. All of these incidents flashed through his mind briefly from time to time. He tried, as did everyone in his line of work, he surmised, to keep such grisly memories at bay.

Part of the job was to forget what you had witnessed the day before, and start fresh with each shift. The psyche wouldn't accept dwelling on such graven images, or you'd find yourself managing a McDonalds or stocking items at Wal-Mart very quickly. He slowly rose to his feet, flushing the remains of what had to be the last of a Fish sandwich and fries he had consumed earlier that night, and sat down with a weary sigh next to his locker. He could hear the news media hounds scurrying outside in the department lobby like roaches in the dark. He would have to go out and face them eventually. The public relations officer could only hold them off for so long. Captain Williams had told him to take as long as needed to clear his head. His response was a nod, although the temptation was to query the good Captain on exactly how many years that might take; how many nights waking up screaming with arms flailing about madly, swinging at an unknown assailant; how many night and day mares that would affect not only his job but his marriage, his relationship with his kids, his parents, every human he would ever come into contact with.

Why him? That question kept repeating over and over. Why did route forty three have to be his tonight? Why not city limits patrol? Why not interstate? Lady luck had sure insisted he bent over and grab his ankles on this day. Watkins leaned back and closed his eyes. He knew he had to coordinate his thoughts for the taped report he had to transcribe within the next few hours.

He grimaced and held his head in his hands while attempting to recall everything that had transpired in some kind of sane order. Sane, a word he might ever quite grasp the true meaning of again.

***

It had been a slow night. He had been on shift four of his scheduled six road hours. Two speeding tickets and an improper lane change had been the only boredom breakers to that point. He had pulled over an elderly couple on their way to Florida a few minutes earlier. The husband, 74 years young according to his license, had been doing 44 MPH in a 65 zone, providing ample opportunity for road rage from his fellow drivers. The man, gripping the wheel as though he were trying to avoid plunging off a cliff top, promised to 'keep it over 55' and rambled off with a denture-enhanced smile.

Fifteen minutes later, Watkins spotted the bus. It was one of those Greyhound double- decker jobs, sitting slightly crooked and off the shoulder of the road. He pondered why the driver didn't have the hazard's displayed as he exited his unit and walked towards the hulking vehicle. He noticed no inside lights shone as he neared the door, and quickly deduced that it must be deserted. He yelled out a quick "hello in there" before pushing the door open, and found himself reeling back as if struck by a tidal wave.

An intoxicatingly strong odor of copper, along with other pungent, unrecognizable smells forced Watkins to back out of the door in disgust. For moment, Watkins was remembering when he was a kid of eleven or twelve, observing his dad gut a pig on their farm. He recalled the odor when the hog's intestine was punctured by his father's blade. One quick whiff and he found himself throwing up in some nearby weeds. This was a similar stench, but magnified tenfold. Watkins climbed back in, this time reaching the bus drivers' console and finding the inside dome lights. He hit the switch and turned to face the source of the odor. Watkins had no idea how much time expired before he forced himself to take a step forward, or how much longer before the local cops were picking him up off of the ground, where he had been sitting outside his unit, the mike still grasped tightly in his hand.

The Heads were missing. Just...gone. All the bodies were horrifically present and accounted for, however.

Torsos intact; legs, arms, feet, all stacked neatly like cordwood before a fireplace, but the space usually taken up by the skull was surrealistically transparent. He had thought crazily for a moment that it was a joke, a gruesome prank left for the first person unfortunate enough to discover the bus. But the grisly odor left by the bodies pushed that theory away quickly. Most of the victims were still in their seat, some still sitting upright as if calmly awaiting to arrive at their destination. A few were lying in the bus isle, legs splayed out in awkward fashion, the fragmented bone stubs protruding from their ravaged necks. There were massive amounts of blood, mostly covering the bus windows and the parts of the seats that weren't inhabited by a body. Watkins couldn't recall checking the bus's upper deck for more carnage.

Somewhere about decapitated body number seventeen, his brain had initiated the automatic shut-off switch.

Watkins' dad had raised cattle and pigs for a living, and upon request also performed the slaughtering and the meat packing, so young Watkins had seen his share of bloodletting. Over the last eight years, he had also seen plenty of gore and spatter. One particular incident had always stood out in his mind when he visualized such unpleasantness.

It had been the day he came home from high school and found his deceased mother. There had been no blood; her heart had simply gone out on her at the reasonably young age of 44. She had always carried an extra 70 pounds on a small frame, and the years of unhealthy eating habits and habitual smoking had simply caught up with her.

Watkins had been frozen at her bedroom door, unable to break his gaze from her open, seemingly aware eyes.

Her left hand gripped her right breast and had apparently been locked into position since death. His dad, almost 10 years her senior, took her passing as a sign the end was near for him as well. They had been married over 25 years, and only knew and trusted each other.

Watkins had been their only child, and at age 20, just two years after his mom's death, his father also passed. Watkins had been away at college, his sophomore year, and hadn't been home in months.

His dad had gotten up one fall day, walked into the barn he had built with his own hands 20 years earlier, and shoved the barrel of a twenty gauge shotgun into his mouth. When Watkins went to identify the body, only the lower half of his father's head was spared the force of the blast. He identified him by the old faded bird tattoo on his chest that he had received while serving in the Navy during WWII. Now over nine years since that day, the sight of his mother's open eyes still haunted him, inducing sleepless nights that even the gruesome memory of his father's sheared off head couldn't match.

Now here he was again, faced with heads. Missing heads.

Watkins leaned down and placed his own head into his large hands and began to cry softly. He damned himself for letting this situation transform him from a stoic, professional lawman into a shivering mass of shattered nerves. His low sobs halted a few moments later as he realized how jarringly quiet his surroundings had suddenly become. The echoing voices of the media hordes had ceased outside the bathroom doors. Watkins stood up and took a few deep breaths, running his fingers through his mangled hair to straighten it, and prepared to exit his personal safe haven and face the music. He figured the media had all been shuffled off to the department's conference room, and were probably waiting with itchy fingers on their respective tape recorders to be filled in on all the grisly details on what exactly had found on that lonely stretch of pavement. Feeling somewhat calmer, Watkins walked out into the department's spacious lobby, preparing to ward off at least a few would be Dan Rather's, but instead found the entire floor deserted. Even the desk officer's chair was vacant, the computer screen positioned there flashing current calls awaiting investigation. His legs still feeling a bit shaky, he walked stiffly towards the conference room, which was down a lengthy, narrow hallway on the east side of the building. As he stood just outside the large oak door entrance, Watkins was again puzzled by the eerie silence enveloping the entire structure. He heard several phones ringing down both sides of the hallway, but none were being answered.

Shrugging his shoulders and sighing deeply, he stepped into the conference room and felt his eyes begin to sting and burn in total denial to the scene developing within their bloodshot confines.

Watkins fell back against the closed door, his mouth attempting to form a scream, although the oxygen required to perform such a function remained frozen in his lungs.

There were bodies sitting upright in the conference room chairs, at least twenty, maybe twenty-five of them. There was also a human form leaning half-bent against the podium that faced the chairs. Watkins left foot slid forward involuntarily, almost causing him to topple backwards.

After regaining his balance, he glanced down and noticed the thick trail of blood on the tiled floor, his own shoe print clearly outlined.

The majority of the bodies were sitting upright, some even looked as though they had been posed there like department store mannequins. Watkins noticed in disbelief that one held a tape recorder in one hand and was holding it out in front of his crimson coated chest, seemingly in preparation for an upcoming statement.

Blood jelled in thick streams all along the floor and onto any unoccupied seats. Watkins noticed a drying line of dark red liquid running down the projector screen behind the podium. It resembled a neatly laid line of maroon dap, but Watkins knew better. His chapped lips formed the word "heads" as he scrambled backwards out the door, momentarily tripping onto his left side into the hallway. He leaped to his wobbly feet and ran as quickly as his shaken legs would allow. He streaked past the deserted desk officer's cubicle, and straight back into the serenity of the bathroom.

He tried to throw up again but failed, managing only a few futile dry heaves before the convulsions subsided.

Watkins stumbled to a mirrored sink and began splashing his face frantically with cool water, his right eye beginning to tick spasmodically.

He screamed as he threw the water into this mouth, and onto his head and Chest. "Where the hell are all the heads?"

He repeated this until it became a ritualistic chant. The scream became a whisper, and as he turned off the water and glared at his reflection in the water sprayed mirror, he first noticed the change. His badge was missing. His name tag was no longer over his right pocket. His shirt was orange instead of blue.

There were numbers stenciled onto the shirt over his left breast pocket. He leaned in closer and read what was typed in tiny letters underneath the numbers.

Watkins began to vigorously shake his head from side to side; first slowly while still glaring into the mirror, then faster with increased force.

Watkins ran from the bathroom, his arms flailing like a man fighting off a swarm of bees.

He turned sharply and ran for the front exit, and was tackled to the pavement almost instantly. He attempted to fight off his attackers, who seemed to be in great numbers, although he was unable to register anything about them due to the swiftness of their movements. He heard one of them telling another 'not to hurt him', and another yell for someone to 'hand him the syringe'. He felt a slight pricking at his left shoulder. Sweet, merciful darkness swept over his senses mere moments later.

***

The two men leaned with their backs against the cool corridor walls, their whispering voices barely audible, although all room doors were closed tight and the hallway totally vacant. The older of the two held a clipboard in his left hand, and was scribbling on it as the younger man spoke.

"I'm really at a loss, Wayne. I've prescribed everything we have available, and at doses that are above what I normally allow. This last episode was the worst by far. I'm afraid constant sedation is all we have left at this point."

The older man placed his pen into his right coat pocket, lowered his clipboard, and stared straight ahead at the bare white walls.

"I would definitely keep him out for a few days. I'll order Mac to run additional neurological tests by the end of the week. Bill, give me a brief history here. I read his file, but it's been a year or two since I've reviewed anyone on this floor."

The younger man turned to the older, rubbing the obvious fatigue from his eyes before replying.

"He's been treated since he was thirteen. Just counseling at first, followed by more intense psychological sessions. He was taking sedatives by age fourteen. Tragic car accident. As bad as it gets. They were coming over a hill doing about seventy and ran under the back of a stalled commercial bus that was still in the road. His mother was killed from the impact from blunt trauma to the head. His dad was decapitated. Little Mike was bruised but fully awake when they found them. He was in the back seat with his seat belt on and his dad's severed head at his feet in the floorboard. His dad was a decorated State Trooper that had been on the job over 25 years. He was only three weeks from retirement, poor guy. Well, Little Mike is twenty-two now and still can't get over what he saw. Just when we thought he was responding, he'd get picked up on the interstate attempting to pull people over with a flashlight on his dash. We always deduced he was, in some way, trying to carry on his father's legacy.

He always told me he was going to be a trooper. He turned in applications at the station constantly. That's where they grabbed him this time. He was running around inside the old deserted trooper building downtown, the one his dad spent years working out of. He still had his patient gown on over a pair of stolen blue jeans.

There was even smeared blood on the shirt, origin unknown. We've already disciplined the night shift guard that allowed him to wander off the grounds. Wayne, every known treatment has been attempted on this young man. His foster parents pretty much let the state have him a few years back. They just couldn't cope with his breakdowns anymore. I don't mind saying I'm damn frustrated on where to go from here."

The older man put his hand on the younger ones right shoulder and smiled amiably. "Dr. Wilkes, you are starting to sound like a veteran of the ward.

He will respond in time. He will never completely heal or live what we consider a 'normal' existence, but he will settle. Believe me, I've seen them almost comatose for years, then observed in amazement as they slowly, painstakingly pulled back into reality. Be patient, doctor. It will transpire."

The other man shrugged and started down the dimly lit hallway.

"I hope so, Doctor Clark. I just fear there's a breaking point for Mr. Watkins, and someday he'll reach it without anyone around to properly prevent his inner demon from lashing out."

The young doctor reached his ground-level office a few moments later and was greeted by two men standing outside the locked office door. The men wore the obvious look of veteran police detectives; tired eyes, rumpled suits, sour dispositions.

The larger of the two stepped forward as the doctor neared. The 'Ward Visitor' badges they wore hung crookedly from their jacket pockets.

"Doctor Wilkes?"

"Yes?"

"I'm Detective Martinson, 22nd precinct. This is Detective McKay. We need to talk to you about a patient of yours. A...Mike Watkins. I believe he was brought in this evening after a short bout of freedom."

The doctor unlocked his door and the men followed him inside, their shoulders collectively slumped. The doctor thought it looked like they hadn't slept in days.

"Yes, Mike got off the grounds for a few hours.

He was picked up by some of your officers and a few of the hospital staff, why?"

The second officer either grimaced or smiled, the doctor couldn't tell which. He sat down in a chair usually reserved for patients or staff directly across from the doctor's desk. "Well, doc. Let me ask you this. Has Mr. Watkins ever displayed a tendency for physical violence in his stay here?" The doctor, now sitting at his desk, turned on a desk light and started shuffling through some unfinished paperwork.

"No, I've been treating Mike for four years, and he has never hurt himself or anyone else. He is manic depressive and socially inverted, but not prone to violent acts." The doctor leaned back and lit a cigarette. "My I again ask why you inquire specifically about him?"

The detective still standing reached out and placed a Polaroid photograph on the doctor's desk, atop the other papers already taking up ample space there.

"Take a look, doc, then I'll explain." The doctor glared at the photo, letting the scene it portrayed sink in, before a low gasp escaped his parting lips.

"What…wha-why are you showing me this?"

"Because, doc. A nine year old kid who had been hiding under a seat survived to describe the suspect. The kid said the man was young, wore eyeglasses, brown hair cut very short…and wearing some kind of hospital gown. Sound like your boy?"

The doctor swallowed hard, handing the photo back to the officer somewhat shakily. "Are those….?"

The seated detective stood back up and glanced around the office with a look of distaste.

"Heads, doc? Yeah. Found 'em stashed in the trunk of an abandoned eighty-eight Lincoln. Found the old couple who had been the owners of that specific vehicle in the back seat. The old man's arms were cut off. The old women's head was sitting in the front seat, cradled in the severed arms of her husband."

The doctor's face turned instantly pale. His scalp began to tingle.

"Those heads there..." The other detective pointed at the photo on the desk, "those were once owned by 6 unfortunate folks who had the bad luck to 'Go Greyhound' on the wrong night. Hell, we found the driver's head in the buses bathroom, stuffed in the toilet. Now, exactly how the guy got access to the bus wearing nothing but the hospital gown is still a mystery. I'll ask you again, doc. Is your boy our boy in this case? Cause if it is, you better make damn sure he is strapped down with iron chains in your violent ward and shot full of the best shit you got, or....," the detective smiled sarcastically, "heads will definitely roll..."

The doctor reached into a bottom drawer of his desk and pulled out a full bottle of Jim Beam. He found he didn't even need a glass. He politely offered the detectives a belt before turning the bottle up and gulping a mouthful.

***

The clock read 5 AM; a young man wearing a white coat and name tag that read 'Dr. Wayne

Clark' strolled past the guard at the main entrance to the ward and gave him a friendly nod. The guard returned the gesture, then turned to enter the numerical code that released the lock on the thick steel door.

The man walked casually through the parking lot of the McMurry Institute for the Mentally Challenged with a wide, sickly grin covering his pale face. Besides the Doctor's coat, he also sported horn-rimmed glasses that seemed a bit large for his slim face, and black dress shoes that, upon close inspection, looked to be a size or three too large for the feet they sheltered.

He waived cheerily at a plump female nurse who had just parked and was exiting her vehicle. She greeted him with a sheepish smile. The man reached inside the coats inside pocket and felt the sharp edge of the scalpel against his fingertips.

He allowed the nurse to stroll by him and then leaped onto her back. He brought the blade across her throat so quickly and with such precision that not even a single scream had escaped her now trembling lips. A stream of crimson sailed across the parking lot, a portion of it spattering the window of a nearby mini-van. As she wriggled and shook, the man pulled her behind a line of parked vehicles and kneeled down to complete the task. He began sawing at the corners of her neck with the blade, his expression a mixture of nervous excitement and insane anticipation. A wide, thick spray splashed onto his face and into his open mouth. The man began to giggle as he licked around his mouth with a tongue that seemed ravenous to the scent and taste of the coppery, sticky substance.

As he continued sawing away at the dead women's ravaged throat, he caught a glimpse of his own reflection in the outside mirror of a nearby car.

***

Doctor Bill Wilkes woke with a scream, knocking the empty Scotch bottle from the top of his desk with a loud thump.

"My G-god...it was...my face. He was visualizing....m-my face," he mumbled, frantically wiping the sleep from his blood shot eyes.

"Jesus, just a dream...thank god."

His knees popping noisily, he practically jumped from his office chair and half-jogged down the corridor that led to the elevators. He glanced at his watch and saw it read 5:16 AM.

He reached the third floor a few moments later. Stan Moore, the morning security guard, was leaning against his makeshift console, fighting off a yawn. Wilkes waived at him through the thick glass window outside the ward entrance. The guard waived him off as the doctor began to pull his badge free from his coat jacket.

"Not needed, doc. I know ya by now, unless I'm dealing with a true master of disguise, that is," the guard managed just before the yawn overtook him.

A buzzer sounded and the door clicked open loudly.

Wilkes stepped through and patted the guard playfully on one shoulder as he headed down the dimly lit hallway.

"Quiet night, Stan?" he asked lazily.

The guard tipped his hat back and again leaned against the guard stand. "Just the usual, doc. A few night screams and the normal amount of babbling nonsense. Dr. Clark must have come down during the night to check on a few of his. You just missed 'im."

Wilkes froze in mid-step, then whirled around so quickly he almost slipped on the recently waxed tile floor.

"Dr. Clark came down this morning?"

The guard pushed himself erect with a sigh.

"Yep. Day shift head-shrink, right? Must have come in before I got here. Man, you guys put in some hellish hours."

His chest suddenly pounding madly, Wilkes breathing came in labored gasps as he ran full bore down the hall towards the room known as the 'Night Crypt'. It was a room designed to store patients who were being segregated from the others due to pending disciplinary actions or adverse, violent reactions to medication. It was also where Michael Watkins had been placed approximately seven hours earlier.

Wilkes fumbled with the key chain that was hooked to his belt buckle.

His eyes were wild and bulging as he finally found the correct key and inserted it into the door marked 'OBSERVATION ROOM'.

He faintly heard the guard asking him something in a high-pitched, shrieking voice. He threw the door open violently and practically jumped inside the dimly lit, shadow-laced room.

He could see a form lying still underneath the

sheets of the bed. He reached over with a shaky hand and clicked on the lights.

The body was completely covered by both the bed sheets and two thick wool blankets. Wilkes took three cautious steps forward as if he were in the center of a live minefield.

He reached over and grabbed the edge of both blankets and slowly pulled them back.

Doctor Bill Wilkes heard a low grunting noise quickly transformed into a siren-like whine originate from somewhere in the small room. It wasn't until he visualized his own reflection in a tiny mirror mounted over the sink that he realized the source of these animal-like emissions as being himself. He felt a hand grip his left shoulder a moment later, and the screeching sounds ceased. He turned to greet Stan the guard, who was holding a crinkled, brown-paper bag in his other hand.

He was holding it out like a man waiting for a tip. Stan the guard's face was milky white. His lips moved but no recognizable words escaped them.

Wilkes turned from the headless corpse on the bed and took the bag from Stan the guard. He heard Stan the guard mumble something about 'finding it on the other side of the door, by the trashcan'.

Wilkes peeked inside the bag and saw the eyes of a fellow physician staring back up at him.

The head in the bag was unable to scream.

Doctor Wilkes, soon discovered, however, that he unable to stop doing so.

***

213

"To this day I find it hard to believe that Michael did those things. My ex and I took turns blaming each other for years, then we finally called it quits on our marriage. I find these days that I wake up greeted with fear and depression. Fear that Michael might show up at my doorstep with the same blame, and depression that he might not ever show up at all. I also find it hard to believe the board set him free after such a relatively short treatment period, but hey, they're the so-called experts, not me."

She walked off the stage unceremoniously, not even bothering to issue a salutation.

The lights remained at low ebb, and Jerry rubbed his eyes lightly after placing his notebook on the seat to his left.

The hand that struck his shoulder caused Jerry to leap forward a step, and he barely avoided flipping over into the next row. He instantly felt the anger flush his reddening cheeks.

Jerry turned, frowning at the frail looking, acne-ridden young man that had been the latest to make him look foolish.

"Barnes, do you mind not scaring the hell out of me next time?" he whispered grimly. "Sorry, man. Hey, have you seen the Prof?" the man asked while continuously adjusting his thickly-framed glasses.

"No, I haven't. Not my day to keep up with him," he barked back, a bit more cockiness in his tone.

The other boy sighed, his shoulder's slumping.

"I can't find my roommate either. He went to

the shitter about thirty minutes ago. I just checked and he's nowhere to be found."

Jerry smirked, although the obvious concern on his own face was now evident. He suddenly realized how long the blonde girl had been gone.

"Maybe they're all outside sharing a joint, or having a roman orgy in the school gym. How the hell should I know?"

The other young man's eyes darted all around the room, and a small bead of sweat was clearly visible dribbling slowly down the left side of his pimple –ravaged face.

"You're a pain in the ass, Lamar, you know that? Thanks for nothing."

Jerry shrugged playfully and said nothing else as the other man briskly walked away. Lamar? Who the hell is Lamar? "Damn. I hope I don't come off that dorky. King Geek himself," Jerry whispered, casually making his way up the empty rows of seats towards the auditorium exit. He had a sinking feeling in the pit of his stomach that if Gary Barnes was 'King Geek', he himself might possibly be the Jester of said Kingdom.

As he walked into the brightly-lit hallway, he turned and noticed the men's bathroom sign about halfway down on the left.

There was a long line of metal lockers on the right side, several standing wide open and empty. Only three years out of high school himself, Jerry began consciously strolling down memory lane as he passed them. The thought only lasted an instant however, once he recalled that high school, what he could remember of it, had been an endless session of humiliation. As he turned the knob and slowly pulled the door open, a whiff of something metallic filled his senses. Jerry positioned himself over the nearest urinal and had just unzipped when he was startled by the flushing sound coming from the lone toilet stall within the bathroom. He turned his head just as the man pulled open the stall door and stepped out wearing a satisfied smile.

"Good evening, young man," Doctor Dante said as he stepped to the sink and began mechanically washing his hands.

"G-good evening, doctor. Interesting stuff out there," Jerry replied, his normal flow of urine halted by the start he had experienced. He realized in frustration that whatever amount had not yet escaped his bladder felt like it had made a b-line back to his kidneys, and wasn't likely to return anytime soon.

The doctor pulled a paper towel from a dispenser next to the sink and dried his hands while viewing his own image in the mirror.

"Ah, the best is yet to come, young man. The last two tales of the evening, sadly, are my own. You won't want to miss either."

Zipping his pants carefully, Jerry backed up from the urinal and flushed what little waste he had managed to squeeze out.

"Doctor, have you seen Professor Carpenter in the last hour? A few of the students are wondering about him."

The doctor shrugged as he tossed the paper towel into a nearby trash can.

"I'm afraid I've been backstage except for this little excursion. Maybe he's taking a tour of the school. Professors have that instinct, you know."

The doctor opened the door to exit and turned back one last time, gesturing towards the direction of the auditorium.

"Hurry back in there, now. Your study material won't be complete without my entries. Missing them would be like reading a fantastically vivid novel and then discovering the final page has been pulled free from the binding."

Jerry nodded and waited for the door to shut completely before washing his own hands. He scrunched up his nose at the persistent odor, and left the bathroom waving his right hand in front of his nose.

He noticed as he cautiously made his way back to his seat that neither Barnes nor the blonde girl had returned, and the professor was also still among the missing.

Doctor Dante grinned devilishly as he stood behind the podium a few minutes later. His eyes seem to be glowing with wicked glee, and the optimistic body language and tone of his voice was a direct opposite from his patients. He came across more like an actor performing a one-man play than a professionally trained psychologist.

"I'm sure you will all be thrilled to know that I am the last of the storytellers for tonight's little seminar. I, as well as my patients, appreciate your attentiveness and the simple respect you have shown. I, alas, do have two more sad but true events to pass on to you before we close it down. The latter is the story of one of my colleagues who fell from grace in both his chosen profession and in his personal life as well. The first deals with a young man haplessly wandering a warped, surreal dreamscape within his own dementia laced mind. His case might well be the saddest of them all…"

CHAPTER NINE
Loner

Leaning back, waves of smoke rising from the cup of steaming coffee perched in his right hand, the Man stared without blinking as the sun slowly arose over the surrounding hills. Sipping cautiously, he lit a cigarette, this one slightly stale, and took a long draw.

He didn't even bother to monitor the landscape for movement, allowing his eyes to pan without actually focusing. Subconsciously he wasn't sure how he would react if a moving object was ever spotted, since it had been over a year since such an event had occurred. Sipping the first day's (but at least ten cups from being the last) Java and sucking on the first day's cancer stick while watching the sun rise had become a ritual of sorts. The fact that both the smokes and coffee were growing more flat and stale respectively, with each passing day, was not relevant. It was a habit the man would have liked to skip occasionally, but it seemed his inner workings had come to the conclusion long ago that his nightly allowance of shut eye would be limited to a maximum of five hours or less.

Months before he had tried popping over the counter sleep aids, enough to cause his midsection to rattle and his bowels to rage, but this had only resulted in daytime grogginess and constant headaches; not a minutes more slumber.

He had attempted to sleep later, to sleep earlier, and even to stay up all night to alter the pattern. Finally he succumbed to the resignation that the days of seven or eight hours a night were as much a part of the past as Cellular phones and the Internet.

As he slowly, almost mechanically opened the can of Vienna sausages that were to be his breakfast (he had long tired of packaged 'breakfast bars' and stale Pop-Tarts), the man pondered, as he was wont to do, exactly why he had chosen the base for his permanent home. It wasn't as if the place held some sentimental space in his heart. He had been stationed there while serving in the Air Force in his early twenties, some fifteen years earlier.

Being a native of Georgia, the heat of West Texas bothered him less than some, true, but there were obviously more attractive spots to inhabit. He guessed it had to do with the sense of security the fences and gates provided, although any type of threat from an outside source was highly unlikely.

As far as he could tell, there wasn't anything left medically alive other than himself and the sparse vegetation on the surrounding landscape. He strolled into the spacious foyer of what used to serve as a lounge area for Bomber and Tanker pilots on alert status. The walls were thick tinted glass that allowed for a panoramic view of the shrub-covered hills that made up the perimeter of the building. Being that it was mid-July; the blowing dust coming off the overly dry terrain was easily visible on all sides of the structure.

The man placed one of the sausages on a cracker and chewed without expression. He longed for fresh bacon and eggs, maybe some hash browns on the side. The inside of the kitchen cabinet was lined with every canned food imaginable, and he had grown sick of both the smell and flavor of each one eons ago. He spat out a portion of the cracker, it's staleness rendering it tasteless.

He realized a road trip would be useless since there was no fresh meat to be had in the great wasteland beyond. A few months earlier, while downing the eighth of what would be twelve full beers before sweet unconsciousness had intruded, he had christened it "Void World", and had thought that quite appropriate.

He sipped coffee and winced as the hand holding the cup shook wildly before ultimately stilling. It was THE THOUGHT that caused the nervous ticks. The thought that he tried like hell each day not to allow into his slowly but surely deteriorating mind.

He was indeed the last. He was all there was.

He was the last breathing organism on the planet. Or so it seemed, at least.

He had discovered no substantial evidence to prove otherwise.

He would, as was par for the course, mark the wide wall calendar that hung in what had been a control room with a large X, thus eliminating another totally unnecessary, depressingly worthless day from existence.

It was July 12th. Three hundred seventy six days had passed. He laid the black magic marker on the oak desktop and sighed, glaring at the smiling, leggy supermodel in the calendar photo. He never tired of staring at her pouting lips, her perfectly shaped breasts, or those seemingly never-ending legs.

"Wish I could bring ya to life, sweetie-pie. I'm a king without a queen. A Kingdom without a people," he whispered, smiling weakly.

Three-hundred seventy six days since he woke up on that mountainside in Murphy's Ridge, Kentucky, still oblivious to what was to come.

***

He had made it a summer habit of renting a cabin in the hills and allowing both his nerves to settle and his blood pressure to get back to a more stable level. His outward persona of icy coolness was one he had perfected since childhood, but it took its toll on both his constantly aching gut and his slowly receding hairline.

Throughout his life, he had chosen jobs (an actual profession having escaped him) that seemed to specialize in providing solitary tasks. Security Officer, which usually found him at a remote site guarding items he personally thought were less than desirable for even the most desperate thief.

Groundskeeper, where his only company was usually the weed-eater he lugged at his side or the riding mower parked beneath his rear end.

Janitor, the field he had toiled in for the past six years, where the only other souls he encountered were the occasional late workers and overtime mavens. The cleaning agency he had worked for had often sent him to completely deserted high rises, and the man thoroughly enjoyed roaming the maze-like hallways, zigzagging between cubicles like a rat searching for a block of cheese. He spent a fair amount of time ogling the family portraits displayed on the worker's desks, secretly wondering just how different their daily lives were from his own, and at times of weakness fantasizing about having the men's wife or his kids. The Man was in his late thirties and had never even dated seriously. Only three times in his entire life span had he partaken in the joys of sex with the female of the species.

Once in high school, a miserably embarrassing spectacle that had barely lasted forty- five seconds with a girl that outweighed him by sixty pounds and had substantially more chest hair than himself.

His second liaison occurred while he was stationed at his present location while serving his country wearing the Air Force blue. She had been a homely, buck-toothed Airman Basic just out of basic training, lonely and confused at her new surroundings. They had dated, mostly attending movies at the base theater and eating burgers at the Base Exchange food stand. The Man had never been much of a drinker, and the three beers he had downed on that particular evening, along with the four or five she had consumed resulted in a quick but very intense roll in her barracks room bed.

The next day he noticed her aloofness, and soon they barely spoke. He transferred to a different base without ever even saying goodbye to her.

His last attempt at sexual gratification came the day he turned the big three-oh. A few of his co-workers at the Security company he worked for (and was soon to leave for his new career of emptying trashcans and buffing floors) gave him a birthday party at a local dive. By the end of the evening, they introduced him to a prostitute they had chipped in and purchased for the night. Despite the awkwardness of the situation, he found the initial tenseness fade away as they undressed in a nearby hotel room. She had been a big breasted but slightly chubby black girl/woman whose age was undistinguishable due to the thick makeup and eyeliner she wore.

The act itself had only taken a few frantic moments, but the Man realized with an overwhelming sadness now that it was the best sex he was ever fated to have.

He could look in a mirror and know with complete clarity that he wasn't handsome or even what some women referred to as 'cute'. He also wasn't a hunchback who rang church bells or a candidate for a circus freak show. He was one of those men that fall into the category of 'completely plain' and 'remarkably normal'. He was five-feet nine, and had always kept his weight (until recent months, anyway) in the one-seventy to one-eighty range. His hair was brown and thick, a bit on the curly side on the edges, and he had worn a thin mustache on his narrow upper lip since he was seventeen.

Most women had taken his natural shyness as a sign of weirdness in school, and this pattern seemed to follow him as the years passed and he became more and more socially uninhibited. He had attended the companies Christmas party a few months before the world changed, and worked up the nerve to ask out one of the secretaries, a buxom blonde with a pretty smile. When her alcohol-induced response to his invitation for dinner was met with a giggle and the remark "We all thought you were a fag," the Man decided the whole idea had been just another in a long line of mistakes never again to be attempted.

His parents were long deceased, and his only sibling was a brother he hadn't spoken to since his early days in the service.

His salary hadn't amounted to much, but he had managed to pay his bills in a timely manner, residing in a cheap one-bedroom apartment and ownership of a ten year old Ford Escort that burned oil like a wino chugging down Thunderbird wine. His meager savings allowed him to live pretty much worry free, and his yearly treks to the mountains was the one luxury that was allowed without question.

A. THE SHOCK

He had shaken himself awake that particular morning and felt an uneasiness that, at the time, was definitely bizarre but at the same time mildly exhilarating.

After packing his meager supplies into the back of his worn out, slightly rusty but still reliable Escort, the Man drove down the hill towards the cabin rental office.

He had already paid his bill upon arrival, so when he found the office mysteriously locked up tight at ten A.M. on a Tuesday morning, he simply laid the cabin key in a wooden box provided near the door and drove away.

It wasn't until he rode up the ramp to the

225

completely deserted interstate that he realized something was horribly wrong. He drove for ten straight minutes without seeing another moving vehicle before exiting when a line of gas station and fast food signs beckoned.

The Shell station's lot was vehicle-less and the interior of the small building itself dark. Ditto the BP station. A local restaurant/gas station with a sign that read "Billy's Good Grub" above the double glass doors was lit up on the inside, but remarkably, void of movement. A few scattered vehicles, mostly old pick-ups and four door sedans, were parked at its entrance. The Man exited his own vehicle and cautiously felt the hoods of the others. All were cool to the touch. He entered the restaurant like a cat burglar tip- toeing through an unlocked door. Two large metal coffee pots, one for decaf and the other regular, were half-filled but the contents cold. The hum of the coolers seemed shockingly loud in the surrounding dead air. The Man snatched a bottle of Juice from the closest one to him and also a large bag of potato chips from a display, then strolled out while scanning the still landscape. He leaned against the hood of the Escort and tore into the chips, only half-heartedly chewing them, his eyes unblinking as he glared at the interstate ramp a few hundred yards ahead.

He waited for the familiar sound of humming engines or a distant horn. As the sound of the brittle chips exploded with each movement of his jaw, he noticed the strangest oddity of all. Despite the rural surroundings, not a single bird chirped, and there was not even the slightest breeze striking his face. He halted his chewing momentarily, and the eerie silence engulfed him. Throwing the chips to the ground frantically, the Man practically leaped into his vehicle and turned the ignition switch, then twisted the worn radio knob to the on position. Greeted by loud static, he tuned it up and down the dial with the same maddening results. He fell into the passenger seat and braced his arms, now covered in a layer of fresh sweat, onto the wheel, vigorously batting his eyes as if this would magically alter the insanity that was slowly building a solid perimeter around his fevered mind.

Just twenty-four hours previous, he had been sitting in a rented bass boat, sipping cold lemonade from a cup, providing the lake's ample mosquito population with a fresh lunch, and loving every minute of the process of not catching even a single fish.

His quickly rose from his slump and exited the car, the radio still blaring low static. Standing in the center of the trash-strewn parking lot, he waved his arms in a semi-circle and turned a complete three sixty, then let his arms fall to his sides, his head falling back in surrender.

No bugs either. Not a single fly buzzed nor moth fluttered. He walked over to a large, open lidded trash can that sit near the restaurant entrance and peeked inside. The stench of rotted meat and decomposing vegetables hit his nostrils in a nauseating wave, but not a single fly fed on the origin of the aroma.

He stood motionless for what could have been as long as five full minutes or as brief as thirty seconds, then his blood-shot eyes locked on a nearby pay phone.

Digging into his pocket for loose change like a junkie might for a loaded syringe, the Man scooped up the receiver and nervously placed three quarters into the slot, then dialed '0' for an operator. There was ringing, eternal ringing, a never-ending echo of ringing that threatened to push his panic meter towards the red line. He hung up roughly, then inserted three additional quarters and tried his work number. He wasn't sure a buck-fifty would cover the charges, but his mind was beyond figuring phone rates. Again, the persistent ringing ensued until he simply let the receiver drop uselessly from his sweaty hand.

He walked grimly back over to his vehicle and suddenly a weak smile developed at the corners of his mouth, each of which sported a thin line of white spittle.

"Drive further, you moron. Yeah, might be different down the road," he had whispered, although the obvious lack of belief in his own tone had him close to shedding tears as he pulled away with tires screeching. It hadn't been any different down the road. The next exit he found (a good eight miles of more deserted, lifeless highway) took him to the front entrance to a large Holiday Inn hotel with a parking lot full of vehicles, the building itself eerily empty of the car's owners. The power was on in the spacious hotel lobby, a large screen TV displaying nothing but high-pitched, blurry lines and the low echo of elevator music humming in the background. He aimlessly roamed each of the hotel's five floors, slinging some doors open and pounding madly on others.

After spending over two hours dialing random numbers from the Yellow Pages into a lobby pay phone and hearing nothing but more endless ringing, the Man departed the hotel grounds in a state of shell-shocked disbelief.

The events that took place in those next few days are a grainy blur in the innermost reaches of his mind. He recalls driving into Nashville and screeching to a tire-smoking halt in the center of Interstate 65 when he spotted the large sports coliseum and what he thought was a group of people sitting in a top row of stadium seats.

They turned out to be cardboard cutouts of humans advertising the latest in 'ice- brewed' beer, and the Man spent a few moments on the dead grass of the fifty-yard line, crying into his own palms like a scolded three year old.

He recalled driving into the brightly-lit city of Birmingham at around midnight and spotting a police station just off the interstate. In a state of both weariness and complete frustration, he had driven the Escort through the double-glass door entryway, slamming full force into a large wooden oak table in the center of the lobby. Sometime the next day he had driven away towards New Orleans in a shiny Ford F150 pick-up with just over five thousand miles on the odometer. It had taken him all morning to find a vehicle with the keys in the ignition, and just the thrill of being mobile again had put him in a short-lived state of euphoria that at least resembled happiness, although dementia might have been a more appropriate definition.

The shimmering neon lights of Bourbon Street

were chilling beacons of the macabre without benefit of the tightly wound crowd that normally accompanied them, and his stay in that particular city was mercifully short-lived.

As the days and weeks passed, his travels led him first south and then sharply west, to portions of the country he had only seen or heard about through the TV media, newspapers and movies.

He spent a day and night in Biloxi, Mississippi, staring into the mostly Wave-free ocean from the balcony of a honeymoon suite that had, only days earlier, costs it's inhabitant at least one-fifty a night. He had stopped off at one of the city's many gambling resorts and played a few slots, losing what little loose change he possessed. He considered finding a crowbar and breaking into a few selected machines, then reconsidered after the tragically comical overtones of such a plan had kicked in. He marveled still at how the power had stayed intact although there didn't seem to be anyone turning the dials to keep it in running order.

He filled up the truck at a BP station just outside the city limits and headed West, his mind numbing from the eerie, non-threatening tranquility that encircled him like an invisible cocoon.

B. THE ACCEPTANCE

Within ten hours the truck was parked haphazardly outside Texas stadium, the Man peering down onto the shiny astro-turf below from a spacious, air conditioned luxury box, a chilled glass of Champagne balanced in his left hand while his right gripped a half-lit cigar.

He had grown up hating the Cowboys, being a Steelers fan made that come naturally, and had never entertained the idea of stepping foot in the state itself, much less in the stadium that housed what had been referred to as "America's Team". He had kept up with sports religiously as a young teen, but like many aspects of his solitary existence, that interest had faded like fog in the morning sun as he had grown into adulthood.

When the night fell, he made his way down onto the field and found the main circuit switch in the southeast corner. Moments later, the stadium's lights blazing down, he imagined himself receiving the opening kick-off five yards deep in the center of the end zone. Picking up a few fantasy blocks along the way, the Man fantasized himself breaking through an opening down the center of the field and sprinting free for a one-hundred five yard return for his beloved Steel city team against the dreaded Cow pokes.

He ceremoniously spiked the ball in front of the enemy goal post, then turned and waved to the ghosts that filled the empty seats of the coliseum. He could feel their presence, their eyes glued to his every move. He sat on the end zone line, gasping for breath, and grinned devilishly. He had just scored the first and definitely last touchdown in this world's league history. It wasn't until he reached Phoenix that it became evident electricity was slowly being lost. The eastern part of the city was pitch dark, and the phone lines, which had been about as useful as a two cups tied with a string regardless, were now without a dial tone.

He spent his one night in Arizona in a large

grocery store (powered) and ate ribs (still edible, although the expired date on the package was two days hence) and potato salad (ditto). He consumed an entire baked apple pie with a full half gallon of vanilla ice cream for dessert, and washed it all down with a quart of chilled orange juice.

A half-hour later and feeling like he had swallowed a semi-truck tire, he wondered from the grocery store to the large brick business next to it in the shopping center. It was packed with sporting goods, and seemed large enough to fit more than one football field inside. He grabbed a basketball and found a goal display next to a back wall. The Man shot and rebounded until literally pools of sweat dripped from his forehead and chin. He picked out a selected group of 'official league size' footballs and practiced his short and long tosses, surprised at how many items he could pluck off the shelves with ease, his aim almost flawless from a reasonable distance.

After a few leisurely games of pool, his eyelids feeling extremely heavy, he strolled back into the grocery store to find a place to crash.

He found a large break room in the back of the store complete with leather couch and feathered pillows. The next morning he stocked the truck with as many canned goods and drinks as it could hold, and drove back towards the east.

He had awoken that morning with a renewed purpose. A quest, if you will. He had realized where he was supposed to be, but not exactly why.

He decided to drive straight through until he arrived at this land that was somehow destined to be his permanent home in a world that time had forgotten.

C. THE HOMECOMING

He arrived at the main gate of Westmoreland Air Force Base, Clarington, Arkansas (ninety-four miles to the north of Little Rock, one-hundred six miles to the west of Memphis, TN) approximately eighteen hours after leaving Phoenix. The F150 had averaged eighty-five MPH throughout, and he had only stopped for fuel twice (and also to drain his bladder). He was unsure why he had driven like an obsessed madman to a place that held nothing but the same dead landscape as the ones just left behind, but there was a strange, almost hypnotic drawing sensation that had propelled him there in a frenzy of apprehension.

Nine years earlier, in what seemed like someone else's lifetime, he had been stationed there. It was his second and last permanent assignment, and easily the better of the two. After completing basic training in San Antonio and a quick Tech School (four weeks) course in Food Service in Colorado, he had been given orders to Abrams Air Force Base, Florida. He hadn't enjoyed his year and a half stay there. It was ruthlessly humid, and there wasn't a day he could remember not having to literally peel his uniform free following a shift (the added heat of working in a kitchen all day increasing the overall weariness). He hadn't made many friends in the barracks and had suffered through a roommate that had two very distinctive and incredible nasty habits. The boy had sucked his teeth constantly and urinated into empty coke bottles.

The latter was due to the kid's laziness at refusing to walk the twenty feet it took to reach the floor's community john. The Man had chalked up the first habit to some sort of abnormality at birth.

His job had been tedious and boring, and the people he worked with either power- hungry dictators (the Master Sergeant that spit when he talked) or simple-minded cretins (the Airman First Class whose choice of subject matter was 'getting laid' or 'getting wasted', and little else).

He was transferred (after months of filling out "dream sheets" in blind hope) to the base he chose to return to, standing inside the open front gate with a warped grin on his reddened face.

The Man pulled slowly past the empty guard shack and made his way down the main strip, past the Base Exchange and Commissary, as well as the base gym and Consolidated Base Objective building, which had served as headquarters. He parked between two large brick buildings that were each four floors high, railed balconies marking each level.

The building number he entered at ground level was marked '1902', as it had been over nine years past. He took the stairwell to floor number two and soon stood on the outside of room number 212, which had been his home for two and a half years in another, much more hectic but at least partially interesting life. He had been a borderline loner even then, but had at least made a few acquaintances and a true friend or two during that span.

His heart raced as he reached for the metal

doorknob, and he had to laugh at himself for such dramatics. It wasn't as if he was going to find a younger, more vigorous version of himself sitting inside.

What he did find was a neatly made bed and a dresser lined with family photos of the young Airman who had been the most recent occupant. The Man sipped from a cool bottle of water he found in the mini-fridge, and laid down on the tightly blanketed bed. When he did wake, it was fourteen hours later.

The power to the base chow hall had obviously been out for days, the sharp, nauseating aroma of ruined meats and rotted vegetables assaulting his nostrils as he entered through an unlocked dining room window, as the front door had been tightly locked.

He found a well- stocked cabinet filled with canned soups and meats, as well as large cardboard boxes stuffed with crackers wrapped in cellophane packaging. He used a metal two-wheeler to load up his supplies, then rolled them back to the barracks building. He pulled a wooden chair out onto the outside railing and enjoyed a lunch/dinner of tuna on crackers, cheese spread on crackers, and potted meat on crackers, chugging it all down with more bottled water from his old hacienda.

His less than panoramic view of the adjoining barracks across the lawn did little to keep him occupied, so he sat out to tour the base and see what changes had been made since his almost decade old departure.

Deciding a long walk might help him shake the

cobwebs induced from the lengthy slumber session; he left the truck sitting and took off towards the Base Exchange.

The base commissary was also void of power, and he could smell the result as he walked through the wide open doors of the brightly lit BX. He playfully tried on a few shirts and shoes from the clothing section, then browsed through the music section for a few CD's to take back with him. The F150 had a brand spanking new Sony CD stereo system with one-hundred watt speakers that he was growing to appreciate, and he planned on setting up his new digs with the best the former makers of such technology had to offer. That was when it hit him. He paused at the jewelry counter, where he had been eyeballing a shiny new watch and leaned down onto one knee, his eyes wide and his forehead furrowed in thought.

Where was his new home to be? He could have picked any mansion in any city in the U.S....in the world for that matter. Why had he chosen the limited resources of the base and it's small town surroundings to settle into?

He fast-walked, then rapidly jogged back towards the barracks, a sudden burst of energy fueled by the answer to his earlier question echoing in his fevered mind.

The Pad. This was the final, permanent 'command post' in his new existence, the final piece of the puzzle that remained. There was nothing out there to seek out, just lifeless, ghost highways with matching phantom buildings surrounding them. He hadn't been certain of much in his life, especially in the last week, but this decision was a no-brainer. He had been led here for a reason. His old stomping grounds were going to be his last.

He held out his arms while standing in front of the main entrance like a man awaiting a hug from a rarely seen relative.

"Honey…, I'm home!" the Man had bellowed at the top of his lungs, the echo bounding back to his ears like he had been submerged in a deep, stony cave.

D. THE FINAL OUTPOST

From the outside, the SAC Alert Facility resembled a middle-priced hotel, it's wide, glass-walled lobby and the solid brick and concrete of its perimeter providing an appearance unlike anything associated with the military. Only the ten- foot high chain fence with curled razor wire at the top disclosed its past life as a restricted area requiring a coded line badge to enter.

The Man found the lobby door open, and a wave of déjà vu poured over his senses as he strolled inside the dark entryway.

The lack of electricity, along with a minimum of windows to allow daylight inside the structure prevented him from investigating more than a few feet past the lobby and into what had been the facility control room.

He smiled, recalling the training and actual hands-on experience he had received operating the huge, truck-sized emergency generator that had been utilized during times of stormy weather (usually thunderstorms and tornadoes) and war-time exercises.

He doubted the generator procedures had been altered since his time as a Controller, and even if they had, he knew the Operating Instructions on exactly how to kick it on would be posted on the machine itself.

The Man leaned on the driver's side of the F150 and made a mental list of all the items he would need to make his new digs complete. He sipped from a water bottle he had pulled from a cooler in the bed of the truck, and stared beyond the facility itself to the desert landscape in the background. Dried up looking shrubs and blowing tumbleweeds gave the illusion of the old west, and he pondered again why he felt that setting up shop at this particular spot felt so right somehow. As he pulled away from the main gate and headed towards the small but once prosperous town of Clarington, he decided to stop questioning the decision and simply live by it.

The city limit sign read "CLARINGTON – Pop. 5012...and Still Growing", most of which had been associated in some way, shape or form with the base itself. The main street held small shops and the usual 'Credit problems? No PROBLEM at all!' shops that were the norm when a base was nearby. A mile or so further would bring you to the 24 hour Wal-Mart, a Home Depot, and (something added since the Man's days) a shopping center whose parking lot would make one think Yankee Stadium was just around the corner. It contained two restaurants (one Tex-Mex, one Chinese), two separate Video stores, a small clothing shop, and a McDonald's. All looked as though they had been constructed in the last two or three years at the outset.

From the powerless Wal-Mart, where he obtained a large flashlight to see his way around in, he spent the next five hours packing seven different carts, and parked each just outside the exit for loading. He had obtained (although not in any specific order): - The aforementioned flashlight with eight packs of 'A' sized batteries. - Four small battery operated lamps (nine nine-volt batteries for each) - Large box of matches - Fifteen gallons of bottled water (just in case) - Assorted towels and dish rags - One large master lock (he had already measured the base main gate, which had been missing it's manual lock since it was normally secured electronically) - Six cases of assorted potted meats and canned vegetables from the food section - A cart full of bottled juices with expiration dates that were still current - A twelve gauge shot gun and shells (although he felt a bit puzzled why he had felt compelled to do so) - An 'Official size NBA' basketball (he had seen the goals still intact just behind the supply building) - A cart full of assorted CD's and Video movies - A Sony CD Player/Cassette with six separate speakers (it had been the highest priced in the store) - Various bottles of Vitamin supplements and pain medications with current dates - A Walkman cassette recorder and packages of blank tapes - A poster of Jennifer Lopez (grabbed it as he went by, grinning mischievously) posing in a two-piece bathing suit, her seeing eyes and pouting lips displaying what seemed to be a genuine passion that caused his heart to palpitate slightly. - A 12 cup

Mr. Coffee Java brewer and filters - Two cans of spray paint (one black, one red). - Eight large cans of Maxwell House Special Blend Java - Three ten pound bags of 'Sweet Tooth' Granulated Sugar - A chart half-filled with magazines and paperback books he had collected without bothering to check subject matter or specific titles. - Three pairs of Nike 'Super Sport' tennis shoes that were all priced at or above one-hundred fifty dollars each. - Packs of T-shirts and underwear, and bundles of ankle-high socks.

Realizing the F150 was simply too small to carry such a load, and not wanting to make various treks back and forth, the Man casually strolled through the lot until he found a large white Chevy Storage van with the keys laying just underneath the driver's seat. Despite its rusty, mud-covered outside appearance, it bolted to life on the first turn of the ignition, and he backed it to the store entrance with a satisfying grin. He figured he'd drive back to get the F150 later on after 'housekeeping' was complete. He never bothered.

Around midnight on that first evening spent at the pad, the generator fired up without incident, flooding the offices, rooms and hallways of the building with a nova-like brightness that forced the Man to walk the entire structure, flipping off switches.

He had found a dozen ten gallon containers of generator fuel in the supply room, along with the previously mentioned OI handbook taped to the inside door of the main generator panel.

He had danced a short jig (his ample gut jigging madly over the belt of his jeans) after the engine had roared to life and the lights flashed on, and again felt the positive vibes that had been his guide since making the trip from the west.

After a late night snack consisting of grape jelly and peanut butter on crackers, he fell into a coma-like snooze on a break room sofa, the wall-mounted TV above him blaring static.

By noon of his third day at the pad, he leaned back in a soft leather chair with his hands at the back of his neck. His feet were softly propped on a wooden table that also held his lunch (heated chili, Ritz crackers and Beanie Weanie) and an ice cold Budweiser beer. His eyes were trained on the movie (via VCR hook-up) playing on the large screen TV, but his mind drifted in an altogether different direction. In his entire existence on the planet, he had never felt more splendidly settled or at peace than at that very moment. He had spent the last forty eight hours wiping, sweeping, dusting, and remodeling.

He had made the obvious choice for his permanent sleeping quarters; the former "Ranking Pilot's" room, which was twice the size of the enlisted rooms, and had its own spacious bathroom with a wide marble sink and oversized bathtub.

That morning he had placed the two-pound Master lock on the base's front gate. He had already sprayed painted over the 'Westmoreland AFB' sign with the can of black and spelled out 'THE LAST OUTPOST' in bright red directly over it.

He had considered this the official christening of his new homeland, what he now thought of as the only living, breathing section of the planet. He would waste no time in fantasizing that others like him existed. The time he had spent in the deathly silent cities and the bare, solitary highways of the west had provided him a blueprint of planet earth.

For whatever reason only the gods knew, he was left as the lone sentry of a planet that had been literally begging for early destruction for untold centuries. He knew an answer to why was forthcoming, and in the meantime he would avoid depressing thoughts of 'the old ways' and just how truly alone he was in a world that once held so many varied life forms.

He felt the gods watching him, watching and waiting. As he stood underneath the sign he had just altered, he smiled and tossed the half-empty spray paint can to the pavement.

"I'm here when you're ready to show yourself. I'm home now, and here is where I'll stay until you give me a sign otherwise," he whispered calmly as warm tears began to form in the corners of his eyes.

After the initial sweeping out and dusting of what would be his living quarters, the large break room which would become his entertainment center, and the kitchen, the remodeling had begun in earnest.

The break room, which he had measured at six-hundred square feet, was equipped with the stereo system (the old unit that had been taking up space there was hauled off to the downstairs break room), while the DVD and VHS players were hooked to the large screen (the old VCR hauled away).

He used a two wheeler to relocate three Video game systems from the east side break room, which he planned on using to store extra canned goods and water once the kitchen cabinets were filled.

He first emptied out then filled a large, mostly plywood bookshelf with the collection of Videos and CD's he'd collected. The bookshelf had come from the pad's library room, which he decided would stay mostly intact. He had never been much of a reader, but understood he might well become a literary scholar out of sheer boredom over time.

With Billy Joel's 'Greatest Hits, Volumes I & II' echoing through the narrow hallways (the Man had always been a connoisseur of classic and soft rock), he went about the arduous task of cleaning the chow hall. He swept and mopped in both the kitchen area and the dining room, and spent over four hours washing the utensils he had hand-picked to be his personal stock, along with the assorted pots and pans he would use.

With Cat Steven's 'Another Saturday Night' playing in the background, he meticulously separated all the canned goods (meat and veggie) and stocked them into their chosen cabinets.

With Survivor belting out 'Eye of The Tiger' as his motivating theme, he spent the rest of that particular day transforming what had been the Control Room into his own corner office of sorts.

He had spent many an hour taking calls from the flight line Tower and Command Post, handing out equipment to the crew members, and editing then typing various command documentation in the twelve by fourteen room he now worked feverishly to redecorate.

He built a pile of items he deemed utterly

useless in his new world; an eight line phone system; a two way radio hook-up; an electronic manning board which had been used to track crew members locations. All relics of an era gone by that were as useless as the lumbering aircraft that lined the flight line outside the building like futuristic dinosaurs. The Man glanced out at the C135 Tankers and the B-1 Bombers and felt a twinge of pity, both for himself and the machines themselves. What once had meant so much was good for nothing now but providing shade to the asphalt below.

He hung the Jennifer Lopez poster on a far wall that metal filing cabinets had been covering. He shoved the Pentium 4 computer into the center of the room and ensured the unit was still workable. He was determined to keep a log of his daily existence, maintaining a mental diary of his thoughts and moods.

He was unsure of what exactly he hoped to accomplish in what seemed to be a fruitless task, but if there was one thing he had plenty of until the day he breathed no more, it was time to kill.

Bad Company's 'Holy Water' ringing in his ears, he brought up the Word Perfect system and called up a new file, saving it as 'LONER.DOC'.

His first typed sentence read "Void World: A New Beginning."

"Void World. Yeah, that's appropriate," he giggled, winking playfully at Jennifer, whose seductive glance would greet him from that day forward.

E. RITUALS

The downstairs gym was stocked with eight different Nautilus machines and over twelve-hundred pounds of free weights, along with two electric treadmills and three stationary bikes. A small Jacuzzi and sauna were just a room over, and a racquetball court just down the hall.

The Man stared down at his jiggling gut and thick love handles, at least thirty pounds of which had been gained since he hit the magic three-o. He came to the decision that a few hours in the work out room could most definitely be fit into his hectic daily schedule.

He would begin reshaping his body (his mind would be forced to follow, he deduced) after the dinner meal that very evening.

Within a month, a definite pattern was beginning to be religiously adhered to. The same habitual regiments that had once been what 'normal' life consisted of were adhered to within a world where the only trend sitter remaining set the pace.

Wake around sunup; eat breakfast. Light up the first smoke of the day (within the next few months, he would go from almost three packs a day to less than one. Within a year, he lit up only twice a day) Sip coffee; insert CD's in stereo for listening day.

Stretch and begin morning workout. Hit the nautilus machines, then the free weights (careful never to place too much weight on the bench press bar since a 'spotter' was nowhere to be had). Thirty minutes at a fairly casual pace on the treadmill, then ten hard- pumping minutes on the stationary bike.

Five hundred crunches later (worked up to from a pathetic fifty those initial pain-filled days), he spent at least forty-five minutes in the sauna, then fifteen more in the Jacuzzi.

After a quick shower, lunch was prepared (he noticed a dramatic increase in his appetite since the workouts had become second nature).

He would devour lunch while listening to Kansas, Boston, Chicago, Styx, or any of the other countless classic rock bands from his slowly dwindling collection.

For a full week, he immersed himself in the works of a group he had always dismissed as 'too spacey' in his earlier life. He soon discovered and understood the appeal of such classics as 'Learning to Fly', 'Another Brick in the Wall' and 'Wish You Were Here', but these familiar singles only scratched the surface of the band's undeniable talent for reaching into one's mind and clutching the inner eye.

After the "Floyd Period" as he thought of it, his mind and ears were ready for something less cerebral and with a harder edge. Soon southern rock mainstays such as Molly Hatchet, .38 Special, Atlanta Rhythm Section, and Lynyrd Skynyrd lived again, at least inside the walls of the pad.

His feet tapped and his hands played invisible drums for days on end.

After putting away the dishes, he would retire to the entertainment room for a flick. Again, he had gone through the majority of what he had haphazardly scooped up while on the shopping spree a month earlier.

Some of the selections had turned out to be

rather on the crappy side as well, he had discovered. He decided to plan an additional 'supply run' into town soon after.

After the movie ended, which was usually around two PM by his watch (although he found clock-watching sure wasn't what it used to be), it was usually time for the afternoon nap. He would crash in his quarters for an hour or so, and normally wake up feeling shockingly refreshed, as if he had just got a full night's slumber.

He would toss on a pair of shorts and his jogging shoes and take a brisk walk/job around the massive flight-line. When excess energy allowed, he would shoot hoops on the outdoor court just beyond the perimeter of the flight line. On most days, however, this activity was skipped. Forty-five minutes to an hour later, showered and growing ravenous, dinner preparation would be in order.

Scouring the cabinets for just the right combination of canned meat and veggie, both swimming in preservatives and mostly void of the nutrition he needed since his workouts became more strenuous, the Man could feel his appetite begin to fade with each meal. He gulped down his multi-vitamin (expiration label assuring freshness for another year and a half), an extra five-hundred milligram Vitamin C (two more years of effectiveness, so said the label), and a B-12 Vitamin to keep him energized for his daily physical torture sessions.

After an hour or so playing video games (none of which he could ever seem to master. Growing up, even 'Packman' had kicked his butt on a regular basis), he would snack on crackers and cheese and watch another flick, then retire usually between eleven and midnight.

His second trip into town occurred at the two month point of his self-imposed exile. He raided the local Blockbuster and also a smaller video outlet named "Land of Video". Approximately four hundred tapes and discs were piled into the back of the van from Blockbuster, and since he hadn't been much of a movie-goer or renter back in the old days, the majority would be viewed for the first time. The flicks he snagged at the other store were of the topic that Blockbuster refused to carry, ones with titles like "The Sixth Sex", "Star Whores; The Booty Menace", and "Blonde Sluts Volume IV'.

He had felt a few twinges of sexual urgings within the past week or so, yearnings he chalked up mostly to his vastly improved physical condition, but also to the fact that he hadn't bothered even thinking about such matters in months. That night, sitting nude in front of the large screen, a buxom blonde moaning, groaning and grinding as she was being serviced by two men beside a sun-drenched swimming pool, the Man felt no guilt as he began to pleasure himself. There was, however, a strange realization that he was visualizing acts that were now nothing more than a faded part of man's past. Like 'surfing the net', attending social gatherings for status purposes, or 'shopping at the mall', the mating game ritual was, simply put, as dead as a hammer. The old saying 'it takes two to tango' never held more relevance.

F. THE DREAMS

It wasn't until around the fourth month that the dreams began. Up until that point his nights had been reasonably peaceful and vision free.

His was awakened by his own harsh gasp, the bed sheets soaked with not only the warmth of perspiration, but also of urine. As he washed the remnants of his body's waste from his groin and legs, the dream did not fade from his consciousness as normal, but seemed to become clear and more tangible. He had been preparing himself a breakfast of powdered eggs and milk when the woman approached him from the kitchen entrance. Her face was that of Jennifer Lopez, beautiful, radiant and completely flawless. The body was at least fifty pounds heftier, however, than the sleek, voluptuous one normally associated with that face. She spoke only Spanish to him, calmly as if he understood every word. Although the meaning of what she said escaped him completely, he seemed to instinctively know what subject she spoke of.

They casually ate together, then she smiled and took his hand, leading him towards his sleeping quarters. He felt no fullness from the meal just consumed, and as they began to kiss and fondle one another, it was as if this was a daily ritual between them, an unspoken agreement to share their passion and feel the closeness, to warm their collective souls.

Her hot, moist tongue in his mouth triggered an erection that to him felt like a solid steel, foot long bar between his legs. Her breasts were larger than they should have been for her suddenly sleek upper body, and as he glanced down at her naked legs, they had been transformed into a dancer's legs, muscular and perfectly toned.

As with all sex-related dreams he had experienced in the past, the sequence was interrupted before his climax (the last 'wet dream' he had successfully completed was around age fifteen, he surmised) and suddenly the scene shifted and he was again in the process of preparing a meal; a freshly cut up chicken baking in the oven, along with mashed potatoes and white gravy. The aroma of these items burned into his nostrils (causing more than a small amount of drool to form at the corners of his mouth as he slept), causing his stomach to sound off accordingly (in dream and reality). The Jennifer girl was sitting at their dinner table, her swollen, circular belly almost sitting flat on the edge of the table, propped like an oversized globe. She kept pointing at her belly and then at the slim gold watch at her right wrist, a look of exasperation masking her otherwise radiant face.

In the next sequence they ate, the Man consuming slowly, chewing each bite of the slightly greasy, indescribably delicious chicken purposely, meticulously, like a condemned man savoring a death row delicacy. The Jennifer girl dove onto her plate like a ravenous wolf on recently slain prey.

She disregarded her utensils and tore the meat off the bone with bare hands and gnashing teeth, teeth which seemed unusually long and sharp from the Man's standpoint. When she finally glanced up at him from the ravaged plate, now covered with tiny pieces of jagged chicken bones, her mouth was smeared in grease and white gravy, her eyes now sedate, her movements leisurely. She again took his hand and this time led him not to his sleeping quarters, but into one of the upstairs men's rooms. Hand in hand they entered one of the toilet stalls and the Jennifer girl raised the lid on the toilet while instructing the Man to lock the stall door behind them (this time her English was perfect and spoken with a bit of a southern drawl). The toilet itself widened until it resembled a Jacuzzi tub, and Jennifer, her midsection apparently widening more by the second, dived in headfirst, the warm, bubbly water splashing the Man on his crouch and legs. When she didn't resurface a few minutes later, the Man felt no panic, but instead followed her lead and dove in with pointed hands and arms.

He emerged from the pool into a large, well lit room that was filled with metal tables covered with white sheets and trays supplied with medical instruments of all shapes and sizes. The Jennifer girl was lying on the nearest table, her face beaded in sweat, her eyes huge. Her legs were propped in the air, each strapped at the ankle. When the Man peeked underneath the sheet that covered her groin, he felt the hair on both his head and arms stand on end as if he had just been handed a live wire.

Her vagina had been replaced by a perfectly shaped human mouth, the lips shapely and plum red. The massive maw opened like the entrance to a dark mountain cave, a warped parody of a human scream, and a moment later the child crawled free on all fours, a lily white diaper already attached around his pouched midsection. The Man held out his arms to embrace the trembling infant, who peered up into his father's eyes as he neared.

The hands and arms of the Man withdrew in a spastic jerk, his own mouth now standing open but unable to omit sounds of any kind. The child stood on its feet, initially wobbly but soon with a steadiness that indicated a youngster of maybe five or six years of age.

It placed it's chubby, fisted hands on its sides and looked a bit insulted at its father, who found his feet frozen to the suddenly icy tile floor. It's voice was that of the Man's, only a touch nasal, like he had been suffering from a still present head cold.

"There are more. So much time, so little to do," it mumbled, a sarcastic, strangely malevolent grin forming on its purple lips, which were dripping goo that wasn't clear but blood red.

Another child crawled free from the chasm, and the Man could now clearly hear the angst ridden cries of the mother producing these smaller versions of himself. Her shrieks bore an eternal pain that surely only damned souls ever experience. It was as if someone was tearing her apart from the inside. The cave entrance/exit widened even more, the tearing of flesh and the cracking of bone filling the Man's overwhelmed senses.

Within moments the entire room was filled with babies whose faces were eerily adult, horrifically his own. They stood in a semi-circle around their apparent father, who was now sitting atop a metal table himself, completely nude and unable to refrain from shaking uncontrollably.

Standing almost a military formation, shoulder length apart, he thought they resembled a swarm of fat white maggots preparing to feed on a decaying slab of rotted meat. They started forward almost at once, the lead child's jaws trembling with apparent rage.

"They will come for you, father. They will look similar to us. They have plans…oh yes. The plans they have for you..," it spat, crimson liquid flying in tubular streams from its slug-like lips.

As they crawled like nesting roaches onto the metal table, their tiny, moist fingers attaching to his skin like leeches, he saw their mouths open. He could barely make out the tips of the miniature fangs that protruded from their pink gums. The Man began to scream then, his arms slinging wildly and tossing a few of them off, but not enough to prevent the prickly, wasp-sting like bites from covering his body like a rash.

He opened his eyes and saw the children were gone, but realized a solid form still had him pinned to the table. He placed his hands against the massively thick, sickly-soft flesh lying atop his chest and shoved with all his remaining energy. The body fell from his and landed with a muffled thud onto the floor to the left of the table. The Man felt the stinging after-effects of the child-bites, and glared down at his torso, which was covered in red dots from his breastbone to the bridges of his feet. Crazily he thought of the 'connect-a-dot' games he used to play as a kid. He rolled off onto the right side of the table and stood on weakened legs that seemed to almost be floating on the hard surface.

He walked around to the other side of the table and saw the Jennifer girl laying on her back, her chunky legs propped high into the air, this time without benefit of the binding straps.

He kneeled down over her and placed his right hand gently on her forehead while leaning the other softly onto her still grotesquely bloated midsection.

Two things happened simultaneously; her eyes popped open like a switch had been flicked, and something very solid slapped his hand from inside her womb.

The Man backed away as the shape inside her pushed its way through her throat like an Anaconda swallowing and digesting a large animal, the sound of ripping tendon and shattered bone filling the otherwise empty room. Her jaws split like a melon struck with an axe blade, and the full-sized man that crawled from the ruin of her rolled onto its own gore covered back and lay still for only a moment before leaping forward aggressively.

The Man again stared at his own face, but this one was not younger like the children, but much, much older. It's ancient eyes seemed to be holding back a terrifying secret it was unable or unwilling to convey, it's wiry body bent over and mangled like that of a ninety-year old man who had been bed ridden for at least the last decade of those.

It reached forward and gripped his shoulders in a vice like grip, the Man again paralyzed. When it finally managed to speak, it was through a toothless mouth that when glared into flashed images of pure madness, frenzied scenes of primal insanity not meant to be viewed by anyone or thing not presently residing in the within the deepest, darkest pits of hell.

'Don't allow their intrusion. Don't let them do what they desire. End it before they get the chance. End it or you will......pray for eternity that you had. It's worse than anything you could...ever... imagine. Listen to me. Heed the words of your older...wiser...self. End it before they....arrive."

He watched the massive maw open wider as he was hypnotically drawn into it like a starving beast to a loaded trap.

Just before he awoke, he witnessed the collective faces contort, melting like candle wax held over a raging campfire. They all screamed in unison, the young and the old, and all were acutely aware.

***

The Man attempted to shake the dream from his mind first by instigating a workout that bordered on the sadistically cruel (thirty extra minutes pounding weights, fifteen extra on the treadmill, and added a mile to his jog around the flight line).

By the time he pawed his way through his second bowl of buttered popcorn and the closing credits to 'The Naked Gun: From the Files of Police Squad" rolled (Leslie Nielsen made him laugh simply by being on screen) , he had chalked up the origin of the dream to all the horror flicks he'd ingested of late. He was definitely going to stick to comedies and light dramas for a while.

A few nights later, he shook himself awake at around 2 AM, literally falling off the bed onto the carpeted floor and subsequently crawling towards the door a few feet before waking.

He quickly decided that additional slumber wasn't necessary, and headed to the kitchen for some very stout Java.

Rubbing his temples as firmly as his tremor-raked fingers would allow, the Man sipped the steaming liquid and retraced the contents of this latest trip into the land of lunacy.

***

In the latest episode, he had awakened (so realistic a fraction of his foggy mind continued to doubt it's falseness) and felt a dull ache at his left side, just below the rib cage. He had strolled into the kitchen to start the 'most important meal of the day' and was almost doubled over with pain while reaching for a coffee pot sitting on the stove eye.

He had forced down a few sausages with his coffee, then laid down on one of the entertainment room's long couches. It was then, probing with the fingertips of his right hand, that he found the lump.

It was about the size of a quarter, and as solid as a ball-bearing. Rising from the couch, he felt both panic and his gorge rise as the pain didn't subside but increased ten- fold from the effort.

He stood over the bathroom sink and shoved various handfuls of pills (some recognizable as simple Tylenol and Advil, but others were as large as billiard balls and sprinkled with every color of the rainbow) into his mouth until his jaws were grotesquely bloated. He swallowed them down in clumps, his throat growing raw from the constant pressure.

He lay back in a large tub, the water within dangerously close to the boiling point, all but the tips of his toes and his head submerged.

The lump was now the size of a softball, the skin underneath his rib cage swollen like a special effects bladder from one of the 'Alien' films. He ran his hand across it and felt it's slightly jagged edges. He suddenly, unexpectedly threw up into the bath water. The substance was dark red, almost black in color, and he noticed a few small, partly congealed chunks floating about the water's surface.

He lay on the metal table, seemingly the same one as his last dream. His right hand grasped a small scalpel; his left a pair of needle nose pliers. Both instruments were coated in rust and shook uncontrollably in his sweat coated hands. The growth, now melon-sized, throbbed visibly underneath skin stretched to the splitting point. A vein as thick as a phone cord ran across the top of the growth, and when he placed his hand near the surface of the object, the pulse rate seemed to increase and he would feel himself grow instantly faint.

He had no choice but try to carve it out himself, although he realized even in a dream state exactly how ludicrous such an attempt was. He peered over at a metal tray to his right, which was piled high with bandages, gauze, and various bottles filled with hydrogen peroxide and rubbing alcohol.

He gnashed his teeth tightly over a slim metal rod pulled from the tray and placed the scalpel blade just over the top ridge of the growth. Closing his eyes and setting his jaw so hard on the rod he thought he heard a back molar crack, the Man slid the blade horizontally in a single, forceful slice. He felt the warmth of his own bodily fluids cover his midsection, along with just the slightest twinge of pain. The rod fell from his mouth onto the tile floor just as he raised his head to investigate the self-inflicted wound. Pleasantly shocked that excruciating pain wasn't racking every fiber of his body, he executed a half crunch and peaked downward at his waist.

The skin of his lower stomach was peeled back in two narrow, even flaps. Not a single drop of blood was present, even at the corners of the gash, and the mutant tumor sat on his bare chest like a cuddled house pet.

It was dark brown and roughly the size of a volleyball, although it's surface was far from smooth. It held the shape and texture of a human brain, with what looked strangely like fish gills on each of its sides. He reached to grasp it, wanting desperately to slap it away from his already crawling skin.

His fingers were inches from making compact when the growth shifted, as if it were trying to avoid the contact. The Man's hands froze in mid-air, hesitant to complete the act.

He glanced over at the metal tray and pulled a handful of gauze packages free with his left hand. He looked back to the growth. It had flattened itself like a semi-cooked omelet, a surging oil spill that now enveloped his entire waist and was painstakingly making a B- line for his chest, throat and face.

He found himself paralyzed to escape it's ascent, and just before it poured over his face like a solid sheet of warm, moist tar, the Man had just enough time to emit a low, pathetic whimper.

The Man arose after his fourth stronger-than-usual cup of coffee and immediately took stock of the medications stashed away in the pad's Infirmary. Since all previously produced antibiotics were long expired, he would have to rely solely on over-the-counter medicines for the duration of their freshness, which in most cases was at least another few years.

The dreams became more clouded and obscure from that point, much to his relief. He began to sleep a bit more, and spending less time trying to deduce their inner meanings. Yes, he was scared indeed scared shitless of contracting a painful, slow-working cancer without the benefit of doctors and proper medication. Consequently, there was a loaded twelve-gauge sitting in the control room that was ready for use if need be. He would not be eaten alive by a flesh-consuming, life force sucking parasite. It push came to shove; he had no doubts he would somehow discover the inner fortitude to pull the trigger.

G. THE LONGEST DAYS

At around the eight month point (and feeling fully recovered after a scary bout with what turned out to be nothing more than a nasty head cold), the Man made only his third trip into town since his self-imposed exile. He had been running precariously low on canned goods and generator fuel.

He found the fuel at a local Home Depot after searching several others locations. He dropped by the local market and snagged several boxes of canned veggies and powered milk and egg mix, along with a few cases of toilet paper and napkins. He thought about stopping by the video store for a new load of flicks, then decided not to bother after all. He was simply burnt-out on watching dead folks filling the screen performing mundane acts that no longer pertained in his world. The porn flicks had also grown tiring once the Man realized the animalistic acts being portrayed were as out of place in the present as a billboard advertising safe sex or warnings concerning the AIDS virus.

He noted while chewing a granola bar (seemingly invented to literally last through eternity itself) that the calendar on the wall read November 28th. A crude drawing of a turkey crossing a pumpkin field was drawn in the date block that also read 'Happy Thanksgiving! Gobble! Gobble!' in bright red letters.

The only emotion he initially felt was a sudden craving for fresh turkey dressing and cranberry sauce to sink his choppers into. His personal memories of both the Thanksgiving and Christmas holidays were one of dogged loneliness and dark blue depression.

He had attended a few family gatherings during these times, and could only recall how hard he had tried to become invisible within his kinfolk's presence.

He'd always preferred a sharp stick to the eye rather than those reunions, or large social gatherings of any kind. The bottom line was, the

Man rarely trusted nor liked very people in his lifetime. He had spent more time with his pets as a boy, and preferred solitude as an adult, the more isolated the better.

Now he was the ultimate loner, though not of his own choice.

He used to laugh at the somehow symbolic irony of his predicament, but after three fourths of a year spent in his own company and no one else's, the humor had gone the way of most of his body fat. His workouts now lasted between five and seven hours a day, and a quick glimpse in the mirror confirmed that the transformation was undeniable. He weighed a sleek one-hundred seventy pounds of pure, toned muscle. A five mile jog was now equal to a casual stroll to the toilet. He could bench press three-hundred ten pounds for three fairly strain-free reps (seven months ago one-hundred pounds made him feel like his entire body was a pulsating hernia).

He realized with no small amount of sorrow (there was that word 'irony' again) that he'd trade every future moment of solitude for a single five minute conversation with another human being. He had found people in general rude, boring, uncaring, selfish, hateful, gullible and downright stupid. They got on his nerves with their annoying mannerisms and their never-ending plethora of useless information.

The Man continued to gaze at the calendar and its numbers and holiday announcements that meant absolutely zilch in the modern scheme of things. He wished with every fiber of his body for someone to regale him with made up facts and out and out lies until his face turned as blue as his mood.

One particular evening, his nightly movie screenings complete, he sat down and made a list of 'pros and cons' about the old world, just to compare what he had despised the most to things he had actually enjoyed.

The Pro List:

a. Cool fall days (perfect coffee sipping mornings and afternoons)

b. Spending an entire evening doing nothing more than watching a sporting event (usually baseball on ESPN or the Braves on TBS in the middle of summer, popcorn and cola , or the occasional beer, by his side)

c. Seeing a comedy that actually made you laugh until y our ribs hurt (usually involving Steve Martin, Robin Williams, or an old Richard Pryor flick)

d. Being greeted with a sincere smile by a perfect stranger (an occurrence that was few and far between at the beginning of the 21st Century)

e. Spotting a beautiful girl that didn't act like she knew it.

f. Hearing a classic rock song you had forgotten about that caused chill bumps to form on your arms with the way it stirred memories of better times.

g. Days when you just knew things were going to get better (even if deep down, you realized it was the BS section of your brain communicating the message).

h. Being a kid and not giving a damn about the whole shooting match.

i. Being left alone.

The Cons:

a. Politicians who bowed down to every whining group of assholes that came along just to get a vote (politically correct had quickly grown to mean politically incoherent).

b. Taxes (see Politicians) that seemed to increase daily, although low income people who it affected most never saw an improvement in their standard of living.

c. The educational system that bowed down to (see Politicians) every simpering parent who bitched and moaned about their precious mutant offspring receiving any form of discipline. In his time, you got your butt skinned at home and at school. It taught you right and wrong through pure, primal fear.

d. Those same whiny, chicken-shit, lazy as the day was long parents who let their kids run the household.

e. The younger generation, ruined by non-caring, government check collecting parents who couldn't teach their kids right and wrong because they were never taught the meaning themselves. Kids had no respect or fear of their elders. People older than them were written off as cranky, out of touch dinosaurs instead of looked up to as more knowledgeable and experienced in the ways of the world. Again, see Politicians. He had worked with a few twenty-somethings at his last job, and it was like spending time with an alien species. Their disrespect for practically everyone and everything around them both shocked and pissed him off royally.

f. MTV television. One of his few goals in Void World was to trek to their production location and dynamite it to the ground. He had always called it CTV ('Crap Television'). What had begun back in the '80's as a showcase for good solid rock music was now a swampland of ear-splitting, cringe inducing Rap garbage and 'Reality' programming that made his stomach churn. He had many times fantasized about walking onto the 'Real World' set and killing them all with a chain saw (hockey mask optional) just to shut the little shits up. Since when did a 20 year old know anything?

g. Rap music ('nuff said). The day this crap caught on, quality music had one foot planted firmly in the grave.

h. Rosie O'Donnel. Simply listening to her gave him gas.

i. Traffic. He had become a quite astute at using sign language on a daily basis on the interstate. The morons wonder why insurance rates went through the roof when they drive eighty miles an hour, two inches from another car's bumper. Old people driving down the wrong side of interstate or driving 'up' an 'off' ramp (some of them not even sure they're behind the damn wheel). Young drivers digging in the back seat for their favorite rap CD ('Snoop Doggy Shit or Kid Rocket or some such disaster) and plowing headfirst into an eighteen wheeler, inducing a twenty car pile-up that takes twenty men with shovels to clean up.

j. Teenagers wearing their pants halfway down their butt cheeks. What the hell was that all about?

Quicker access to their ass-cheeks maybe? j. The state of sports entertainment in general had driven him away as a fan, though he had grown up an avid follower of both Pro and College Football, as well as Major League Baseball. Sports reports sounded more like "America's Most Wanted", or 'Lifestyles of the Greedy and Drugged'. You had all these guys getting filthy rich playing kid's games and not having the damn sense to appreciate it, and owners who bitched and moaned that they were going broke, then shucked out ten million a year to a player who was only marginally talented.

k. Not being able, at least up to the point that things had ended, to find that 'special someone' to share his views, likes and dislikes, and life with. If indeed there was 'someone for everyone', he sure as hell had never found her.

l. Being left alone (funny how those three words can have such a diverse meaning depending on one's situation).

Yep, the cons had won out that night in a landslide, but a recount in present time would more than likely produce a turnaround of sorts. No doubt about it.

Back to the 'useless info provided by most people' issue, he placed a request to whatever God saw fit to play this unspeakably cruel practical joke on him that the originator of these tales be blonde (who was he kidding? Bald would suffice), about five- two and one-ten, with a nice round butt and breasts that defied gravity, and have the anatomically correct body parts of the human female.

He had, on a lark, picked up a fifth of Jack Daniels from a liquor store on the last trip into town. He had never been much of a drinker (more like 'the drink had him' instead of vice versa), but poured himself a shot on the anniversary of his introduction to "Void World." After the fourth such drink was downed, he was at least relieved to find that some things hadn't changed much from the olden days. First he got sick and vomited, then passed out and awoke with a horrendous hangover.

Soon afterwards, The Man seriously considered abandoning the pad for a road up the east coast. He had always wanted to see New York City. He abandoned the idea once the magnitude of such a trip and the fear factor considered in seeing a city that once held millions reduced to miles and miles of empty skyscrapers and hundreds of thousands of motionless motor vehicles. Phoenix and Dallas/Fort Worth had been bad enough, and that had been over a year previous, when his mind was still in the initial shock stage.

Moreover, the perception that he needed to stay put would not completely exit the recesses of his mind. He realized that he was the sole gatekeeper of the hellish post, and that there had to be a valid reason, a unique purpose, for such an individual to exist.

He only hoped that specific secret was disclosed to him soon, as he felt his slim hold on sanity slip away like a child swinging from a tree limb layered in melted butter.

Departing the control room with a resounding

sigh, he decided to spend the rest of the day snoozing, hoping he could at least dream of kind human contact.

He had given the poster of Jennifer a sad nod as he left, and could have sworn even she looked a bit down in the mouth.

Late that night, in his own pathetic homage to the former second most celebrated holiday in American history, he ate canned turkey slices with instant mashed potatoes and gravy, and canned pumpkin. He tried but failed to hold back the tears afterward. A wave of utter helplessness transported him back to the six to eight year old range, assaulting him with such force it had caught his emotions haplessly off guard. Wiping the moistness from the corners of his bloodshot eyes, he then whacked himself on the right side of the face with an open palm.

He slapped in an old John Wayne movie ("The Shootist", his personal favorite of the Dukes), muted the sound on the TV and cranked AC/DC's "Black in Black" album. He whispered and then repeated one sentence under his breath until he was convinced it had actually sank into his subconscious.

That sentence was "You are not alone'.

He not only wanted to believe the words. He simply realized that he had to.

H. THE VISITORS

The Man saw her first on day four-eleven on 'Void World'. He had been walking the flight line wearing a thick denim jacket and leather gloves, scanning the overcast sky. He had seen a few random flakes of snow drift past his eyes, and was surprised to discover how excited and childlike he became at the prospect that more of the white stuff might be forthcoming.

His steps first slowed and then halted in mid-stride as he spotted the still shadow propped behind the rear landing gear of the KC-135 Tanker.

He removed the glove from his right hand and rubbed both his eyes as if clearing them from blowing dust that did not exist.

When the shadow clearly shifted to the left, the Man felt his heart palpitate. He stumbled a few feet ahead, dragging his feet noisily over the cold asphalt.

When the figure stepped out from behind the aircraft and greeted him with a warm, sympathetic smile, the Man urinated in his pants for the first time since approximately age three.

When he awoke the next morning, his entire face swollen from over nine hours of uninterrupted slumber, she was gone. It came as no surprise, however, for he understood from the beginning that she had never really been there. He sipped his first coffee of the day and squinted at the bright mid-morning sun shining through the glass walls. The ground was white in patchy spots from an overnight flaking, and he smiled despite burning his upper lip with the steaming drink.

His mother had passed away at age fifty-three when he was twenty-eight and stationed at Westmoreland. She had been driving a used Ford Mustang that his dad had purchased just a few weeks before. A semi (the driver blitzed out of his skull on speed, it was later discovered), ran her into an oak tree doing about sixty on a narrow two lane road just a few miles from their house. She only drove the car back and forth to the Winn-Dixie once a week and to Wednesday night services at the local church. His father had told him there wasn't enough left of the 'Tang to stick in a number ten envelope, so there hadn't been any reason to pass on the physical condition of his mother.

His mother had been a meek, somber woman who had taught him right from wrong (her version of such, at least) with the aid of one of his father's belts.

He was forced to attend church until age seventeen, when he left home for the first time, and other than smoking non-filtered cigarettes by the handful, she had otherwise possessed very few vices.

His father worked at a sawmill until he died three years after mom's passing. His vices were (in no particular order); drinking, smoking, overeating, chasing other men's wives, and wrecking a different car every other month (see drinking above).

The Man was certain his mother had endured a lot of horse manure living over thirty- five years with dad, but divorce was something not so easily accepted in their generation, so she stuck with it right until the end.

His long-deceased mother had taken him to the kitchen after a quick flight-line hug, commenting that he resembled 'one of them TV muscle men'.

The Man sat and stared at her, mouth agape

much of the time, while she prepared an early supper. Chicken strips (dark meat) swimming in egg noodles, along with fresh from the garden black-eyed peas and fresh cabbage were devoured in record time, followed by three of her home made from scratch biscuits with butter and honey. He gulped down at least three full glasses of iced tea (sweetened just right), and finished the meal with a large slab of baked apple pie with a scoop of vanilla ice cream.

She tucked him into his bed a short time later, their conversation a mystery to him when he awoke. Her smile had been radiant as she leaned over his bed and whispered 'Dream only of good things, son. Bad dreams in the night can lead to bad thoughts in the daytime', just as she had when he was a youngster.

Upon inspection, he found four empty cans of Spam, half-eaten angel hair noodles, and three empty Apple Ding Dong wrappers scattered about the kitchen table.

He lowered his head and laughed softly. The laugh soon turned to a whispering sob.

He worked out like a Banshee that day, his bench press at an all-time high of three- twenty-five. He did an hour on the treadmill, and spent almost two in the Jacuzzi afterward, sipping ice water out of a large glass pitcher.

He spent the next few days in a walking haze, unable to concentrate on any task that required more than a few moments attention. He ate sparingly, slept constantly, and felt his mind deteriorating like a moist leaf lying in hot desert sand.

He woke to the feel of her warm hand against

his bare chest.

He rolled over and the sweet wetness of her tongue invaded his mouth like some alien probe. He started to struggle, but her grip was surprisingly strong and held him fast onto the mattress. She straddled him and leaned up to sling her long black hair out of both their faces. He recognized her face as one of the adult film stars he had viewed over the past few months. Her lips seemed to be set in a permanent pout, and in her dark brown eyes there raged a fire he had not seen in her movies. The bland, 'going through the motions' look was gone. He felt her genuine desire for him, and something inside his soul clicked. A wave of suppressed emotions he had long since dismissed as permanently 'out of order'.

He could smell the light scent of perfume on her slim neck as he caressed and kissed first her face and lips, and then downward to her firm, perfectly shaped breasts. A moment later he felt her surrender to him. He gently slipped her onto her back. He heard her giggle seductively as he made his way lower still.

When it was over, he fell back and puffed like a man who had just ran the Boston Marathon on stilts. He felt as though a long-festering illness had been cleansed from his very soul. He kneeled up onto his elbows to speak to her, and found the lower portion of the bed empty, the sheets still bundled and curled in her shape. He felt a cold chill enter the room and his arms were instantly coated in gooseflesh. Out of the corner of his right eye he detected movement.

He turned with a jerk and she was there, crawling onto the mattress like a predatory beast only moments from devouring it's cornered victim. He fell back against a far wall, and from a few feet away saw the obvious physical changes in her.

The luster that had made her hair resemble spun velvet was gone, replaced by lifeless, flat wiry fibers. She reached up to adjust it and a sizeable clump pulled loose from her scalp with a ripping sound.

She smiled then, revealing a mouth void of teeth, only moist, purple gums with empty sockets that smelled of rotted vegetables.

Her breasts sagged almost to her belly button, the nipples shriveled and black. She reached for him with fingers that were no more than inch long nubs that were grotesquely bloated and seeped yellow pus at the tips. The Man had backed himself against the wall and was cornered. He felt the mutilated hands on each of his shoulders as he clamped his eyelids shut. The words he heard her speak seemed to originate from inside his head.

The icy coolness of her soured breath slapped his skin and caused him to cringe and a release a small, helpless cry.

"You will never be alone, my love. We will keep you company always."

***

When his eyes reopened, he was lying just inside the bedroom door on his stomach. It took him a full minute to find the strength to pull himself up onto his knees. He felt the throbbing pain at the back of his skull, and winced as he first noticed the fairly deep, horizontal slash marks across his upper

272

chest.

He dragged himself to the bathroom and took a shockingly long look into the wide mirror over the double sink. A trickle of blood ran down the top of his forehead, obviously from the head wound, and the two slash marks were at least eight inches long, and perfectly straight across from one nipple to the other. He studied his own fingernails for a moment, found them crimson free, and resumed his search for further damage.

He wiped his chest with rubbing alcohol and cut up a sheet to make a bandage wide enough to cover it, securing it with a thin strip of gauze and tape. He washed his head with soap and carefully patted it down with a rag dipped in alcohol. It felt like someone lit a match to his scalp.

Before digging a fresh pair of underwear out of the bedroom dresser, he stood next to the bed to investigate.

The sheets were in disarray, and the room held the passing scent of her perfume.

For the final test of whether or not he had been in the throngs of the most vivid dream imaginable, or possibly losing his remaining marbles, The Man reached down and massaged his genitals. Realizing the moistness he felt there might possibly be nothing more than his own sweat, he raised his fingers to his nostrils and cautiously sniffed. The scent was husky and definitely not his own. His mind racing, he felt the pulse in his temples thunder. Figuring (and faintly fearing) she was still in the building, he jogged (still totally nude) to the control room and retrieved both a loaded thirty-eight and a combat knife with a seven-inch, serrated blade.

After hours of searching the pad one room at a time, his initial nervousness slowly faded as the realization that he was again alone in the structure became obvious. He had even walked the flight line (tiny spears of sleet bouncing off of his exposed cheeks) and found no evidence of her ever being on the premises. He showered, re-bandaged his chest wound, and ate an entire twenty-four ounce container of canned peaches.

Late that night, he locked every entrance into the building, including his own bedroom door (even pushing a heavy oak dresser tightly against it), and was still too petrified to do anything other than drift in and out of sleep. For days he performed daily (armed) 'security checks' (as he had begun to think of them) both inside and outside the pad, something he had done on a regular basis back in his days of actually working there.

The underneath of his eyes were dark and swollen, and the stubble of a beard he usually shaved off after no more than three or four days had become thick and wiry with small patches of gray along the jaw line and chin. He hadn't lifted a weight in five days, nor had he eaten a full meal. He sipped water occasionally, but more and more he preferred to gulp down intensely stout, pitch black coffee. From dusk to dawn he was averaging twenty-five to thirty cups a day, and his smoking had increased from the ritualistic two a day back to almost two full packs (despite their slightly bland, at times almost crispy condition) .

The TV/VCR hadn't seen power in days, and the music had stopped. The halls were silent and ominous, but the Man had decided he required total silence in order to hear even the most minuet sound that preceded a possible visit and/or assault attempt.

His chest wound had scabbed over and was now itching like mad. He had ran out of alcohol and peroxide days earlier, but didn't even consider the possibility of leaving the grounds.

He sat perched on the flat surface of the pad's graveled rooftop, a twenty two rifle propped on his left shoulder and a loaded forty-four magnum gripped lightly in his right hand.

His badly trembling right hand. It wasn't the sub-thirty degree temperature that was causing the shaking, however. Nor was it the chilly climate that induced the severe facial tick that caused his right eye to blink one-hundred plus times a minute.

What rational part of his mind that remained (most definitely a minority) knew she hadn't been real, just as his dead mother had never served that turkey dinner. The paranoid sector of his mind (winning the battle in a landslide) countered that the scratches hadn't just appeared on his chest, and his fingernails had been clean and bloodless, just as the husky female aroma hadn't been beamed onto his groin via some alien laser.

This was the third straight day he would spend playing rooftop sentry. He swallowed the last of the coffee from his thermos cup and stood slowly, his knees popping like brittle kindling.

He had taken only two steps down the ceiling ladder when he halted as if someone had just poked the side of his head with a cattle prod. He jerked his head up and scanned the dead plains just outside the

275

perimeter of the base, to the left of the pad. He felt a surge of instant comprehension.

Someone was coming.

It wasn't the girl this time, either. It was something infinitely worse. Drawn to the yet unseen visitor like a magnet to steel, the Man re-manned his post and kneeled down onto one knee. He could hear nothing but his own harsh breathing.

Moments later, they came clearly into view, engulfing the horizon from every direction he twisted his bleary vision towards.

They had form, but cast no shadow in the bright morning sun beaming down it's rays directly onto their backs.

The first thing the Man noticed was their size difference. The initial form was no more than three feet tall, his steps taken with the obvious gait of a pre-teenager. The second body in line was taller, long legged, and the walk was steady and sure. The third was a bit shorter, but wider in the midsection. His steps were slightly stiff, the arms swinging mechanically, robot like. The last form (followed again on its left by the small, childlike body already described) was a bit hunchbacked, the steps taken gingerly. His bright gray hair shone like a flare set off in the pits of a cave. As they grew steadily closer to the pad's locked gates, the Man calculated their numbers in the thousands.

They seemed to be strategically surrounding the pad itself from all directions. They emitted no sound other than the muffled thuds of their footsteps. He was about to swing around and re-enter his safe haven when he finally got a clear look at their faces.

The Man began to unconsciously nod his head from side to side in fierce denial, as if the motion alone would drive the vision from his sight.

They were him. All of them. The first was age eight or nine, ten at the most. Until approximately age thirteen, he had paraded around with one front tooth, it's twin knocked out by a baseball when he was just ten. When the form opened its mouth (seemingly talking to the teen Him?) he saw the familiar gap where the tooth had been.

The second was the teenager version (perhaps seventeen). He recognized the gawky, undisciplined stance and the wavy, out of control hair.

Third was a mirror image of how he had looked when his body had so dramatically transformed, mid-thirties pouch intact.

But it was the fourth form which would forever inhabit his future Nightmares (what few mercifully remained). A vision of himself in his seventies or eighties, slumped over and gasping, simply a wasted husk walking on stick-like legs that made him resemble a roaming granddaddy spider in search of prey. The eyes were hollow, the head sunken at the sides as if they had been shoved inward with great force. The elderly Man (men, as the evolutionary scene replayed on the surface time and time again) grinned, raising his bony right hand and waving directly in the Man's direction.

The Man broke from his daze and practically leaped into the opening to the control room.

He scooped up a loaded thirty-eight while shoving boxes of ammo into his jacket pockets. He ensured his combat blade was attached to his belt, and quickly jogged to the nearest stairwell.

They were after him. He was after himself.

As he locked himself (two deadbolts and a master latch) inside what had been the alert crew's conference room, a sly smile crossed his horribly chapped lips.

They were supposed to get me the first time, the bastards. Well, I ain't giving up without a hell of a fight, no sir. This was their mistake, their miscalculation, not mine. Tough titty, I say. Kiss my lily white ass. I never was a joiner, and I'm not about to change now.

He leaned up against a far wall, past the long oak conference table (now coated in a half inch thick dust), and popped the top on an icy bottle of beer. He had stocked the room with three coolers full of food and drink. The Man had known this dramatic 'last stand' was coming days before. He had prepared well, as was the norm.

He had locked the gate entrance (the ONLY entrance to the pad itself) the day before, securing it with the largest master locks he had left in storage. The gate was also held electronically, and although he had set and checked it himself, finding it impossible to budge, he had no idea how to release the lock. He had decided to worry about such details when and if he survived the present situation.

Whoever the bastards where, they had sent his own likeness, in different stages of life, no less, to eliminate their greatest mistake.

Like a forty pound sea bass snapping a twenty pound fishing line, he had simply been 'the one that got away', a prize catch that had somehow slipped the universal noose. No one was supposed to walk the earth, and he had somehow defied the order. Now it seemed as if the bill had finally come due.

He waited. He drank.

He drank and he waited. He smoked, drank, and waited still.

The silence that engulfed him was both undeniably terrifying and strangely soothing. He passed out hours later, the thirty-eight hanging limp from his right hand.

Once he awoke, it took him a full thirty seconds to deduce his exact whereabouts. He stood in front of one of the wall mirrors in the pad's gym.

He wore nothing but a thick sweatshirt with the words 'I'm A Wanted Man' stenciled in red over his chest, gray sweatpants and white socks.

He rubbed his head, first slow and gentle, then fast and furiously hard, with both hands. His scalp itched like mad, and his mid-section began to bloat like he had just swallowed a honey dew melon whole. His hands, now coated in a fresh coat of oily sweat, left his head and reached for the bottom portion of his sweatshirt. He lifted it slowly, as if opening the curtain on a stage play. The face that protruded from his midsection was the elderly Him. The toothless smile housed his belly button directly in the center, and the eyes utilized his nipples for pupils. The shape of the head (bulging just below his badly shattered collarbones) was that of slowly deflating football.

He attempted to push the pulsating shape back into his chest, but the growth was strong, unrelenting.

It spoke to him in an evil, maniacal whisper that seethed with devilish glee.

"You cannot escape yourself, boy. Sooner or later you would be your own undoing. Sooner has finally arrived..,"

His chest exploded onto the mirror as if a grenade had detonated beneath his breastbone. Splintered bones, blood and internal organs mixed with flying shards of glass ricocheted from the ruined mirror back into his own eyes.

The Man remained standing, his torso hollowed out like a Halloween Jack- O-Lantern, and watched like an unconcerned bystander as the older Him crawled from the ruin that was his midsection like a bloated maggot. The old Him was screeching, his bald cranium swinging back and forth so quickly it seemed it would detach from his neck any moment and literally sail across the room.

The screaming stopped, and the old Him, blanketed in crimson gore, turned to him and smiled shyly.

"You can't escape yourself, boy," it croaked, waiving one finger back and forth defiantly. The Man awoke with a shriek of his own. He was curled underneath the conference room table in a fetal position. The thirty-eight was tucked underneath his side, jabbing his ribs.

He felt his chest hurriedly, ensuring all the parts were still intact.

"J-Jesus god. What a TZ'er that was," he muttered while standing up stiffly and reclaiming the revolver. TZ'er stood for 'Twilight Zone' and was the reference he had always used for particularly bizarre dreams.

He stuck his left ear to the metal conference room door and held his breath, listening for even the slightest hint of uninvited guests in the hallway.

By his watch, he approximated he had been adrift in coma-land for at least four full hours.

He sighed heavily, secure that he was still the structure's lone occupant.

He unlatched the locks and walked slowly towards the stairwell that led upstairs. He planned on a warm meal and some hot coffee, then a lengthy shower immediately after checking the grounds. From the most recent dream, he was accepting the theory that the never-ending formation of 'clones' of himself, both past and present, had also been a figment of his overstressed, horribly fatigued, and woefully under rested mind.

He made his way onto the roof without a hint of panic or apprehension, seeing what he expected to see on the gray, dead landscape, which was absolutely nothing.

No marching armies of himself; buck toothed boys or hump backed old men waving his way.

Sighing with resigned relief, he made his way back into the control room and headed into the kitchen, leaving his guns behind.

He was a step away from the kitchen entrance when the door slammed shut just a few inches from the tip of his nose. He became acutely aware of the shuffling noises to his left. He heard them clearly, but for a split second refused to turn in the originator's direction.

When he did, he found his vocal cords had been turned to the off position, perhaps permanently, and his knees transformed into fast-melting rubber.

The girl led the way, only two long, stringy black hairs hanging onto her mostly flesh-free skull. Her tongue hung from the corner of her mouth like a leather belt strap, hissing at him as she got closer.

His mother was behind her, her facial expression displaying sincere parental sorrow despite soulless eyes. He noticed with some dismay that mom had no arms and hopped towards him on her one surviving limb, a skeletal left leg. Behind mom was the old version of himself, dozens of them. They rammed and shoved each other like they were in the middle of a club mosh pit. All smiled the same toothless, gummy smile that instantly chilled the blood within his veins.

"Stay...Stay the hell away from me, damn it!" the Man managed to croak, backing clumsily towards the control room.

"Dear, we just want this to end. You've suffered enough. You've been alone your entire life. You don't...deserve this," his mother's voice blared, although he never actually saw her lips even slightly quiver.

He turned and sprinted into the control room, roughly grasping the loaded twelve gauge.

He started up the steps to the roof and halted when the legs coming down the ladder caught his attention.

It was teenage Him. It reached the control room floor and turned to him, placing remarkably strong hands on his shoulders before he was given a chance to flee.

"I hated you, you bastard. Look how our miserable life turned out. Not a single friend. Not one. Not a single lover that cared for you or vice versa. It's time for this shitty life of ours to call it a day, don'cha think?" it said to him, the voice calm but the eyes horribly bloodshot with unrelenting anger.

The Man pleaded, dropping the gun to the floor without notice. "N-not my fault. I...we were just...different than everybody else. Don't you all understand? I liked being alone. I cherished it. But...but now I..I.."

The old Him leaned over his left shoulder and finished the sentence with an older, wiser voice, but a voice that was undoubtedly his own.

"..you despise it. Time to be released from this hellish existence, boy. Time to go.."

The Man felt the hands, some small and almost incapable of grip, and some old and inhumanly stout, grip every fiber of his tattered being. He felt no pain, however, only an inner peace that brought forth the most genuine smile he had ever experienced. He would have certainly laughed aloud if only one of them had merely released his throat.

I. THE KEEPER

Spitting dirt from his lips and half-chewed leaves from the roof of his mouth, the Man rolled over onto his back, hacking and coughing for a full thirty seconds. He was lying in a dark, cool shade created by the circle of high oak trees he centered.

He glanced down at the dark blue jeans he sported and noticed a wide tear at the kneecap with dried blood along it's jagged edges. Leaning up until he sat on the balls of his feet, he reached up and gingerly rubbed the swollen knot just above his left ear. His graphite fishing rod and tackle box lay a few feet away, both half-submerged in moist leaves.

Rising to his feet, unsteady and wavering, the Man noticed the clear trail he had cut through the leaves as he had apparently tumbled from the edge of a steep hill just to the right of the small clearing.

A rock the size of a basketball lay beside his left boot, a spattering of his own blood coating it's rough edges like spilled syrup.

The Man brought his hand down from the wound on the back of his skull and specs of dried blood fell from his fingertips.

He began to laugh as he stepped over to retrieve the fishing gear.

The laugh soon became a piercing howl that literally bent him over, clutching his faintly aching ribs.

"You've gotta be kidding! A freaking dream? This shit is priceless...priceless!"

He raised his left fist towards the clear blue sky and shrieked joyously.

"Great joke, man! You really got me with that one. Really fell for it, ya might say. But it's not gonna change who I am, if that was your intention! I still hate people and their moronic, selfish ways, and no freaked out nightmare from the closet of Rod Serling is gonna alter my attitude one damn smidgen! Got it?" He bellowed, the jubilation he felt at simply hearing a passing bird chirp from a high oak limb indescribable.

Feeling his senses return to full power, he cautiously made his way through the clearing to the dirt road a few hundred yards to the north. As he sidestepped overgrown shrubs and briar bushes, his head wound throbbing and his hip aching from the fall, the smile never left his face. In times like these, he almost wished he had a close friend to confide in about the dream itself. Almost, but not quite. He even surmised it would make a great television mini-series, surpassing anything even Stephen King might cook up, if he could manage to recall all the sordid, surrealistic details.

He turned left on the narrow dirt road, now less than a half mile from the cabin. He was hungry, thirsty, and in dire need of a handful of Tylenol, but nonetheless felt elated that the unbridled madness that had seemed so real, so vivid, had simply been a rather warped creation of his subconscious. Just the idea that such inane thoughts were buried there was unsettling, but the Man tried not to dwell on the negative as he picked up his pace.

Negativity was something he had experienced his fill of, thank you, at least for now. Presently, he would revel in the simply joy of just being awake. Awake and aware on a plain of reality that could be smelled, tasted and touched.

The faint sound of a vehicle engine snapped his train of thought, and he whirled around just as the front end of the old pick-up rounded the sharp curve he had just covered moments earlier.

The Man stood like an interstate hitchhiker, his fishing pole propped on one shoulder like a marksman's rifle, the small tackle box in his hand resembling a child's lunchbox.

The old blue Ford truck, which had been in

dire need of a paint job possibly fifteen years earlier, pulled slowly through the curve and began braking about twenty feet before reaching him.

The Man had seen the shapes of three figures inside the cab, but the sun's reflection on the windshield had prevented him from clearly seeing the faces contained within.

He leaned towards the passenger window just as the truck screeched nosily to a halt. The smallest of the three met his smile with a warm grin of his own. The Man's smile quickly melted into a series of facial tics that prevented the words he tried desperately to form from ever materializing.

The small hand landed on top of his own, gently stroking like an elderly woman petting a feline, and the Man felt like he had been instantly freezer burned by the icicle coldness of the thing's fingers.

The child Him didn't speak, but nodded to the two other figures in the truck, both of which were giggling uncontrollably.

The Teenaged Him had one arm around the child Him, his other hand gripping his penis and masturbating wildly through the hole his sweatpants provided. His mad giggling persisted unabated, like a stuck needle atop an old vinyl record.

The elderly Him was behind the wheel, his blank, albino eyes staring straight ahead. He was completely nude, his bloated stomach covered in brownish shaped age spots and also what appeared to be polyp-type tumors that were growing outside his skin, enveloping his lower stomach and groin in a horrific rash.

The old man pointed at the road ahead, which

the Man now saw no longer cut a trail through a wooded mountainside, but a barren flatland with a single building standing alone possibly a mile ahead in the distance. It was the pad, he knew. His pad. His home. The only home he would ever know.

"Get lost, son?" the old man asked sarcastically. The teenage Him continued shrieking, his free hand now massaging the old man's sagging, hairless breasts.

The child Him was now leaning with his head just outside the truck's window, chewing on the Man's fingers. Blood flowed freely but he felt no pain whatsoever. He even thought, just before the old man spoke for the final time, that it even tickled a bit.

"You have to get back to your duties, son. Don't you understand yet? Ain't no escapin' 'em. That place...hell, that planet, is your destiny, your fate. You are the one. The only one."

The old man was nothing more than a blur as he leaped towards the window, his sinewy neck stretched impossibly long.

The Man tried to flinch back and failed. The old man's face was just inches from his own. The old man's breath was like a whiff of decomposed pork that had been baked in the desert sun.

The old Him reached over and rubbed the present Him on the cheek in a gesture of pure, all-forgiving parental love.

The old Him then jerked forward like a cobra and swallowed the present Him whole.

***

287

The Man fell back with a spastic dance of shock and confusion, landing just to the right of the metal barbell rack that might have cracked his skull wide open upon contact.

From his seated position on the sit-up pad, he stared at himself in utter disbelief in the walled mirror of the gym.

His shirt was still pulled up around his chest, where he had been attempting to push away the mutated face from his torso.

He crawled to his feet and began to undress. His movements were mechanical, his expression bland and lifeless, as if deeply entranced.

The corners of his mouth crept upward as he walked down the hallway towards the control room. He ignored the stash of loaded artillery at the base of the ladder that led to the roof, not even bothering to pick up the parka jacket that he had placed on the ladder's bottom rung sometime that morning (afternoon? Perhaps a week from last Thursday?)

He sat crossed legged, his arms resting on his naked lap. No need for a coat after all. He found the icy spears smacking against his bare flesh refreshingly comforting, in fact.

There was no more horizon to stare blankly into.

His eyes saw only the outer reaches of space as the new perimeter of his pad.

He had learned the names of the planets as a child. Maybe over time he would recall them. He had plenty of time for such trivial matters, obviously. He felt no anger now, not at being chosen. No, that emotion, as well as the frustration and confusion that had been its constant allies, were no longer a part of his fragmented thought process.

He was obligated to this task for a reason. Who was he to question why? Billions of people, and he was the keeper of all that remained. The Sentinel of a dead world inhabited solely by the ghosts of his past life. A life that had been, after all, horrifically lifeless.

He would remain here, yes, for what choice did he have? He was the Sentinel, after all.

He was isolated.

He was solitude personified. He Was.

Within hours, his statuesque frame pelted by a lethal mix of freezing rain and astonishingly thick snowflakes, the Keeper sat permanently frozen atop his self- proclaimed kingdom like a recently erected gargoyle, the smallest of smiles painted across his slightly parted lips for all of eternity.

＊

"Jonathan Osgood was the patients name. He died in my care just a few short months ago due to congenital heart failure. Poor boy was my sister's oldest son. He had recorded the aforementioned tale while under hypnosis, although while doing so he managed to maintain the same stoic, mechanical expression as was his trademark from day one of treatment.

Poor Jon truly lived within himself, the self-proclaimed sole survivor on a world that no longer existed within what we deem normal perimeters. He never responded to medication nor any other avenues of therapy. I can only hope the world he now inhabits bears little resemblance to the nightmarish landscape his subconscious had so cruelly created for him."

The doctor cleared his throat and seemed to gauge the crowd's reaction before resuming. When greeted only by a few coughs and several muffled yawns, he then spoke with a renewed vigor; the volume of his tone raised a few decibels in an attempt to refocus their fading interest.

"Alas, the final chronicle of the evening is a painful one, on both a personal and professional level. It involves a mysteriously traumatized young man and a former colleague of mine, and is a textbook example of how a man can easily be entrapped and enslaved within the borders of his chosen profession. It is a story filled with unparalleled madness and fatal obsessions. Listen up, young people, and you may just learn a valuable lesson in the importance of balancing one's sense of priority…,"

CHAPTER TEN
Psychobabble 27 Feb

As a Senior Resident Psychologist, I've experienced and encountered countless troubled, mentally unstable individuals over the past seventeen years. As of this date, however, all past situations pale in comparison. At 8:15 AM today, a young man was brought by ambulance to the violent ward of our facility. After the initial in-processing procedures were completed, during which time it was reported he had managed to injure two staff members; he was duly sedated and physically strapped down. I was the first to interview him upon his regaining consciousness at around one PM. According to his chart, his name was Dillon Kaufman, age twenty-five; five feet eight inches tall; weight of one hundred seventy pounds. He worked as a video store clerk at the 'Video Expo' downtown. It seems he had been harassing various citizens at their homes, sometimes going to the extremes of breaking into their residences during the early morning hours, screaming at them and warning of imminent danger and even death. The police had, after the last of the seven families he harassed contacted them, decided Dillon was a prime candidate to come visit our little facility.

I found him to be still slightly groggy from the medication, but coherent enough to interview effectively. His eyes were wide with terror as I attempted to begin our initial session. When I inquired as to the reason he had contacted these total strangers to warn them of danger, Dillon would never respond with a clear answer. He continued to insist to me, as he strained against the tie-down straps to the point of actually loosening them a bit, that those people simply had to be warned. I was about to call for an orderly and have him again sedated, when I heard the first of the upper body straps snap. I whirled around from where my chair had been facing the door, and just as my eyes fell on his, I noticed the colors.

Dillon's eyes bulged as he fought to snap the second of the chest restraints, and they were engulfed in a shiny red aura, a swirling circular light that at first I thought I had imagined.

I vigorously rubbed my own eyes even as I leaped from my chair and stumbled to the door. I heard the second strap rip free just I turned back to him. He was tearing frantically at the bands that held his thighs and ankles, and the red aura encircling his eyes still hovered there, possibly even brighter than a moment before. I recall he was screaming something, repeating the same words over and over as he attempted to escape his bonds. It was something like "get out of there! He's behind you! Look out!" or similar to that. The orderlies ran in just as I slung the door open. I sprinted into the hall as they had entered the small room. I heard the struggle as I picked up my clipboard from the hall floor, as I had dropped it in my haste to exit.

It took them a full three to four minutes to get him strapped back down, and not without a price. It seems he had torn the straps off his legs just as the orderlies had arrived. Jimmy Deiken, a huge man who weighs in at close to two-hundred seventy-five pounds and has arms as thick as phone poles, was, unfortunately, the first to tangle with Kaufman, he was a full foot taller than and outweighed by over one hundred pounds. According to Wayne Lueders, the other orderly present, Kaufman leaped from the cot and, before Jimmy could even strike a defensive pose, dug the fingers of his right hand into Jimmy's eye sockets. Lueders claims that before he could even get around his partner to get at Kaufman, the smaller man picked Jimmy up until his feet dangled off the floor a few inches, then tossed him like a bag of laundry into the far north wall. I re-entered the room just as Lueders was joined by three more orderlies, and they finally managed to hold Kaufman down long enough to sedate him. One later claimed a partially separated shoulder for the effort, and another says Kaufman broke three of his fingers by merely grasping them and squeezing. Lueders himself has bruised ribs and a severely broken nose.

Lueders informed me that he has worked in mental institutions for over a decade, dealing with dangerous and psychotic patients of all kinds, but had never seen an individual as small in stature as Kaufman manhandle so many larger men. All the orderlies involved also reported seeing something they couldn't even begin to explain while dealing with the patient. All reported Kaufman's eyes were glazed over with some sort of red neon light all the while they were struggling with him, and that the light subsided once they sedated and re-strapped him, using a stronger banding material.

Leuders told me he had never seen anyone,

regardless of their size or strength, actually snap tie down bands. Jimmy Deiken is, at this moment, still in a coma. He has broken vertebrae in his neck and back, and the trauma that was done to his eyes may prevent him from ever seeing clearly again. He will be scheduled for surgery as soon as he responds to medication.

As I pour my third glass of brandy since arriving home this afternoon, I find myself mesmerized by the mystery that is Dillon Kaufman.

2 March

Had my first in-depth discussion with Dillon Kaufman this morning. He had calmed down somewhat. After the initial violent behavior and actions the day of his arrival, he was tested for hallucinogenic and other drugs, and the results were negative on all counts. His almost supernatural physical strength that day can only be attributed to a remarkable surge of adrenaline fueled by inner fear.

I have no other logical explanation.

His story has all the elements of your basic paranoid delusion, but is so detailed that I can't help but feel there is something more to it. He informed me that the visions had begun a few weeks ago, and that from the beginning they were inundated with scenes of brutal violence and grisly death. Dillon explained the visions came to him randomly and without warning at any time of the day or night. He said his movements would become spastic and uncontrollable during these episodes, and that the visions themselves were viewed through his eyes clearly and without blurred or faint imagery of any kind, as though watching a TV or movie screen. Dillon explained he just attempted to 'blow off' or ignore the first few, despite the obvious effect they would have on him afterwards. He was fired from his job after one such episode occurred during the middle of his shift. His boss accused him of drug use and told him to pick up his final check the next day. Dillon told me he had stayed mostly isolated at his apartment following the loss of his job, scared to confess his problem to any of his friends or family for fear of their reaction. He told me that the scariest part of the visions were not the brutal scenes of carnage and death, but the clue he was given just as the vision faded. A clue to the murder's possible location. Sometimes it was a street sign, or a marked mailbox, and although the actual perpetrator of the crime was never revealed to him in any of the scenes, the faces of the victims most definitely were. Dillon said that after a particularly gruesome episode, he decided the only logical course of action to take was to screen the local TV news and newspapers to see if the killings taking place in his mind were actually occurring, since all the addresses in his visions were local ones.

He made a trip to the city library and checked back as far as six months earlier. He found nothing to substantiate his nightmares.

His second course of action was to actually visit the addresses themselves and, feeling his visions must be true signs of things to come, warn the victims he had witnessed murder.

Dillon explained that he truly understood the fear and distrust he was met with at each home. He said as he stared into the faces of people he had seen torn, battered, and mutilated in such episodes, the loud thudding at his temples threatened to drive him to his knees. He said it was as if he wasn't meant to warn them, that something, someone, was causing him physical and mental anguish for his efforts in warning the potential victims. Dillon tells me he knows what he sees will transpire eventually, he just cannot pinpoint a date or time. As we conclude our interview, he closes his bloodshot eyes and immediately dozes off. I believe Mr. Kaufman will be with us for quite some time.

8 March

Mr. Kaufman had to be sedated and restrained once again this afternoon. He was in only his second day of freedom from constant supervision, and had another episode in one of the dayrooms. He managed to break the arm of another patient during the fit, and also smashed a television with a thrown chair. It must be noted that the chair was the large couch type and weighed in excess of ninety pounds. Since all dayroom TV's are mounted on brackets six feet off of the floor, this means Mr. Kaufman had to get the large chair airborne. His strength during these visions is three times that of a normal man his size. It took 150 milligrams of Pentobarbital to put him down.

10 March

Dillon Kaufman was finally able to speak to me semi-rationally this morning. He looks at me as though I am a ghost from his past. He tells me he saw my face in his most recent vision. I ask him if I have been added to his list of victims. He will say no more to me, just looks away, his eyes filled with paranoia-driven terror.

A copy of Dillon's medical records from the Hospital arrived this afternoon. Over the past twelve years, he has only been treated for influenza and other common viruses. No documentation of any mental problems from State records as well. It never ceases to amaze me how a seemingly normal, physically fit and mentally stable person can be transformed in a matter of days or even hours, into someone as troubled as Mr. Kaufman. It is why I entered this field initially, I believe. There is nothing more fascinating to witness or study than the collapse of human sanity.

14 March

I was called into my superior's office this morning. It seems my position, as well as my career itself, is being threatened by the accusations of three families who had relatives I have treated in the past. I go in front of the board in one week. It will not be the first time I've faced such a situation. I have complete confidence in the decisions I make for the patients I treat. I will not lose any sleep over it.

22 March

The board challenged not only my professionalism but also my personal judgment. It seems I am being made the facility scapegoat for some unfortunate events that transpired some time ago.

The father of Broderick Mills, a tortured young man who spent his every waking minute traumatized by violent hallucinations, and who had a troublesome habit of biting staff members until he drew blood, was the source of allegation number one, case C-1342.

I had the patient fitted with a rubber mouthpiece, of my own design, that fit over the top and bottom rows of teeth, thus eliminating the biting problem during treatments. Approximately a week after he had been utilizing the piece, which was held onto his face with straps around his neck to prevent willful extraction, he got into an altercation with some of our staff orderlies. A violent struggle ensued, and the mouthpiece straps snapped free. The rubber piece was subsequently swallowed, and lodged into the patients throat. Once discovered, It took an additional five minutes or so before the piece could be dislodged, and it was later determined (questionable at best) that the blockage it caused in that time had cut off the oxygen to Broderick's fevered mind. The poor boy remained on life support for eight months before his father decided to pull the plug a few short weeks ago. Now the man is pointing the finger at the facility and specifically me for what he is calling 'unjust cruel treatment' to his son, which led to his death. The board seems more than a little shocked that I would allow a 'homemade' device like the mask I designed to be used in a real life situation. I make the supreme effort to aid in my patient's safety, and this is how I am repaid. After all, the boy had degenerated dramatically in his short time here. Untimely and admittedly tragic as it was, his death might have indeed been a godsend for such a doomed soul.

The second case, listed as C-1459, concerns the

parents and older sister of Shelia Wilbur, a young woman brought to us last year suffering from a chemical imbalance that resulted in her going through unpredictable, seemingly uncontrollable fits of nymphomania. She would, without warning and often times in public facilities, begin wildly masturbating. At times she would also beg, sometimes from family members as well as complete strangers, for sexual gratification. She was caught twice in the act of bestiality, once copulating with the family canine and on another occasion with a neighbor's pet horse, with which she was orally servicing.

I studied and treated her for many agonizing months, never discovering the source of her behavioral abnormalities. Ritalin and other anti-depressants were tried to no apparent avail. One day she would seem like a typical teenage girl, speaking of pop music and her love of the piano, and the next she would have to be restrained from harming herself almost to the point of self-mutilation by violent masturbation. She had went almost a month without an incident, and seemed to be responding to the anti-depressant regimen I had prescribed, so I made the decision to release her from constant supervision. Within days of her release from the violent ward, she was found outside the recreation yard, the wooden handles from a set of pruning shears protruding from her bloodied and torn vagina. The family is seeking my ruin for their daughter's demise. Again, I made a decision. I stand by that decision. That is what I'm paid for.

The final case, number C-1661, involved a set of twins that were placed under my care over two years ago. Their names were Michael and Marty Calin, white males, seventeen years of age. They were admitted into our midst by their parents and grandparents after years of various problems. The twins, according to the parents, were 'born evil' and their devilish ways had become increasingly worse as they had aged. They had both dropped out of school at the ages of thirteen, and were constantly in trouble with the local authorities. Michael and Marty were troublesome when separated, but their prowess for mischief increased ten-fold when together. At age fifteen, they had taken a neighbor's retarded eleven year old daughter into a wooded area and raped as well as sodomized her, taking Polaroid photographs of the victim as they had their way with her. They had left her beaten and bloodied in the weeds, and both brothers, according to police reports, "proudly" confessed to the crime, and were sentenced to undergo observation at the facility for an undetermined time period. During my initial interview with the family, they expressed to me that whatever needed to be done to help the boys was acceptable to them, and as I recall, they signed the necessary release forms stating so.

I studied and treated the twins for over three months, and during that time period, I found myself frustrated that not only was I unable to pinpoint the origin of their decadent and violent anti-social behavior, but also I found a suitable treatment escaping my grasp. I tried anti-depressants as well as controlled stimulants. Their deviant stances and attitudes remained intact regardless of the medication. I have never believed in the Dark Age theory that there is 'pure evil' born into this world, but I have to admit my opinion on that subject was being sorely tested by those two. On the day they were caught sodomizing a paralyzed patient in a storage closet, I found my only recourse, regarding not only the safety of the other patients but of my staff as well, was to turn over the twins to the State Corrections Department. In my report, I explained I found no specific psychosis present in their cases, at least none that were treatable by our standards. They were both sentenced not only for the earlier rape of the retarded girl, but of the patient at our hospital as well. Both are serving twenty to thirty years in the state penitentiary. Their family has waiting for fourteen months, and now have decided they did not give permission for me to turn the boys over for sentencing without first attempting some sort of treatment in an alternative facility. The paperwork they signed giving the institution the right to turn the boys over to be sentenced as adults by the State Corrections Department has been misplaced or filed incorrectly, therefore, I find myself backed into the proverbial wall as the scapegoat. I was told the board would decide my fate in two days.

23 March

Checked in on Dillon Kaufman today. Staff members say he has been without an episode since my last interview. He was released back into the non-violent ward today. He is being monitored closely, however. I find out tomorrow if I will still be around to supervise further treatment.

24 March

Those hypocritical bastards have suspended my license to actively practice. I never thought such a thing could actually transpire. They called me "negligent' in my duties, and 'careless' in my treatment methods. The families were outside the boardroom when I exited. I will never, ever forget the smirking, smug looks on their collective faces. Not only did they find someone to sacrifice for their own parental shortcomings, but also all will most likely become quite wealthy from their respective settlements. Meanwhile, I will have a most difficult time obtaining employment within the stringent perimeters of my chosen field. My god, my colleagues treated me like a raw, pimply-faced intern. Seventeen years of caring professionalism, dedication and devotion to human caring, gone. Dust in the wind.

13 April

Swallowed my pride and for the first time in my life, walked into an unemployment office. Blackballed in my own field, I found I had no choice. Was informed by a balding, sarcastic piece of civil servant dog-shit that I cannot draw unemployment due to the facility claiming that I had 'resigned' and was not fired from my position. I tried to explain to the mental midget that I was given a choice of being fired or turning in a mock letter of resignation. He said the best he could do was 'recommend' a few job opportunities for me, one of them as a social 'counselor' for welfare mothers. I was told this would pay the hefty sum of fourteen dollars an hour. I laughed in the smarmy imbecile's face and walked out. I have money saved. True, it is dwindling at a frightening rate, but I can still make the house and car payments. Fourteen dollars an hour? My god, my lifestyle is accustomed to over four times that amount. I have to believe that things will turn around for the better. Again, I have no choice. It is now, sadly, a matter of survival.

2 May

Traded in the Volvo. The eight hundred dollar a month payment, along with the additional hundred-plus a month for insurance was becoming too much of a burden, especially for a man who hasn't brought in a single dime in a month and a half. Driving a used Cadillac now. In layman's terms, it's a piece of crap on wheels. I spend my days watching the endless TV talk show drivel on the tube. It's no wonder facilities like the one I once served are never at a loss for patients. I could make a career just from the brainless imbeciles that frequent Jerry Springer. I believe primal madness is setting in, and I'm not just speaking of the outside world. Went for a job interview at a local VA hospital. Another counselor's position that paid around $35,000 a year. The man took one look at my resume and just shook his head, telling me I was 'preposterously overqualified' for the job. I saw the look in his eyes. I've seen it quite often recently. It says, 'what exactly did you do wrong, mister?"

I may end up flipping burgers before this nightmare ends.

17 May

The families were awarded their settlements today. Saw it on the local news, in between Rikki Lake and Montel Williams. Also saw an old photo of myself with the words 'malpractice' hanging over my head like a noose. I didn't listen to how much the state awarded them. My size eleven shoe had quite an effect on my TV screen, I'm afraid. The unemployment office called me today, inquiring as to whether or not I would consider applying for a position as a counselor for Juvenile Offenders at the local County Jail. I politely declined their pathetic blue-collar waged offer. I have decided I have better things to do, actually. I find myself secretly wishing I had married so that I would at least have someone to vent my frustrations on. I thought about buying a dog or cat to torment. I do believe I can remedy my tension in other, more satisfying ways, however.

21 May

Good old Frank. He's been on night shift security ever since the facility opened. He didn't even question me when I told him I needed to get into my former office to pick up some files I had accidentally left behind. Such a trusting soul. So hard to find these days. I easily avoided being spotted by the staff nurse on duty as I quietly slipped into Dillon Kaufman's room. I felt no personal gratification in this act. This was not part of my original plan. I had been fortunate to run into Ed Walker, who is now running the show in my absence. Ed was never too good with patient confidentiality. But unlike me, he will probably never suffer the consequences of his acts. It seems Dillon had begun having visions again, and the strange red glow that accompanied them was reportedly growing brighter with each episode. He had informed Ed that he had finally seen and could positively ID the face of the killer in his visions.

That face had belonged to yours truly. Old Ed had thought it hilarious that I could ever be mistaken for a maniacal butcher who could slice and dice innocent people. I laughed along with him, hoping he wouldn't notice the uncontrollable facial tics I've recently developed. I had been coming out of a local medical supply store, using the name of a recently deceased MD I had taken some courses with years ago, when I ran into and almost over Ed. The scalpels and bone saw I had just purchased came dangerously close to sliding out of the plastic bag that held them and falling at old grinnin' Ed's feet. That would have been tragic...for Ed, that is.

Dillon's eyes opened just as I plunged the loaded syringe into his bony neck. I placed the rag over his mouth and he bit into it hard. His eyes were huge, aware. He might have envisioned this little scene as well and found the reality of it more terrifying than the nightmare itself. Totally understandable, that. In another time and another setting, I would have probably inquired about this, doctor to patient. Unfortunately, I am out of that line of work now. I have found a new calling. The valium accomplished its mission. It will look like a simple overdose. A nurse will more than likely lose her job. I can truly sympathize.

23 May

I have decided which of the family's addresses to visit on my initial mission.

I will come to their door while they lounge in their living room chairs, stomachs full from a fine dinner, their eyes drooping with relaxation. My instruments have all been honed to perfection. I haven't used some of them since my med school days, but the practice I've done on soft watermelon hide and rock hard slabs of roast beef and pork have me itching to take on the real deal. I will make them rue the day they dared to ruin my life. I love to say that....rue the day....sounds so medieval. I just hope Dillon's mad pleas to them are long forgotten. I'm certain they shrugged it off as soon as the authorities dragged him away as he attempted to save their worthless, pathetic lives.

I feel my energy returning to me, revitalizing, rejuvenating energy. I feel useful again.

Time to go to work.

CHAPTER ELEVEN
Severed Bloodlines

The doctor cleared his throat and coughed lightly, then leaned back with his hands propped delicately on his hips.

"I know what you all have deduced from this little tale. The man is obviously insane. The man has 'lost his marbles' or has 'only one paddle in the water'. This would seem to be the most logical reasoning as to why he would go on such a homicidal rampage, but I am here to debate that way of thinking. Now, I am not saying he was totally justified in the merciless acts he performed, but as cruel and warped as it may sound to the laymen ear, I do understand the vendetta itself."

Jerry fought off a yawn and rubbed his weary eyes while secretly wishing someone would turn up the lights. The blonde girl had been a no-show for the last story, but he had figured she was more than likely sitting in a back row somewhere just to avoid being near him. His luck with women had always been of the bad variety, so he wouldn't have been the least bit surprised if she had ducked away just to avoid his company.

Jerry figured once he became a full-fledged MD that the women would change their perspective of him, and the opportunities to get laid on a regular basis would be plentiful.

He tucked his notepad underneath his right arm and placed his ball-point Bic pen into his left pocket protector, then fell back in his chair and focused back in on the good doctor, who suddenly seemed more animated than he had been while telling the previous story.

"...and when a life is ruined, there must be retribution of some kind. Revenge is not something I would normally condone, but I read this man's personnel file, and his work at that institution had been outstanding up until his dismissal, which I found to be completely unjustified to begin with."

For the first time that evening, a voice from the audience broke through, causing Jerry to bristle. He rolled his eyes and groaned.

"I knew it. Now it's question and answer time. I'm never getting out of here," he mumbled.

The interrupting individual was a black female sitting three or four rows behind Jerry, her tone shrill and sarcastic.

"Doctor, this man must have butchered a dozen people, and had ruined their lives before killing them. You saying such an abomination is acceptable?"

Doctor Dante opened his mouth to reply but was cut off again. "Did they ever catch this lunatic?" the girl added.

Dante grinned, his mouth stretched comically wide. "No, my dear, he is still among the general population, I'm afraid. He is on the FBI's ten most wanted list, I understand, but seems to be a master of not leaving clues as to his exact whereabouts. The man was a trained professional in a field where a high IQ is a must, so capture by the authorities might take years or even decades. Remember that in this great country of ours, serial killers and 'lunatics' as you called him, are a dime a dozen. They are somewhat like city buses; a new one comes along every few minutes."

Squirming in his seat uneasily, Jerry glanced over and noticed a young man he only knew as "Larry" standing in the isle with his chin raised high as if he were searching for something on the ceiling. He noticed the man had his nose upraised and his nostrils seemed to be flaring wildly, although Jerry wasn't sure of this detail due to the overall dimness of the room.

A moment later, as he watched Doctor Dante back up a few steps from the podium and gesture towards backstage, the first scent of smoke aroused Jerry's own senses.

Dante turned back towards the audience, who were now mumbling and whispering among themselves.

Turning back towards the stage, Jerry noticed Doctor Dante and the man in the wheelchair who had spoken earlier pulling the stage curtain closed.

The other man wheeled his way towards the Doctor with the right side of the curtain, and they met in the middle and subsequently tugged both dusty, slightly stained sides together.

"What the hell now?" Jerry grumbled, joined in the seat to his left by the guy he knew as Larry, whose face was contorted in a mask of confusion.

"Jesus crow, are we ever getting out of here? I've got a date, for shit's sake," Larry moaned without ever actually glancing at Jerry.

Jerry was about to asked him if he smelled smoke when Doctor Dante's voice blared over the auditorium's speakers in a voice that seemed twice as loud as earlier.

"If I may have your attention one last time, dear students of medicine, I believe there is one last detail of our little seminar that has yet to be covered."

The doctor glared over at the man in the wheelchair, who looked to be close to bursting out in howling laughter, and nodded agreeably.

"Please come down from your seats and line up in front of the stage," the doctor continued, his hands wringing together somewhat nervously.

Jerry followed Larry slowly down the aisle, and saw that the other students around him seemed strangely cautious as they made their way down.

They gathered and made a single straight line in front of the stage, some leaning onto the stage with their elbows resting on the hardwood edge.

Jerry had Larry on one side of him and a tall black man with shoulders as wide as Nebraska on the other. The black man looked like he had just been awakened from a deep coma. He had a fairly deep sleep-crease on the right side of his face just below the eye. He turned to Jerry, who smiled weakly, a bit embarrassed at being caught staring.

"You smell smoke, man? I swear something's burning?"

Jerry nodded as Larry responded before he ever got the chance to.

"I thought I did a few minutes ago. As old as this place is, it'll go up like a straw in a bonfire once it catches."

Again Jerry opened his mouth to reply but was cut off, this time by the good doctor, who now stood at the side of the podium, facing them.

The man's face practically gleamed with

enthusiasm, as if he were about to present his personal masterpiece to a group of highly regarded art critics.

"Ladies and gentleman, I would again like to sincerely thank you for your attendance. Unfortunately, all things, both good and bad, must come to an end. Your cohorts tonight did fine. I tried to get more of you to volunteer, talked until I was literally blue in the face. It might have helped you all develop an inner peace before the inevitable, but I do understand your hesitance."

The man in the wheelchair joined the doctor, parking his wheelchair a few inches to his left. When he suddenly arose from the chair and stood perfectly erect with his right arm propped on the doctor's shoulder, his face smothered in a grin that radiated smugness, the student body gasped as one.

"One hell of a job by Matt here, don't you think, people? I must also give credit where credit is due for the rest of our troubled but obviously talented cast." The doctor waived his right hand as if in greeting, and the curtains were slowly, dramatically pulled apart.

A surreal mixture of gasps, screams, and wild, giggling laughter ensued as the full scene was displayed in all its perverse glory.

Jerry felt the air in his lungs instantly freeze. The scream that yearned to escape his throat hung like a stale piece of chalky bread. He noticed in horror that the large black man standing only inches away was laughing so hard that tears literally sprang from his eyes and coated his moistened cheeks.

Doctor Dante stood in the center of the chairs positioned on stage like a master magician posing before the ultimate grand illusion. His wide eyes seemed to be lit in neon, and the grotesque smile parked on his pale, pasty face seemed more wolf-like than anything human.

It took a full minute for Jerry to recognize the man tied in the first chair on the right side of the stage. Professor Carpenter's throat had obviously been cut, and his bloodied tongue protruded from the clean horizontal slash in his throat like the back end of a large snake. His left eye had been cut out, and the dark crimson hole that remained seemed impossibly deep and cavern-like. His upper body was tied to the large oak chair with a thin metal wire of some kind that cut through the clothes and had imbedded itself into the flesh, turning the man's white cotton shirt into a red pin-striped one.

"P-Professor? What the he-hell?" Jerry managed as he fell to one knee. He saw the doctor's lips moving but was unable to comprehend due to the spastic activity all around him.

His old pal "Larry" was curled on the floor beside him, sucking his right thumb like a napping infant.

The large black man was now standing a few feet to his right and had his pants pulled down to his knees. Two of the girls were performing oral sex on him, and Jerry noticed one of the girls had no front teeth and was salivating like a starving animal watching a rib- eye steak cook atop an open grille.

Slowly, like a video switched from pause mode to fast forward, both the audio and visual portion of the macabre stage show flashed into focus.

Dante was now standing beside chair number two, which held the strapped down corpse of Laura Willis, who had been decapitated, her severed head placed in her own lap like a person holding a large melon in a grocery check-out line.

"...and as good as Bernie's performance as the Professor was, I believe our speakers were the true stars on this night. Laura here had ample portions of pent-up rage towards the justice system and the medical profession in general. She begged me for relief from the constant bombardment of nightmares and day sweats due to her deceased husband's nocturnal visits."

Jerry stumbled forward on his knees and practically propped his chin onto the stage's front edge just as Dante casually strolled up to the next chair in line.

It was the old man, Willow, minus most of the top of his head, which looked as if it had been sheared off with a dull hacksaw.

Next came Randall Costner, both of his arms bloody stumps past the elbows, his mouth posed in a grimace of pure agony, one of his hands hanging from between his purple lips, the fingers reaching out of his mouth like the legs of a massive black widow spider crawling from a dark, moist cave.

On down the line came Martha Brackens, her breasts slashed off, leaving two blood- spattered concave holes in their wake.

The next display in the grisly gallery of horrors was Betty Danley, propped in the chair like a mangled rag doll, her legs severed below the hip and tied to each of her arms by the slim wire. Her positioning and the abnormality of her feet standing straight over her head gave the impression that she was the definitive contortionist, the most agile woman alive....or recently deceased.

The last chair on the stage simply held a collection of bloodied, pulped heads.

Jerry recognized Bernard Winthrop's, along with the blonde girl he had been trying to make time with earlier.

"H-hope that l-last pee was a g-good one, g-girl," Jerry muttered to himself, fighting back the giggling spell that threatened to rip away what remained of his sanity with all the will power he possessed.

Dante's voice broke through Jerry's daze a moment later, just as he noticed 'Matt'

leaning over him, stroking his hair gently.

"....I have learned, as with my treatment methods all those years ago when I was actually a legally practicing psychologist, that the only tried and true treatment for mental illness, especially the kind that cheats time and winds its way cruelly through generations of families, is to end the suffering of the patient. If it is a genetically bred madness, this treatment also eliminates any further bearing of bad fruit. It severs the line of insanity. I used to curse the names of patients I held responsible for my demise from my chosen field. If they were still alive, which of course isn't possible, I would now thank them. Poor young Dillon Kaufman saw my future all those years ago, but what was left out of his horrific dreams was the genuine good that has come from it, and all the needless suffering that has been eradicated."

Matt ceased patting Jerry's head just long enough to stand and clap after Dante had paused. Dante nodded kindly in Matt's direction and bowed like a veteran stage actor receiving a standing ovation.

Jerry noticed the thick clouds of smoke bellowing over Dante's head before he ever actually smelled them. He struggled to get to his feet, almost causing the black man next to him to tip over onto the girls that were busy at his groin.

The scream that had been bottled up in his chest was finally released when he saw that the girls were actually eating the man's genitals, not just suckling them. The black man turned and grinned at him, his eyes as wide as saucers. The toothless girl leaned her head back and howled, a chunk of severed testicle hanging like a child's toy on a string from her crimson coated maw.

Jerry attempted to twist away from the stage and run when a strong hand landed on his right shoulder, causing him to collapse back onto his knees. Matt held him down until Dante joined them, billowy tendrils of smoke beginning to caress them from all directions.

"...Lamar my son, just where exactly do you expect to go from here?" Dante asked calmly, the pupils of his beady eyes as soulless as that of a predatory reptile.

Matt coughed harshly, then leaned down while still holding Jerry firmly by his upper arms.

"He always does this, Doc. He gets too far into his role. Last time it took us three days to bring 'im back."

Matt slapped Jerry across both sides of his face with the back of his hand with enough force to burst both the man's pouting lips.

"Snap out of it, boy! We have to be leaving now. We've done our job here. It is finished. Lamar, are you with us, son?" Dante asked, leaning down until the tip of his nose was only inches from the young man's.

"L-Lamar? W-who are you talking...about? M-my name is Jerry...Jerry.." Dante smirked.

"Jerry what? Just what is your last name, boy? Can't recall? This is due to the fact your name is Lamar. Lamar Petry. Your Uncle Matt and I saved you from those mind butchers in Tennessee and have tried our best to liberate your scrambled mind from the tapestry of madness that overtook it all those years ago in that Alabama ice storm. It's painfully obvious that we are failing miserably." Dante stared at the other man momentarily and shrugged his round shoulders.

"Damn it, doc, he's my sister's kid," Matt pleaded.

"He's also a suffering soul, my boy. One that is not responding to any form of shock treatment. Let us mercifully end this hell on earth he wakes with each day and takes to sleep with him each night," Dante replied sadly.

Jerry/Lamar's mind raced. As his struggles from the grip of the larger man began to lessen, his mind was flooded with images that were only then beginning to rise from the foggy mists of his subconscious.

He saw an image of a middle-aged woman

sitting at a kitchen table, wrapped in a blanket and sipping hot, smoking liquid form a black cup. He sees the hand that reached into the kitchen drawer and pulled out the long, wide-bladed knife.

He saw the young, possibly teenaged girl asleep on the carpeted floor, the dimly lit fireplace only a few feet from her exposed, bare legs.

He saw the young man wrapped in thick blankets and passed out on the living room couch.

He saw another young man lying on his back on the other side of the same couch, only his head visible from the clothing that cocoons him.

Finally, he watches the blade tear and render the flesh it penetrates, and his eyes grow blurry from the sticky, wet substance that splatters and soaks them in excess.

He heard laughter from a distance, and then realized that he is the originator.

Now he sees neatly folded clothing lying on a lily white-sheeted bed. The shirt and pants are colored in the same dull gray, and just underneath the lone shirt pocket there is a nametag sewn in. It reads 'PETRY – C4456' in large letters, and just underneath that, in smaller print, are the words "BARTON INSTITUTE."

Lamar smiles peacefully as he snaps back into the present. The hatchet blade opens his skull from the tip of his scalp to the base of his neck. Portions of his brain matter land on his uncle's boots, and the man bows down after the deed is done and cries for his nephew.

Dante, his arms waving madly at the smoke engulfing them, grips the man by his forearms and pulls him up.

"We have to go, Matt. The gasoline has worked it's magic quicker than I expected. We can mourn the dead at a later time. Get outside and start up the bus."

Portions of the auditorium's ceiling collapsed inward just as Matt ran for the backstage exit. Two flaming bodies came jogging by Dante just as he jumped back onto the stage and gave one final look at his latest work.

"I loved you all. I brought you here for one last excursion into fantasy that might relieve you of the terrors you have lived and relived through in your time. I now release you from the horrific burdens you've been forced to endure. Goodbye, my friends, and have a tranquil, peaceful after life!"

He darted from the stage just as the curtains blazed. One of the patients/students tried to follow his lead and was crushed by two others that pulled him into their personal bonfire monkey-pile. The screams of pain were temporary. The screams of sweet relief seemed to outlast the fire that attempted to extinguish them.

***

Half an hour later, the glow of a dying blaze and a dark, smoke-filled sky already miles in the distance, the large yellow bus crested a steep hill that led to a mostly empty stretch of interstate.

The driver of the bus sobbed quietly, wiping his eyes roughly with his shirtsleeve.

The older gentleman sitting directly behind him in the otherwise completely empty bus clapped him softly on the back and rubbed gently.

"I know you'll miss him, Matt, but he is in a better place now, believe me. Now his fevered mind can finally find a measure of peace."

The driver smiled through warm tears.

"I know, doc. But I sure loved that boy. He never did hypnotize like the others. Always do damn hard to snap out of it."

The older man nodded.

"I loved all of them. They were my own children, as I see it. They deserved better than a fiery death, I know, but at least they were mostly unaware. All perished quickly and without the undue pain and suffering that decades of medicating would have initiated.

The final therapy is a necessary evil in order to correctly expunge the soiled roots of their existence. These people were damned, Matt, damned from the day their hearts first beat outside their mother's womb. Their insanity was as pre-ordained as their untimely demises.

Alas, my speakers and dear old Bernie had nothing but escape on their minds at the end. I deeply regret having to resort to such crude methods in therapy, but sometimes brute force is necessary for a successful outcome."

Clearing his throat and sighing, trying bravely to fight off another fresh crop of tears, the driver gripped the wheel tightly and sighed.

"Where next, doc?"

Doctor Dante clapped his hands together and leaned back restfully, a study in contentment.

"West Texas, Matt my boy. There is an institution called the 'Fowler Institute for the Socially Challenged' that is infamous for its inhumane treatment of its patients. My paperwork is in order. I'll have no trouble liberating those poor souls from their hellish captors, and then from the chains of lunacy that binds their souls."

Matt glanced at his mentor and friend through the rear view mirror just as they passed a dented road sign advertising a new anti-depressant drug just made available to the general public.

"We're doing a great thing here, ain't we doc?" he asked gleefully.

"Yes we are, my boy. A service to society that is truly invaluable. We will never receive recognition for it, I'm afraid, but our patients know. Look closely into their eyes just before it ends. Their eyes speak volumes for their gratification, and that's all the thanks I'll ever need."

They began to laugh a moment later, at first softly and a bit subdued, then loud and shrieking like angry barks from a pack of rabid dogs. The howls of the mad echoed through the surrounding countryside, and somewhere along the roadside that led to the interstate, a blooming flower withered and died.

THE END